ATLANTA Blues

ATLANTA Blues

Robert Lamb

HARBOR
HOUSE

AUGUSTA

ATLANTA BLUES
By Robert Lamb
A Harbor House Book/2004

Copyright 2004 by Robert Lamb

For information address:
            HARBOR HOUSE
            111 10TH STREET
            AUGUSTA, GEORGIA 30901

Jacket Design by Jane H. Carter

Library of Congress Cataloging-in-Publication Data

Lamb, Robert, 1935-
  Atlanta blues / by Robert Lamb.
      p. cm.
  ISBN 1-891799-02-9 (hardcover : alk. paper)
  1. Journalists--Fiction. 2. Missing persons--Fiction. 3. Atlanta (Ga.)--Fiction. I. Title.

  PS3562.A429A94 2004
  813'.54--dc22
                              2004015180

Printed in the United States of America
10 9 8 7 6 5 4 3 2 1

For all my sons: David, Clay, Tyler, and Carson

"I'd rather drink muddy water and live in a hollow log
than to be in Atlanta treated like a dirty dog . . ."
- *T for Texas*, by Jimmy Rogers,
The Singing Brakeman

"There are more things in heaven and earth, Horatio,
than are dreamt of in your philosophy."
- *Hamlet*, Shakespeare

PART ONE

Chapter One

1981

I SYMPATHIZED WITH THE WOMAN, but my mind kept ringing up No Sale. Her story was small potatoes. Dog-bites-man news. Her daughter Connie, an 18-year-old community college student, had run away from home. No apparent reason. Been gone a week. No word. No trace. So what? I wasn't a cynical reporter, even after 20 years in journalism, but I was a reporter, not a truant officer.

The woman looked like she'd been crying the whole week. Her eyes were red, her nose looked raw, and she seemed exhausted. I felt sorry for her, sure, but runaways were a dime a dozen. You could read about them on your milk carton every morning over cereal. Barring unusual circumstances, newspapers didn't even bother reporting them anymore, and I saw nothing unusual about this one. Besides, I was busy with other stories. I had agreed to see the woman only because she asked for me by name and because I wasn't busy at the moment. Now that I knew what she wanted, I planned to hear her out and then say, "No. Sorry. Can't help you."

In fact, I figured it was the other stories that had brought the woman and her husband to see me. When you had a hot one going, people came crawling out of the woodwork with story ideas for you, most of them goofy, and you had to listen to them, had to be polite — up to a point. For more than a month, I had been turning out stories for *The*

Phoenix, two or three a week, in an ongoing series about cops and their everyday lives.

We got the idea for the story from a medical study that said police work was one of the most stressful jobs in the world. We had had a lot of fun with that one in our news meetings. One of the other reporters said the most stressful thing he'd ever seen a cop face was deciding between regular and glazed with his morning coffee. A copy editor said, "No. Between blonde and brunette."

The copy editor might have been onto something. The uniform did attract women. I'd seen that for myself in the past month or so of riding with various cops on patrol, mostly at night. The way women, especially the young ones, came on to cops gave a whole new meaning to a policeman's "nightstick."

That aside, my stories so far had shown clearly that the workday of the average street cop was no prom date. It was gritty and grinding, and struck me as hours of stupefying monotony interrupted by occasional moments of gut-wrenching panic. So I and everybody else in the newsroom were surprised when the stories caused a great stir among our readers.

The newspaper's switchboard lit up, letters to the editor poured in, and circulation, most visibly in street sales, spiked like a fever. Readers couldn't get enough of cops and crooks, cops and crazies, cops and geeks of every description. Maybe that was what appealed to readers, same thing that pulled people into sideshows at the carnival. I was only a month or so into my research and I knew this much already: You name it and cops had to deal with it up close, day in and day out, things most people only *hear* about.

The woman must have been reading my mind. "I've been following your stories about the police," she said, primping to cry. "They're very interesting." She clenched her hands several times, clutching a frayed facial tissue in one. "You make the police seem so caring, so dedicated to helping people."

"Some of them are," I said. *And some of them aren't,* I thought. A lot of them, I was finding, were burnt-out cases, just as the medical study had predicted. But I didn't say that. I was determined to keep this talk as short as possible.

The woman sobbed and put a hand to her face, "But they haven't helped me." She shot a pained look at her husband, seated to her left. "They haven't helped us at all, have they, Honey?"

The woman's husband hadn't uttered a sound since grunting when we shook hands. He had just sat there and let his wife talk. He put a consoling hand on her thigh and uttered a somber "No."

"The police don't care about runaways," she said bitterly. "But how can they not care about children?" Her anguished green eyes tried desperately to lock with mine.

I avoided her gaze by looking beyond her, out into the newsroom, an open area about the size of a football field, with hip-high partitions cutting it into departments: news, business, sports, and features, where I worked. In each department, people scurried here and there, or clustered around editing desks, or peered into computer terminals as they typed away, all to a constant ringing of telephones. It was 4 p.m. The paper's first-edition deadline was only two hours away.

I knew there was truth in what the woman had said. Missing persons were a low priority in any police department because most missing persons were runaways. Most runaways, like little lost sheep, came home on their own in a few days. Most of those that didn't simply did not want to. So what was the point of finding them? Send them back home and they'd only run away again.

Screw that kind of story. I liked investigative stories with all the pieces there. Some crucial pieces might be hidden, and usually were, but at least they were there, waiting to be uncovered. In a runaway story the whole damn subject was missing — and might never show up. No. This was the features department, for Christ's sake, not lost-and-found, and I was going to tell the woman that – until she mentioned Joanna.

"I didn't come to you because of your stories about the police. Not altogether, anyhow," she said. "I came to you because of your wife."

I looked at her. What on earth did my late wife have to do with this?

"Forgive me for bringing it up," she said, almost wailing, "but I remember reading about your wife. Her accident. Only someone who has lost a loved one of their own could know how I feel. *That's* why I came to you."

The woman's eyes, shimmering with tears, followed mine with such a hunger for contact that I gave up and looked her squarely in the face.

It was a nice, open face, the kind that is a mirror of the heart, and I could see that as a young girl she had been cute. She was not unattractive now, at about 40, but I had observed over the years that cute didn't age well. I saw it again in her looks. Her face seemed to be going from young to old with no pause in between at mature. Still it was a nice face, redeemed by those green and earnest eyes if nothing else.

Her husband was another story. All I could see in him was proof that opposites did indeed attract. He was huge; she was small, almost petite. She was animated; he was still. She was open; he was closed. But there was nothing menacing or sinister about him. In his own way, he seemed as earnest as she. Some people simply suffered in silence.

Nobody spoke for a moment. I stared into the distance, but I was really looking inside myself. That thing about Joanna, my wife, had sucker-punched me. But what the woman had said about losing someone you loved was true, the kind of true you have to live to know. So I found myself thinking it over.

Runaways, even those with unusual circumstances, were not my kind of story. I wouldn't even know where to start. True, I could check into the girl's disappearance easily enough. I'd be riding that night with a very good street cop, Rick Casenelli, and I knew he could point me in the right direction, help me get started. Too, I was in and out of police headquarters a dozen times a week. A few detectives and even a couple of the department's brass owed me. But what reporter in his right mind would call in favors for a piss-ant story? And why should I risk getting sidetracked from a hot story to go off looking for somebody's little lost darling? Did I look like a social worker? Connie Phillips was probably shacked up somewhere with a campus stud. Or two. Or three. *Jesus!*

So there it was: several good reasons to say no to this woman and no good reason to say yes. Still, her words resounded in my mind, and every time I heard them again, they set off echoes from the deepest caves of my memory. I *did* know what it was like to lose somebody you loved. Grief and, for some reason, guilt pulled you down into a black pit and took turns working you over. And they didn't let up, night or day, for a long, long time. You survived, but you were never the same again. You walked around with something crucial gone out of you; some special little light had been extinguished. Perhaps it was the belief that no matter what life threw at you, you could take it. That was *real* grief — the kind I saw in the woman's eyes.

Aw, fuck it, I thought. I said I'd do what I could to help find her daughter.

The woman burst into tears, causing others in the newsroom to turn and stare. Her husband leaned over to soothe her.

"I knew you would," she said, darting her hand into the purse on her lap and pulling out a fresh Kleenex. "I just knew you would." She put a hand on her husband's massive thigh. "I told Joe you would. Didn't I, Hon?"

Joe nodded and made a murmuring sound.

"I've followed your stories in the paper," the woman said, sniffing and wiping her eyes. "You care about people. That comes through." She sobbed again.

I looked around helplessly, embarrassed. She was causing a scene, but what could I do?

"Thank you, ma'am," I mumbled. But all the while — I couldn't help it — I was thinking: *Please, God, make her shut up!*

She was still breathing raggedly when somebody — I didn't notice whom — appeared at her side, handed her a cup of water, and went away as quickly as he or she had appeared. The woman uttered a quavering "Thank you."

I pulled a reporter's notebook from my desk drawer and got out my pen to take some notes. Connie Phillips had planned her getaway well. Under the pretext of spending a Friday night with her girlfriend and schoolmate Jane Kimball, she packed an overnight bag and left home around 5 p.m. on July 24. Her father was still at work at his auto repair place, and her mother was grocery shopping. The girl was not discovered missing until noon Saturday, when Mrs. Phillips, wondering why she hadn't heard from Connie, called the Kimball residence. The Kimballs hadn't seen Connie.

In the next two hours Wanda Phillips called everybody she could think of, including out-of-town relatives, who might know her daughter's whereabouts. Meanwhile Joe, working on Saturday but home for lunch, got into his car and drove all around Avondale Estates, a small community just east of Atlanta where the Phillipses lived. Both parents searched in vain and by 3 p.m. had grown deeply concerned.

They called the police.

"They were no help at all," said Mrs. Phillips, her voice a high whine of disbelief.

Joe finally spoke, his voice a low rumble. "There was no evidence of foul play, the officer said, and the police won't accept reports of runaways until they've been gone seventy-two hours."

Mrs. Phillips interrupted, her tone of voice an appeal to simple common sense. "But by then it's too late, don't you see?"

"Then," Joe added, "when the officer asked if anything was missing, Wanda went to check, and found Connie's clothes and a suitcase gone. That was it. The officer said there was nothing he could do for forty-eight more hours, and left."

"Yes, and what did he do after the forty-eight hours?" Wanda said bitterly. "He talked to Jane Kimball — Connie's girlfriend," she prompted, "who told him nothing, and then he said he'd file a missing-person report. He didn't act like he wanted to do even that much; Connie was of age, he said, and could leave home if she wanted to. That's the last we've heard from the police. The chief won't even see us or return our phone calls anymore." She dabbed at her nose with the limp, crumpled Kleenex and stared off into space, disconsolate.

I made sympathetic sounds, but I wondered if I could do any better than the police had. To the police, a runaway was a matter of small importance, a sort of domestic fender-bender; you wrote it up and then wrote it off. Now I was thinking that's what I should have done, *dammit*. The girl could have left town going in any direction, and the trail was a week old. I couldn't even find, after some delicate probing of the Phillipses, a reason for the girl's leaving. She seemed a completely ordinary teenager and they seemed completely ordinary parents, maybe more caring than most. The only hint of unhappiness came when Wanda said, "Connie thought she was overweight. She wanted to lose twenty pounds. But it wasn't *that* big a deal with her. It couldn't have been. I would have known. Here," she said, reaching into her purse. "She's a pretty girl. See for yourself."

She handed me a photograph.

"Pretty" was stretching it a bit, but that was a mother's prerogative, wasn't it? Connie Phillips wasn't homely, either, judging from the color Polaroid snapshot before me. She had inherited the large bones of her father instead of the small frame of her mother, and no diet and no amount of exercise was ever going to render her svelte. But nature, maybe in a compensatory mood, had given her big brown eyes in a pleasant face, long wavy brown hair, and breasts at eighteen that an Amazon might envy. That made me ask, and I put it as gently as I could, "Any possibility your daughter was pregnant?"

"No!" Wanda said. "In fact, I'm as sure as a mother can be that Connie's still a virgin." She dropped her eyes. "*Was* a virgin. Now, who knows?"

"Now, honey," Joe said, patting her hand, the meaning clear: don't let your imagination run away with you.

Again Mrs. Phillips started to cry. "My baby may be dead, for all I know." Her eyes locked with mine again. "Please find my little girl, Mr. Blake. Please. I just know she wouldn't leave home like that unless she was in some awful trouble. Or unless somebody made her leave." She covered her face with her hands to muffle the sobbing.

From out of nowhere, a staff photographer appeared at Mrs. Phillips' side, kneeling, stooping, squatting to snap off three or four frames before I caught his eye and shooed him away. "I'll do what I can, ma'am," I told her.

I meant it, but beyond asking the police to help I had no idea which way to turn. I looked around for somebody to ask, maybe somebody with more experience in missing-person stories than I had, but I was the only reporter still there. People who worked in features, the writers at least, cleared out at five o'clock. One of the attractions of working in features was regular hours — nine to five, Monday through Friday. When I had worked for the city desk, which I did for several years, I never knew when, or even if, I'd get home. The job had its exciting moments, but eventually it got old. Joanna didn't like it, either. I never knew what time I could call my own. Now that I did know, I reflected wryly, I didn't have Joanna. But this was no time to be thinking about that.

After answering a few more questions, routine ones about Connie's background, friends, habits, the Phillipses got up to leave.

"I'll call you the minute I know anything," I told them. "You have to understand, though, that I might not find out anything. All I can do is try."

Mrs. Phillips nodded and glanced at the picture of her daughter on my desk. "I need to hang onto that," I said, reading her thoughts, "but I'll take good care of it and you'll get it back. I promise."

I WALKED THE PHILLIPSES TO THE ELEVATOR and bade them goodnight. When I got back to my desk, my boss, David Owens, was waiting for me.

"Anything there?" he asked eagerly.

"Plain vanilla runaway, I'm afraid."

"Damn!" Owens said. It was he who had spoken first with the Phillipses and pointed me out to them when they showed up in the newsroom.

Normally, Owens's news instincts were uncanny. A newsroom wag said Owens could "smell a story upwind across a valley, a village, and a vacant lot." He *was* good. Only 32 or 33, he was one of the best editors I had worked for, and easily the most enthusiastic. When he got wind of a juicy story, his eyes gleamed behind his old-fashioned wire-rim glasses, and he all but danced with excitement.

"From the look of her," Owens said, meaning Mrs. Phillips, "I figured an axe murder at the very least."

"Sorry," I said. Catching ourselves, we smiled at each other in recognition. We had often commiserated over beers about what we called the Newsman's Double Bind. You don't wish misfortune on anybody, but unless it happens, your newspaper, as well as your job, can be awfully dull.

"You're worse than a mortician at a train wreck," I said, laughing. "Actually, killing her might have been kinder than just leaving like she did — her daughter, I mean."

"Hostages to fortune,'" Owens said. He had two daughters of his own. Things like this made me glad that Joanna and I never had children.

"Yeah, she's suffering, all right," I said. "That's why I told her I'd help her."

"You said you'd help her?" His face brightened as if he sensed a story here, after all. But just as quickly it darkened. "How?"

"Well, her daughter, an only child, the light of her life, took off without so much as a by your leave. The Avondale police — surprise, surprise — couldn't care less. I said I'd try to find her daughter."

He gave me a dubious look.

I shrugged. "Can't hurt to ask around."

Owens brightened again. "This *could* fit in with the stories you're doing."

"How can we fit it in if the police aren't working the case?"

A mischievous grin moved across Owens's face. "Let's *make* them work it. Write up a little piece about the girl's disappearance. We've got pictures of the mom." He smiled. "I *knew* it was a good idea to send that photographer over. Don't you have a picture of the daughter? Good. We'll get the story in tomorrow's paper. It's late, but no problem. There's never much news in a Saturday paper anyhow, and if anybody asks why we're doing stories on a runaway, we'll just say it was a slow news day."

"OK, but this is strictly an Avondale story," I reminded him. "No Atlanta cops involved."

He grinned again. "Not anymore." He turned to walk away, but then turned back. "How long has this gal been gone?"

"Since last Friday."

He made a sour face. "God, if she shows up on her momma's doorstep tomorrow, or even Sunday, we're gonna have egg on our faces."

"Yeah," I said broadly, "a lost child returned to home and hearth, a mother's heart made glad. That would be just awful."

"Screw you," he said, turning again to leave.

"Maybe you could stake out the Phillipses' house and tackle the girl if you see her trying to sneak back home," I said.

"Screw you," he sang again, walking out into the newsroom, toward the city desk.

AS SOON AS OWENS LEFT, I phoned Casenelli. The sooner I could enlist his help in this matter, the better. Rick was no ordinary cop. A transplanted Philadelphian, he had chucked a stockbroker's career to move south and join the Atlanta police force. "I wanted some excitement in my life," he said simply. He was intelligent and articulate, and at thirty-one had already made a name for himself on the Atlanta police force. It wasn't a name that stood him in good stead with his superiors. He had flair and he was outspoken — qualities that can make superiors feel uneasy, qualities that had landed him in the media spotlight a few times, which of course made his superiors even more uneasy. I glanced at my watch as the phone rang.

Rick answered on the third or fourth ring. "Yo! Rick Danger here. Make it quick; I'm halfway out the door."

Briefly, I told him why I had called.

"I'll have to think about it, Ben, and ask around." He laughed. "As you know, I am but a lowly street cop. Drunks, punks, pimps, whores, barroom brawlers, burglars, con men, junkies, pushers, drunk drivers, car thieves, shoplifters, enraged spouses, child molesters, the criminally insane — the whole crazy concerto on concrete — those I can tell you about. But people who split are outside your humble servant's area of expertise. I'll ask around and fill you in later. We still on for tonight?"

"Wouldn't miss it."

"Pick you up in front of the news building at 8:06. *Ciao.*"

While waiting to meet Rick, I got on a computer near the city desk and wrote up the story of Connie's disappearance. It was only four paragraphs long.

"It's long enough," said Owens, who was reading over my shoulder. "All we need to do is get the ball rolling. This and the photo should do it."

At 8 p.m. I left the building to meet Rick.

Chapter Two

AT EXACTLY SIX MINUTES AFTER EIGHT, Rick pulled up in front of *The Phoenix* in a black-and-white squad car, a Ford Galaxy that looked fairly new. Some of the squad cars I had ridden in were real clunkers.

"How'd you rate this?" I asked, climbing in and belting up.

He smiled and eased out into the traffic on Marietta Street. "The best-looking cop you'll ever see is now in charge of the garage on my shift. Blonde, sky-blue eyes, surfer-girl tan, a body built for speed. That's where I was running off to when you called me — a bit of afternoon delight, if you get my drift." He gave me a sideways look. "You do get my drift, I presume, but take your time. I know how slow-witted you journalist types can be."

I laughed. "Get real. A Ford tells me what she thought of your performance. A reporter would've come away with a Cadillac."

At Central City Park, a few blocks down from the news building, Rick turned left, cruised through Margaret Mitchell Square, and swung north onto Peachtree, heading toward his regular beat, the city's northeast quadrant.

"This car," he said grandly, "is the best the APD can offer." He sighed extravagantly. "Come to think of it, she is too."

I let it drop. I hadn't been with a woman since Joanna died. Hadn't even thought of it. Monks in a monastery had a richer sex life than I did. "Well, at least this car's got a good air conditioner," I said.

The car was nearly frigid, but the cold felt good to me. Atlanta had been frying in a heat wave for days, and not even nightfall brought much relief. Here it was, nearly 8:30 — still light, thanks to daylight saving time — and the time-and-temperature sign on a bank we were passing flashed 85 degrees.

The humidity was the worst part, though. In the four or five minutes I had spent waiting for Rick out on the sidewalk, sweat had begun to trickle down my back and ooze out of my hairline. As we drove along, the few people still out on the street looked like Edward Hopper figures trapped in a painting by Salvador Dali. Late commuters waiting for buses leaned against storefronts and lamp posts as if too wilted to stand erect, and the few tourists heading back to their hotels after supper or some last minute errand seemed to trudge along in slow motion. Not to worry, though. All of them would get off the street as soon as they could, and it wouldn't be because of the heat. At nightfall during the week, people evacuated downtown Atlanta as if William Tecumseh Sherman were coming again, and on weekends Atlantans didn't come into town at all. It was a sign of the times. The streets weren't safe.

"Sex," I said, leaning back in the seat. "That must be the first word a dago baby utters. I'll bet that's the only reason you became a cop. The uniform attracts women, I hear."

He smiled. "You malign a dedicated public servant and a noble breed, m' boy. Can I help it if these Southern belles are attracted to my Mediterranean good looks, to my Yankee *savoir faire?*"

I said, "Sure," giving it a sarcastic spin, but Rick was good-looking, and single, not a bad combination in a city that drew young women to it like a magnet. He was a trifle short, but body-building had given him a muscular physique, which he carried with a slight but inoffensive swagger. The chiseled face topped with black curly hair didn't hurt either. But his main assets, I thought, were devil-may-care charm, an extravagant sense of humor, and a physical intensity that charged the air around him with electricity. "So modest, too, all you wops," I said. "But tell me how to find Connie Phillips."

"She's on the wire. I checked. So are a jillion other runaways. And frankly that's about all the police can do about people who vamoose:

notify other police departments to be on the lookout. Once in a while it pays off. But don't hold your breath."

We crossed North Avenue and headed up The Strip, a stretch of downtown Peachtree Street that ran for several blocks. In the early 1970s The Strip had been taken over by Hippies. Now the Hippies were long gone and the prostitutes had moved in. You could see some there every night, but tonight they were out in force, heat wave or no heat wave. Friday was payday for many of their clients.

Rick continued, "I also called a guy I know on the Avondale police force. He said they've scoured the town for that girl and are still on the lookout for her. Not much hope there, of course. When runaways get gone, most of them get good 'n' gone. Then, to most cops, it's a case of out of sight, out of mind. Sorry, but that's the way it is. Take me, for instance. My mind — my police mind, that is — almost never thinks outside of Atlanta. Worse, even outside of my beat. Look around you. I got more right here on The Strip than any one man can handle, than the whole damn police department can handle, you wanna know the truth. If I hear that somebody — a suspect, say — has hauled ass out of town, I say 'Good riddance!' That's one less turkey I have to put up with. Tell you something else: That's the way all cops think."

Northbound traffic was now bumper-to-bumper along The Strip and hardly moving. Some of the drivers were merely gawking sightseers, but most seemed to be circling the blocks in a four-wheel version of musical chairs, the better to check out the hookers' merchandise.

The behavior of the prostitutes was the main problem, though. They had grown increasingly aggressive in recent weeks, and from time to time would stand in the street, bringing traffic to a standstill, while they tried to entice motorists or haggled with them over price.

They had also come up with a simple but clever scheme to get the money without delivering the goods. While one girl stood at the driver's window or leaned in to distract him, another entered the car from the other side, slid up beside him, and lifted his wallet while rubbing against him and running her hands all over him. As soon as she got the wallet, she scrambled out of the car, and both girls fled.

Most victims didn't know until later that they had been fleeced, and the victim who caught on quicker saw the hopelessness of giving chase in that throng, to say nothing of the risk of leaving his car standing in the street. The whores didn't call their customers "tricks" for nothing, I mused.

My deeper thoughts were on Connie Phillips, and I was about to ask Rick how to start looking for a runaway, when a female voice crackled over his police radio. I had no idea what she said. The codes were a mystery to me, and most of the words were tangled in static, like a parrot squawking.

But the message got through to Rick. He flicked on his blue light and threw the Ford into reverse. He barreled backwards until headlights behind us looked as if they'd wind up in our back seat. At the last instant he screeched to a stop then whipped the car forward, turning into the oncoming lane, which was clear. The Ford couldn't make the complete turn in one maneuver — Peachtree is too narrow — but Rick knew that. He bounced up over the low curb and onto the sidewalk, swerved around a big oak tree near the street, and hit Peachtree again with a burst of speed that snapped my head back.

"You buckled up?" he shouted.

"Bet your ass!" I shouted back. "This ain't the first time I've ridden with you."

Rick was intense all the time, but under pressure he became a raw force of nature, cyclonic, almost demonic. Danger gave him an adrenaline high, he had told me, and that was what he liked most about police work. It was a fairly common motivation among cops, I had learned — and another of the many factors that led to police burnout.

"Hang on," he said, running a red light at Peachtree and North, and turning left to get over to Piedmont, another major thoroughfare, twice as wide as Peachtree.

"I'll just get out at the next corner." I said, scared witless but trying for humor. "Where are we going in such a hurry anyhow?"

"For coffee," he said, grinning, "what else?" He was so manic that for all I knew he was telling the truth. But he soon added, "Emergency at Pine Manor Apartments. Medic needs help with a patient. No idea why."

The blocks of Piedmont reeled past as if the street were rewinding back into the city right out from under us. Traffic was light, and the few cars in our path darted into another lane like small fish fleeing a marauding shark. Near Broadview Plaza, a shopping center, Rick angled left off Piedmont, tires squalling, shot across three lanes of oncoming traffic, and roared up a hill into a residential neighborhood. Seconds later, spotting an ambulance just ahead, he swerved into a small parking lot and stopped. The car was still rocking on its springs when he hit the ground at a trot, running toward a medic who stood nearby waiting for him.

Scrambling out of the car, I heard the medic yell, "I got a man inside who'll be dead in thirty minutes if we don't get him to the hospital, but he refuses to go." He pointed down a walkway to an apartment where a bare light bulb burned over the door, which stood ajar.

Rick hurried toward the door. "What's wrong with him?"

"GI bleeder," said the medic, a tall, thin man balding prematurely and wearing glasses. He fell in behind Rick. I followed.

"He drinking?" Rick asked.

"No. He's sober, sane and rational; he just refuses to go."

The door led into the back of the apartment, one in a cluster of buildings that all looked the same. With Rick leading the way, we stepped into a kitchen and rushed on through the apartment to a bedroom door, where we saw another medic, a short, dark man of about twenty-five.

Inside the room, on the bed, lay a naked man, rolls of fat puddling at his waist. In the light from a bedside lamp, he glistened with sweat, and fresh blood stained the pillow and sheet beneath his head. More blood oozed from between his legs, smearing his buttocks and thighs. This was a kind of blood I'd never seen before: brown streaked with purple. A billowing stench filled the room. I fought to keep from gagging.

The man's wife, a slender, frail woman whose face was drawn with fear, stood at his side. She gave us a hopeful look, but the man, lying on his back and smoking a cigarette, regarded us as casually as if we stood in his bedroom doorway all the time.

Rick approached the bed. "Sir, we've got to get you to a hospital."

"I'm not going," the man said in a calm, cultured voice, "and you can't force me to go."

"We've tried everything," the woman said, meaning she and the two medics. "He just won't go."

On the floor at the foot of the bed sat a yellow plastic basin overflowing with bloody rags. In spots, the carpet glistened with blood.

The man looked at his wife. "Who are all these people?" he asked, annoyed.

Rick identified himself and then Patrolman Johnny Lee Cook, who loomed now in the bedroom doorway, towering well over six feet. I knew Cook. I had interviewed him in connection with cops and their marital problems, which made for one of the highest divorce rates in the nation. A good-looking, slow-talking country boy from South Georgia, he was Rick's backup man on this call.

"They're here to help you," the woman told her husband.

"I don't want their help; I want them out of my house."

The tall, thin medic spoke up from the doorway. "If you don't get help and get it quick, you're going to die." He looked at his watch. A life was ticking away.

"That's my damn business," the man said. He reached for a glass on his bedside table and lifted his head to sip from it. Then he casually lit another cigarette and added, "I know my rights, and all of you are trespassing. I want you out, and this time it's not a request."

Rick included all of us in a quick look around the room. "Let me talk to him alone."

We went into the living room, where the man's wife began to tell Johnny Lee about her husband. "Checked himself out of the hospital this morning. Just got up and walked out. Stubborn." Her voice was thin and fragile, and she wrung her hands the whole time she talked. "He used to be a heavy drinker. He hasn't had a drink now for six months, but he's very sick. Maybe it caught up with him after all."

Her husband, who was 50 but looked sixty, worked for the federal government, she said, but had once attended medical school. "He knows just enough to be dangerous to himself. He was willing to go on to the hospital until they checked his blood pressure." With a nod of her head, she indicated the medics.

Johnny Lee looked at the tall, thin medic. "How was his blood pressure?"

The man raised his eyebrows and made a face. "Pretty good, considering."

"Considering what?"

"That he's lost a lot of blood — and is still bleeding." The medic looked at his watch again. "We've got to get blood into him. We need to start right away."

Rick charged out of the bedroom, grabbed the phone, and dialed one number. "Operator, this is a police emergency." Reading from some letters he had jotted in ink on the skin of his palm, he said, "Give me the number of the Rev. Claude Casey." Over his shoulder, Rick told us, "He's willing to go if his preacher will meet him at the hospital." He began dialing a number.

"He'll go into shock soon," the short medic said, "then we can take him anyhow, but it might be too late."

The thin medic said, "It might be too late already. People who lose this much blood usually don't make it." He caught himself and turned to the wife. "Sorry, ma'am."

Rick turned back to the phone, listened for a moment then cursed under his breath. "A recording." He left a message for Casey to call Piedmont Hospital, hung up the phone, and turned to us. "That's it," he said. "As far as I'm concerned, the man is out of his head." He looked at the medics. "Move him out. If we have to, we'll slap cuffs on his ankles and wrap him in that sheet — whatever it takes." He moved toward the bedroom door, but then paused and looked at the woman. "Any objections, ma'am?"

She nodded a quick no.

"Get him," Rick snapped.

The medics spun into action, rolling a collapsible stretcher into the bedroom and to the side of the bed.

No longer looking calm and collected, the man said feebly, "I'm cold."

"Could be going into shock," the tall medic said, checking his watch again.

"Move him out!" Rick barked.

This time, the man offered no resistance. Maybe he was too weak. He suddenly looked pale and scared.

The medics rolled him onto the gurney and hustled him outside. By the time they reached the paved walkway they were nearly running, the stretcher clattering loudly between them, its wheels whirring furiously on the pavement, except for one, which spun lazily in the air as if mocking this great hurry to save a life. I wondered if it were an omen.

With Johnny Lee lending a hand, the medics lifted the man into the ambulance. One of them climbed in with him while the other medic, the tall, thin one, hurried around to the front to do the driving. Johnny Lee and the man's wife clambered into the back of the ambulance, too, and Rick ran to his car. I barely got in beside him before he had the car rolling, and as soon as I closed the door he floorboarded it. The tires spun on gravel, sending pebbles flying, scratched for an instant more, and then caught. Seconds later both vehicles, sirens wailing, lights flaring, were hurtling toward Piedmont Hospital with Rick leading the way.

The first wild ride that night had been unnerving, but this one was harrowing. My stomach, already queasy from the powerful odor in the man's bedroom, bounced around like a ball. I had to fight to keep from throwing up. Roaring up and down Atlanta's hills, Rick whizzed around other cars as if they were parked, zipped through intersections without so much as a glance right or left, and ignored stoplights altogether. In our wake, the traffic lights looked like spatters of red, red blood floating away on the velvet night.

Rick handled the car expertly. In his hands, the Ford hugged the road, never losing its footing, and tracked through curves as if on rails. The ambulance driver was no slouch either, staying right on our tail all the way to the hospital, located on Peachtree.

Soon, an orderly was wheeling the patient down a hall toward the emergency room, a bottle of blood plasma swaying on a high hook at the side of the stretcher and leaking into a tube plugged into the man's arm. A doctor and a nurse walked briskly beside the stretcher, the doctor feeling the patient's pulse. The rest of us, except for the medics, followed.

Still conscious, the man said feebly, "I want to go home."

The doctor, a short, bespectacled man with a round, impassive face, replied as calmly as if he were ordering a sandwich, "You do and you'll die; it's that simple."

They pushed through the emergency room's swinging doors and we stopped there. Through a small window in the door, we watched them go to work on him, but soon they pulled a curtain that cut off our view.

Rick and Johnny Lee turned their attention to the wife, trying to reassure her. Anxiety had drawn her face into a tight, gray mask, but she seemed at least relieved that her husband was where he belonged and was finally getting treatment. She thanked the policemen again and again.

Seeing the short medic come out of a restroom down the hall, I walked to meet him. "What are his chances?" I asked.

Looking beyond me at the man's wife, he said softly, "He'll be dead by morning. If he's not, he'll be the first I've seen to pull through after losing that much blood."

"GI bleeder. What does that mean?"

"Gastro-intestinal." He saw my next question coming. "Could be caused by a hundred things. Sorry, I'm no doctor." He walked away just as Rick and Johnny Lee came up. "Thanks," he said to them as he left.

We walked outside and stood a moment on the loading platform just off the emergency room. It was dark now, and still hot and humid, but a faint breeze stirred from some dark corner of the night. Rick drew deep, deep breaths, trying to get as much fresh air into his lungs as he could.

"That smell," he said, wrinkling his nose. "And it's clinging to my clothes." He plucked at the breast of his shirt as if that might shake the odor loose. "I thought I was gonna lose my lunch back there."

"Think how it was, closed up in that ambulance," Johnny Lee said, making a face.

"What was that odor?" I asked. "I've never smelled anything like it."

"Who knows?" Rick said. "Crud. Crap. Disease. Take your pick."

"Yeah," Johnny Lee said. "I grew up on a farm, but man is the dirtiest animal I ever saw."

"Careful, JL," Rick said, joking. "You're talking to a reporter. You could wind up in his newspaper sounding like a misanthrope."

"A what?" JL said.

"A bitter cop," Rick said simply.

"Go right ahead and quote me," Johnny Lee said, incredulous that anyone could doubt his homely wisdom. "Ever smell a corpse?"

"Don't talk about it," I said. "My stomach's still reeling from that roller-coaster ride over here." To Rick, I said, "I couldn't take notes anyhow, thanks to you. I'm too queasy to hold a pen."

Rick laughed. "Maybe you ought to do a story on *reporters* and stress."

As we drove Johnny Lee back to his car, left behind at the apartment complex, Rick told him about Connie Phillips.

"Well," Johnny Lee said before getting out of the car, "let's bat it around over a cup of coffee. The radio's quiet; we better go while we can."

"Okay," Rick said, revving the Ford's engine. "Race you to Pete's."

I groaned and he laughed.

"Just kidding, Ben," he said. Then, to Johnny Lee, he said, "Proceed to Pete's — but at a stately pace. Scoop here has an upset tummy."

Chapter Three

THE MAN BEHIND THE COUNTER at Pete's grabbed three cups and began filling them as we came through the door. He slid them in front of us as we stopped at the counter. Rick and Johnny Lee joked with him for a minute, and then Rick said, "We'd better take a booth this time." The man waved a hand that said, "Take your pick." The restaurant, a few blocks up from The Strip on Peachtree, was all but deserted.

Johnny Lee sat beside Rick, the better to stretch his legs, I figured, and I sat facing them. Johnny Lee spoke first, spooning sugar into his coffee. "Find out if she had a boyfriend. Talk to him."

"Yeah," Rick said, sipping his coffee black. "And that girl she was supposed to spend the night with."

"Jane Kimball," I said.

"She might tell you things she wouldn't tell her local police," Rick added. Sipping again, he winced and called out to the counterman, "Hey, what'd you heat this with, a blowtorch?"

The man smiled.

"Meanwhile," Johnny Lee said, "I'll run a check on the parents. You never can tell. Jot down their names and address for me. I grew up with an old boy who works on the Avondale force; he'll do it real quiet-like."

Rick turned to Johnny Lee. "Get him to see if anybody else lit out that day. Avondale Estates is not that big. If you get two missing from there on the same day, you could be on to something." He turned to me. "Next, don't assume that the girl left town. I mean Atlanta. The term 'runaway' can be misleading. We think of runaways as lighting out for parts unknown, but it's human nature to prefer the opposite: in other words, parts known. Your little lost lamb didn't show up at any of her relatives; could be she's right here in the Big 'A'." He tapped on the plate-glass window. "She can get good 'n' lost right out there on the street."

God help her if she is, I thought. To the young and innocent, the streets of Atlanta could be slide boards to Hell.

"Rick's got something there," Johnny Lee said. "That way, she could leave home and still be right next door to mama — just in case."

"Makes sense," I said. "Her folks made her sound too retiring or too unsophisticated, or maybe even too backward, to venture far on her own. Said she was an old-fashioned girl, a real homebody."

Johnny Lee gave me a dubious look. "I wouldn't place too much faith in any parent's description of their own child. It's something to go on — but I wouldn't take it as scripture."

"And she had no money to speak of," I added. "No bank account, no credit card. So how could she get very far even if she did want to leave town? Even hitchhiking costs money. You've got to eat, have a place to stay, food now and then."

Rick gave Johnny Lee a conspiratorial look he meant for me to see. "Let's pretend we didn't hear Ben say that, JL."

"What? Why?"

Johnny Lee laughed. "She's got a moneymaker in her pants, Ben, same as every woman. Where you been all your life?"

I made a wry face. "Not this girl."

"Streets are full of 'em," Johnny Lee said. "And more coming into town each day."

"Which brings us back to the odds," Rick said. "Fact: nine out of ten Georgians are already in Atlanta — Metropolitan Atlanta, anyhow."

"Yeah, and at least half the rest are planning to move here," Johnny Lee said.

Rick laughed and jabbed a thumb toward his partner. "He ought to know. He couldn't wait to get out from behind that mule down in —" He looked at Johnny Lee and squinted. "What's the name of that tank town you're from?"

Johnny Lee smiled. "Claxton." With a show of mock civic pride, he added, "Fruitcake Capital of the World."

Rick looked at me, rolled his eyes, and nodded toward his friend. "They got that right. Anyhow, my contact over in Avondale says they checked the bus stations. Zilch. The town has got no airport, and nobody, least of all a teenager, takes the train anymore. Did she leave on foot? Not likely. Teenagers don't walk either. It's against their religion. Has she got a car? No. That leaves, one, hitchhiking, which would indicate that she did leave town; two, a friend with wheels that we don't know about yet; and, three, MARTA — a city bus or train. That's another thing to check, but easy enough. I'd put my money on Number Two. What do you say, JL?"

"That pretty much hems it in. We could be overlooking something, and probably are, but you gotta start somewhere, and you might as well go with the odds."

"So much for strategy," Rick said, looking at me and leaning forward. "Now let me level with you: Be prepared to go to a lot of trouble for nothing. Most runaways come home on their own, and most do it within two or three days. That's why the police make you wait awhile to file a report on them. True, your girl is still gone after a week. At least we assume she is. For all we know, she could be hugging mom and dad on their front doorsteps right this minute. Next, if she doesn't want to be found, you aren't likely to find her. Most adults who take off leave a trail a blind man could follow: credit cards, driver's license, job history, life insurance — the whole nine yards. Youngsters don't have all that baggage; they can disappear as if they'd stepped into the Twilight Zone, and at least a million a year do disappear. But almost always it's because they want to, for whatever reason. That's what you're up against."

All of this was even worse than I had expected to hear. Talk about a no-win situation. Against my better judgment I heard myself saying, "I'll give it a try. I gave the woman my word."

Rick flashed a big smile. "Good. What time do I pick you up tomorrow?"

"Tomorrow? For what?"

"To go to Avondale. What else?"

"Naw. I can't ask you to do that."

"You didn't."

"No. Not on your day off."

Holding up a finger, he said, "One, it's not my day off. I haven't had a weekend off since I shot off my big mouth about the department — in your newspaper, as I recall, to a reporter who shall remain nameless, but whose initials are Ben Blake. Believe me, the brass know how to deal with dummies like me. I'll still be in a squad car, still working nights and weekends, when they give me my gold-plated watch." He put up another finger. "Two, I can find out more in Avondale in ten minutes than you could in 10 days. What do journalists know about this kind of thing?" He smiled and shook his head. "What do journalists know about anything?"

"I got a friend in rapid transit, so I'll check MARTA for you," Johnny Lee said. I looked at him and he shrugged. "I've got a little girl myself, ten years old."

"All the more reason to stay home on Saturday," I offered.

"I see her every other weekend; this ain't the weekend."

"I'm sorry," I said. He shrugged again and looked away as if he had not come to terms with that loss, and still wasn't ready to.

His marriage, I recalled, had begun to stall a couple of years back. He was about 34 then, only five years on the force, and already the job was tearing his marriage apart.

"My wife and I are like strangers to each other sometimes," he had said.

It was a complaint I had heard from one cop after another as I got to know them. Their divorce papers used antiseptic language like "incompatibility" and "irreconcilable differences," but such words were merely semantic bandages concealing vocational wounds. Cops' wives lived in the normal, workaday world where human meanness cast only an occasional shadow on the inherent goodness of man. Take it all in all, they believed, people were basically good. But the husbands? Day in and day out, the men patrolled a world of moral darkness, seeing man at his worst — petty, dishonest, treacherous, vicious, and sometimes depraved. *Man is basically good? Ha! Now tell me another.* Sure, a marriage could bend without breaking. Marriages everywhere did that. But not many were elastic enough to spring back from completely opposite views of reality.

As if reading my dark thoughts about his partner, Rick said, "All right, that's enough of that. Back to work." He drained his cup and nudged Johnny Lee to get up. "The city lies defenseless in the night, and here we sit. To arms! To arms! Tally ho and all that."

"How do I thank you two?" I said, getting out of the booth.

"Well, you could start," Rick said, "by paying for the coffee."

I reached into my pocket.

Rick laughed and grabbed my arm. "Men in blue don't pay for coffee," he said. "Don't you journalists know anything?"

Johnny Lee laughed, too, and waved goodbye to the counterman as we left.

Chapter Four

JANE KIMBALL WAS HIDING SOMETHING. In 20 years of interviewing people, you develop a sensitivity to that sort of thing. It's in the eyes, the tone of voice, the way they work together. And when they get out of sync, it's as if a pianist, playing along just fine, suddenly struck a wrong note.

"Was Connie into drugs?" We sat in the Kimball living room, she in an easy chair, I on the couch. Her mother was somewhere else in the house, but I could feel her hovering near, within earshot. Rick had dropped me by the house, a neat, modest place on a tree-lined street in Avondale Estates, and would pick me up in half an hour. He had gone to look up his buddy, the Avondale policeman.

"No," the girl said. "If she had been, we wouldn't have been friends."

That had the ring of truth. I moved on. "Did she have a boyfriend?"

"No. Well, there was this guy at school, a junior, she had a crush on, sort of, but he wasn't her boyfriend. She didn't have a boyfriend. Besides, I heard he was gay."

That didn't sound like a promising lead. I changed the subject. "How long have you known Connie?"

"I knew her, to see, in high school, Crosskeys High, but we didn't get to know each other until last year, in college."

"That's Decatur Community College."

"Right."

"Who'd she date?"

"Nobody much. Her parents are very strict. And Connie is — I don't know — funny about boys."

"Funny in what way?"

Jane Kimball made a face and tossed her head. She had a nice face even when it wore a sour expression. Dark hair and eyebrows set off her bright, gray eyes and pale complexion. Her mouth would be pretty too; once she shed the braces, and I had seen when she was standing that she was trim and shapely.

"Well, one minute she'd like a boy, and the next minute she would-n't. She was very shy, and real sensitive about her size. She is big, but it's solid, not fat, and her figure isn't bad either, in my opinion. I told her so again and again. I think she was just afraid of boys, afraid they'd reject her. For that matter, she didn't have many girlfriends either. But I liked her. She was, *is*, a sweet girl."

"Any idea why she'd run away?"

"No," she said, stirring restlessly in her chair. "You know," she added, looking at her lap. "I've already told all this to the police. And, like I said before, I just don't know anything."

I hadn't believed her before and I didn't believe her now. The urgent appeal, characteristic of innocence, just wasn't there. But I let up any-how. "I apologize for putting you through it again, but I have to hear it myself, for the story I'll write." I was bluffing. I wasn't sure I'd write another story about Connie Phillips, wasn't sure there'd be anything to add to the short piece I'd already written. But sometimes people changed their tune once they knew they were talking for publication.

Her eyes darted back to mine, then to the notebook on my lap. "Will I be in it — the story, I mean? Couldn't we just talk and you leave me out of it?"

She was concerned about having her name in the paper, more con-cerned than she wanted me to know. I wondered why. Most people were tickled pink to see their names in the paper, and Jane Kimball didn't strike me as shy and retiring. She knew how to play the demure 18-year-old, but something in her eyes, in her manner, said she was more know-ing than that. I could easily see her, under other circumstances, as a spoiled and demanding little princess.

I shrugged. "The story will say only that you knew nothing about Connie's disappearance, no idea why she'd run away." Actually, at least so far, I wasn't planning to mention Jane Kimball by name at all. If I wrote about it, I could say merely that Connie had told her parents she'd be spending the night with a girlfriend, but that she had not shown up at the friend's home. I could see, however, that Jane Kimball was thinking it all over, so I gave her all the time she needed.

After a few moments, as if straining for a recollection, she said, "There was this boy she was friendly with, sort of. I never understood why. He was fast. Older. Spoiled rich boy. Seemed to know everybody."

"How long ago was this?"

"Uh, just recently," she said.

"You spoke of him in the past tense, as if he were gone." I let it hang there like a question.

She hesitated and then shrugged. "Well, I haven't seen him since school was out. Couple of months." She made it sound like a year. Maybe to a teenager it was. "But Connie mentioned seeing him, mentioned it not long ago."

"Was this the same guy she had a crush on?"

"No. I don't think that guy even knew she was alive."

"Did she ever go out with him — this fast, older guy?"

"I don't think so," she said slowly, dropping her eyes to her lap. Then, raising her head, she added, "She wouldn't have mentioned it to me anyhow. She knew I didn't like him. No, she probably just saw him out and around. He really gets around in that silver Corvette of his. Has friends over here, too, I think."

"He's not from around here?"

"Not Avondale Estates. Decatur."

Decatur, much larger than Avondale Estates, lay just east of Atlanta. "You said older. How much older?"

"About 25, I'd say." She frowned. "He was in college for awhile, DCC, but he dropped out. I don't know what he does now. Probably nothing."

"What's his name?"

She glanced behind her and lowered her voice. "Uh, do you have to say I said?"

"No."

She breathed deeply and said, "Brooks Creighton. Father's a big banker."

I wrote the name in my notebook. "It sounds as if you and Connie didn't share the same friends. Is that about right?"

She blushed and looked down at her lap again. "No, we didn't. She seemed attracted to, well, misfits. No, not that exactly, but to, well, a different crowd. Faster. People who didn't really fit in. Dropouts, trouble-makers — that sort of thing."

"People like Brooks Creighton?"

Her face brightened. "Yeah. Show-offs and such." She turned serious again. "Now understand, she didn't *run* with such people. Or if she did I certainly didn't know it. No way her parents would allow that."

"But she didn't shun these people either."

"Right. That's it."

I thought for a minute about all that. It wasn't much to go on, but it did make sense and showed me a side of Connie that her parents had-n't shown me, probably didn't even know about. I was assuming of course that it was true, but as Johnny Lee had said: You have to start somewhere. Besides, I could see it in my mind's eye: A young girl with strict parents and big inferiority complex feels left out, while people like this Brooks Creighton seem to have the world by the tail and having a great time. Connie Phillips would be attracted to that. Like a child to a toy store. Wouldn't bother her a bit that these people didn't fit in. She didn't fit in either. In fact, all of that made more sense than her friend-ship with Jane Kimball, obviously a very different kind of girl, one whom I was sure fit right in with all those who shut Connie out.

"Why were you and Connie friends?" I asked.

She gave me a startled, quizzical look, so I added, "You don't seem to have had much in common."

She blushed again and appeared flustered. "Well, she's a very sweet person, once you get to know her. And maybe I felt sorry for her. She seemed to have no other friends."

I got up to leave. "Is there anybody besides Creighton you think I should see?"

She got alarmed. "You're going to see him?"

"Well, that's the next logical step," I said gently. She started to speak again, but I knew what was coming.

"He'll never know it was you who mentioned him. You've got my word." My "word" didn't mollify her all that much, but she'd have to settle for that and seemed to know it.

As SOON AS I GOT INTO THE CAR, I knew Rick had something. "Somebody else did light out on that same day," he said, dropping the Trans-Am into drive and pulling away from the curb.

I was sure I knew whom he meant. "Brooks Creighton."

Rick shot me a quizzical look. "Who's he?"

I told him about Jane Kimball and what she'd said.

"No. This was one Clifford Sims. Nineteen. Same school, DCC. No job, no police record. Still missing."

"Circumstances?"

"I talked to his mom. He left while she and her husband were out for the evening. He has no car, but plenty of friends who do have wheels. She said it wasn't unusual for him to spend the night with friends, so she and his dad didn't get concerned until Saturday night rolled around. Sunday morning they called the police. I asked if they knew Connie Phillips. They didn't, and had never heard their son mention her."

"What do you make of it — two disappearances from here on the same day, I mean?"

"Nothing solid." He pulled up late at a stoplight, looked up at it and laughed. "I keep forgetting that I can't drive this Trans-Am like I do a squad car." He turned thoughtful again. "But I've learned to be suspicious of coincidence. Same small town, both teenagers, same day, same school. Uh, uh." He looked at me and said, grinning, "Now, the AEPD sees no connection, but they wouldn't be the first cops I've known who couldn't find their own asses with a flashlight and an Indian guide."

"Me, neither," I said pointedly. He laughed. Then I had an idea. "Find a pay phone," I said. Seconds later we pulled into a Texaco station and up to a phone booth. Only one Brooks Creighton was listed in Decatur. I dropped a coin in the slot and dialed the number.

"Hello." It was the voice of a woman with a garden-club accent.

"May I speak to Brooks?"

"Junior or Senior?"

"Uh, junior."

"He's away for the weekend. May I say who called?"

I muttered a no-thanks and hung up the phone, explaining to Rick when I got back into the car that I'd had a hunch Creighton might be missing too. He knew Connie, probably knew Sims, too, and he had a car.

"He's worth a look-see," Rick said. "We'll pay him a little visit later." He checked his watch and began to pull out of the parking lot. "We've got to make tracks. I told JL we'd meet him at Pete's at one. It's already quarter to."

"Well, what's the next move, aside from chatting with Brooks Creighton, I mean? Any ideas?"

He nodded no and started to pull out of the lot, then threw the Trans-Am into reverse and backed up to the phone booth. "Spend another dime on Jane Kimball," he said. "Ask her if Connie knew Clifford Sims."

Jane Kimball answered the phone. She wasn't happy to hear from me again, but she listened. Her mother must still have been hovering close by, for her answer was almost a whisper. "He was the boy she had the crush on."

She was about to hang up when I thought to ask, "Did Sims know Creighton?"

"I don't know," she said softly. "Creighton seemed to know a lot of people. But I don't know. Now I really have to go." She hung up.

PETE'S WAS CROWDED, but Johnny Lee was waiting in a booth and waved to us as we came in the door. "Everybody's lingering over lunch," he said as we sat down. "Too hot to rush back outside."

"What did Southerners do before air conditioning?" Rick said. He picked up Johnny Lee's ice water, saying, "Mind?" and drank it down without waiting for an answer. Johnny Lee looked at me and rolled his eyes as if to say, "See what I have to put up with."

"Find out anything?" I said.

Johnny Lee nodded. His friend at Metropolitan Atlanta Rapid Transit Authority had helped him find out who was driving the city bus route near Connie's home on the afternoon she disappeared. "I called the driver at home." He frowned. "Came up empty, though. Nobody with a suitcase has ridden his bus in quite a while. Sounded like the kind of guy who'd remember. I also checked the local cab companies. No calls to her address that day. No memory of picking her up elsewhere, either."

We told him what we'd learned in Avondale Estates.

"Two teenagers missing on the same day, and the police over there see no connection?" Johnny Lee said.

"Maybe they do, but just aren't saying," I suggested.

"Possible," Rick said. "But more than likely they just aren't paying attention. I told you, runaways are a low priority in any station house."

Johnny Lee thought it over. "Yeah. And, besides, we're focused on her. To them, it's out of sight, out of mind." He shrugged. "Maybe they eloped, Connie and our boy Sims." He dismissed the idea as quickly as we did. "Naw. They'd be back by now." We exchanged dubious looks all around, and he added, "OK. I'll check it out."

Just then a waitress slid a hamburger and fries in front of Johnny Lee.

"I got hungry," he said. "No breakfast."

"Sounds like you and I eat the same way," I said. "It's the Bachelor's Diet." Rick and I ordered sandwiches, too, and refills on the coffee. "There are days when it's a toss-up whether to go ahead and starve to death or eat another TV dinner."

"Amen," Johnny Lee said. "My wife, or rather my ex-wife, wouldn't appreciate this, but one of the things I miss most about her is her cooking."

"Not me," I said. "I miss the cook."

"What both of you need," Rick said, "is a new outlook." He pointed toward the street. "It's a bachelor's paradise out there. Listen up. Stop living in the past. Get out there and get yourself some sweet young thing. Best therapy in the world for what ails you two. At the very least, they will take your mind off food."

Johnny Lee swallowed slowly while giving Rick a measured look. Then he looked at me and nodded toward Rick. "The voice of experience," he said. "Never married, but knows all about it."

Rick laughed. "I know enough about it to say, 'No way, Jose'."

Johnny Lee brightened. "Well, I'd say no, too, if a Jose asked me."

"He got you that time, Rick."

"Awright, awright," Rick said, nodding, "let's get down to cases here." He snapped his fingers. "But first. Almost forgot. I called the hospital this morning. Our GI bleeder did go into shock, but he's hanging in there. Intensive Care."

"What's the outlook?" I asked.

"'Time will tell' — and that's a hospital quote."

"He really pushed his luck, waiting like that," Johnny Lee said, shaking his head. After a moment, he added, "You say this Sims is a fag? Why would our girl skip out with a fag?"

I corrected him. "The Kimball girl said she *heard* he was gay. She could've heard wrong."

"Yeah, or he might be, but Connie didn't know it," Rick said.

"Well, if he is," Johnny Lee said, "that points straight to Atlanta. Hell, half the fags in the U.S. of A. are here."

"Yeah," Rick added, "and that points to our beat. They all live in Midtown or hang out there."

I knew Midtown. I lived in an apartment not far from there in Virginia-Highlands. Like my neighborhood, Midtown was a residential area of older, gracious homes that was staging a comeback. Young professionals, dubbed "urban pioneers," many of them single, many of them gay, were buying the houses and fixing them up. Regentrification, the process was called.

"Where do they hang out?" I knew of a gay nightclub or two along The Strip, as well as a couple of adult bookstores on Piedmont, stores with tiny cubicles in back for viewing pornographic movies, but that was about the extent of my knowledge of gay Atlanta.

"You doing anything special tonight?" Johnny Lee asked.

"Oh," I said airily, "the usual. After a leisurely dinner and cocktails at the Pleasant Peasant with a stunning twenty-five-year-old blonde, I'll take her dancing at Studebaker's. Then, in the wee hours, after we're bored with Buckhead nightlife, we'll grab a Delta flight to New Orleans for breakfast at Brennan's."

"Sure," he said dryly. "Ride with me awhile tonight. Pick you up at your place around 10, unless I'm on a call, in which case I'll get there soon as I can."

"Meantime," Rick said, "I'll go by headquarters before I go on duty, and get us copies of the reports on Sims and the Phillips girl. Both moved on the wire with photos, and we might as well have 'em. They may be nowhere near Atlanta, but it won't hurt to flash their pictures around and ask."

Chapter Five

JOHNNY LEE CAME BY FOR ME at 10:30 and headed the patrol car toward Piedmont on Monroe. Before reaching Piedmont, however, he turned down a side street that led into Piedmont Park, a large area of several square blocks that lay in downtown Atlanta like a tiny ocean of green. It had tennis courts, ball fields, swings, picnic areas, gazebos, and a lake no longer used for swimming, but nice to look at, to stroll around. In the summer, evening concerts were staged in the park, which was run by the city and highly prized by Atlantans.

"You know Piedmont Park, don't you?" Johnny Lee asked.

"Sure. Used to jog here."

"Ever go here at night?"

"No."

"Then you only think you know Piedmont Park." He crossed a bridge leading into the park and began to cruise its network of roads.

I had thought the park would be deserted, but people were everywhere, appearing out of the night like ghosts as the squad-car's headlights swept across them. Some were walking, some sitting in swings, and some just stood around on the sidewalks. All were male.

Farther into the park were even more young men, and a couple of places seemed downright congested. The sidewalk was crowded. A line of cars, bumper to bumper, glided slowly past, and here and there, at parked cars, figures stood bent over at the driver's window as if engrossed in deep conversation. I hadn't seen anything like it since a wrong turn one night led me to a busy intersection somewhere in the bowels of south Atlanta. Young black toughs were selling drugs on the street corners to buyers flocking there as if to a fire sale at Rich's.

"This is spooky," I said. "Looks like curb service in Hell."

"It's curb service, all right, but it's right here in Hotlanta. Goes on every night right in your nice little neighborhood park. The ones on foot are male prostitutes. The ones in cars, all men, are here..." he hesitated as if uncertain how to put it "to buy their services."

"Look how young they are." Johnny Lee knew I meant the ones on foot, the ones selling.

"Late 'teens, early twenties." He laughed sardonically. "Any older, they can't give it away, at least not here."

"Why doesn't the city do something?"

"Not much we *can* do. To make an arrest, one that'll stick, we have to catch 'em in the act. Or send a plainclothesman out here to get propositioned. But they're too smart for that; like the gals up on The Strip, they let *you* proposition *them*."

Just then, a subtle change came over the activity we were watching. An air of alertness seemed to ripple through the crowd, changing its behavior from uninhibited to reserved.

"They've made us," Johnny Lee said.

"Why do they care?"

"The prostitutes don't, except that we're putting a damper on trade. The guys in the cars are the ones who spook. Most of them are solid citizens. Good job, home in the suburbs, wife and kids. Get hauled in on a homo rap, and all that's down the drain. They don't even want to be *seen* here by anybody straight, especially a cop. And of course, they never know when we're taking down license plates, just for future reference."

The cars ahead of us began to move out. Johnny Lee did too, then swerved over to the curb and stopped. A few feet away, leaning against the frame of a park swing, stood a short, wiry young man. Johnny Lee rolled down his window and motioned for him to come over to the car. "I know this one," he said.

The young man ambled over and stooped to look in the window. He looked a bit older than most of the others I'd seen, 20, maybe 21, and had dark curly hair. He did not speak.

Johnny Lee picked up a clipboard off the seat next to him, moved it to the window, and shined his flashlight on it. "Seen this guy around? Sims is the name. Cliff."

The young man studied the picture on the clipboard. "No. He hasn't been around here."

"Ever see him before?"

The young man looked around, obviously uncomfortable, and shook his head. "No. Never."

"If one like him just hit town, where would he go?"

"He gay?"

"That's the word."

"I don't hang out with fags. You know that."

"You still got eyes and ears."

The young man looked around again. He thought for a moment and said, "Mom's, The Peacock, Hot Grease – hell, there are a dozen places. You know 'em as well as I do. Depends on what he likes."

"Who'd be most likely to know when fresh meat comes to town?" Johnny Lee asked.

"The bartenders at any of those places. I'd start at Mom's first. See Choo-Choo. He's not a bartender. Just hangs out there. But he keeps up."

Johnny Lee started to roll up the window. The young man said, "Hey, don't leave me here. It's one thing to call me over; it's another to show me a picture in front of everybody else." He looked behind him and up and down the walk. "Makes for bad public relations."

Johnny Lee hit a button that unlocked the back doors. "Get in."

"Just to the other side of the park," the young man said. "Thanks."

Johnny Lee dropped him off moments later and headed out of the park, toward Piedmont.

"What did he mean, he doesn't hang out with fags?" I asked.

"All of 'em out here will tell you that. It's the buyer who's queer, they say. Them? They're just businessmen supplying a need."

"Hell of a way to make a living."

"Most of 'em don't. They're just after a little quick pocket money. But some are pros. The guy who just got out swears he's worked his way through Georgia Tech selling pecker in the park. I never checked it out, but I don't doubt it. After being a cop for 10 years, I don't doubt anything — except maybe 'the inherent goodness of man' that my preacher used to talk about."

On Piedmont, Johnny Lee turned at Tenth Street and headed for The Strip. After driving a couple of blocks, however, he turned down a side street, and then onto Selwyn, a dark, narrow street that resembled an alley. "Know where you are?" he asked.

"Just off The Strip." I pointed. "Over that way is West Peachtree. But what's here?"

"This is Fag Row," he said, moving slowly down the street. Young males seemed to be everywhere, either standing in clusters on street corners or walking the sidewalks two-by-two, some holding hands, as if out for a promenade. "It's a meat market here, too, like the park, but nobody here claims he's not gay. They're hard-core."

"Why this street?" It struck me as odd that the center of homosexual activity was one block over from The Strip, where female prostitutes plied their trade. It was interesting, too, that The Strip was so visible and gaudy, a sex circus brightly lit by neon, while Selwyn was tucked away out of sight, dark and relatively subdued.

Johnny Lee pointed to a dimly lit, low-slung building on a corner we were passing. "There's one reason."

It was an adult bookstore that seemed to run under a hill, giving it the appearance of a bunker. A small sign over the doorway said No Exit, and I slowly realized that that was the name of the place. A dark parking lot around back was filled of cars.

A couple of blocks down, on the other side of the street, Johnny Lee pointed to another building, this one on a corner, too. "And that's the other. Upstairs is a restaurant. The real action, though, is in the bar, downstairs. Anything you want, as long as it's not a woman. A bar, a meat market, a dating service and drug store combined. One-stop shopping. K-mart for queers."

A blue, vertical neon sign identified the restaurant as Mom's, the bar as The Peacock. Johnny Lee stopped at the curb near the bar. He picked up his clipboard, pressed the spring at the top, and slid out copies of the missing-person reports on Connie and Sims. "Here," he said. "You'll need these."

I knew what he meant, but I was taken aback. "You're not coming in with me?"

"I'm not dressed for it," he said. "They like lavender, not blue."

I took a deep breath, folded the reports, stuck them in my shirt pocket, and then, remembering that I hadn't yet taken a good look at Clifford Sims' picture, pulled them out again. The picture, apparently a reproduction of a yearbook photo, showed a good-looking kid with dark hair, even teeth, nice eyes, and a dreamy-looking smile in an angular face. I put the reports away again and opened the car door.

"Forgot to tell you," Johnny Lee said abruptly. "Had a pal of mine in APD records do a computer check on marriage licenses — both names, for the whole year to date, in all 25 counties that make up greater Atlanta. No dice."

My shoulders sank. "So the plot thickens," I said.

"Win some, lose some," he said. He nodded toward the door of the Peacock. "I'll give you 30 minutes inside. If I'm not here when you come out, I'm on a call and will get here as soon as I can. If you're uncomfortable standing around here, walk up to The Strip. It's a better show, anyhow."

I got out.

"Ask for Choo-Choo," he said.

I closed the door and he drove away.

Chapter Six

THE PEACOCK, WITH ITS LOW CEILING and wooden beams overhead, looked like a cellar, and I realized it once must have been just that. The entrance, on Selwyn, was one story lower than the entrance to the restaurant, which was around the corner, on higher ground, and the whole building looked as if it had once been a fine private home.

The place was packed. Larger than it appeared from outside, the room had lots of little nooks off the main room, and all of them contained tables too small for the number of customers crowded around them. The bar was crowded, too, and it was a big one, a massive wooden rectangle in the middle of the room. The air was heavy with the sour smell of marijuana, and a thick layer of smoke wafted lazily among the rafters.

I felt conspicuous even to be in there, and seeing no place to sit made it worse. But I soon noticed that nobody was paying attention to me, and a moment later a stool came vacant at the bar. I took it and ordered a Michelob Light.

I sat there for some time sipping beer and looking straight ahead at a post about six feet away. Eye-contact might give somebody the wrong idea, I figured. Slowly, though, I loosened up a bit and began to look at others seated at the bar. Nearly everybody in the place looked young, no older than 25 or 30, but then I saw a gray-haired man at one end of the bar, and felt better. He looked older than I and just as out of place —

maybe more, for he wore a suit and tie — but he seemed perfectly at ease, which was more than I could say for myself. I hadn't wanted anybody to approach me, at least not to proposition me, but after awhile I felt perversely disappointed that nobody had. Was I that homely? Was I that old? Hell, 41 wasn't so old, was it? Not two minutes later, a man moved up to the bar and stood at my side, sipping from a glass in his hand.

"How are you tonight?" he asked.

"Fine. You?" I turned and gave him the once-over. He stood about five feet eight inches and looked fleshy, as if he might be fighting a weight problem. He wasn't fat yet, but he wasn't missing any meals either. The boyish look was starting to go, too. The face sagged a bit here and there, and the hair, blond, was thinning. I pegged his age at 35 and counting, a little old for the crowd I saw around me.

"Fine. You come here often?"

I saw in his eyes that he already knew the answer. "First time," I said.

He grinned. "Well, there's a first time for everything, they say."

I hoped I wasn't staring, but the more he spoke, the more I noticed something peculiar about him. He vibrated when he talked. I had thought at first that he was simply ill at ease, shuffling about to get comfortable with himself. Now I saw it was more than that, connected somehow with speech. Before, during and after speaking, he shook like a gasoline engine missing on a couple of cylinders. He caught me studying him and said, "I'm nervous. I think I have a nervous disorder." He laughed and stuck out his hand. "They call me Choo-Choo." I started to speak, but he went on. "What do you do?"

"I write."

He giggled. "No. In the bedroom?"

"Lately I sleep."

He thought that one over. "Well, what do you like to do? What turns you on?" He put his hand on my thigh.

"Not that," I said.

He looked confused. "You're not gay?"

"Only moderately happy."

He removed his hand and looked at me more closely. "You're not a cop," he said, shaking his head.

"Reporter."

That took him by surprise, but once he adjusted to it he said, vibrating hard now, "Boy, have I got a story for you! My life! Where can we talk?"

"Maybe later," I said. "I'm looking for somebody."

He put his hand over his heart, and smiled wanly, "Aren't we all?"

I reached into my shirt pocket and pulled out the reports. Unfolding them, I showed him the picture of Sims. "He's a runaway," I said.

Choo-Choo looked askance at me.

"Him, I don't care about," I lied, pointing to Sims' picture. "But it's believed he was traveling with somebody I do care about." I showed him the picture of Connie. He still seemed to be thinking me over, so I added, "Sims is said to be gay, and there's reason to believe he came to Atlanta. A guy in Piedmont Park told me to check with you. He said you'd know somebody new in town if anybody did."

Choo-Choo looked up at me through lidded eyes. "No fuzz?"

I told a half-truth. "The police don't give a damn about runaways. That's why I'm out here looking."

He checked his glass, now empty. "Buy me a drink?"

"Name it."

He signaled the bartender, held his glass aloft to show it was empty, and turned back to me. "I've seen the guy."

A tiny shock rippled through me, but I hid it. "Don't blow smoke," I said. "The last thing I need is a bum steer."

"Look," he said, "If I wanted to lie, I could do a better job than that. No. This is the truth. He was in here..." I held my breath. "Two nights ago. Thursday."

"You're sure?"

"Look, there are two things I never forget; one is a face."

I could guess what the other was. "And you're sure it was Thursday?"

"Yeah. I stayed sober on Thursday. Bad hangover. Mixed beer and wine. I don't stay sober many days. It was Thursday."

"Was he with anybody?"

"That, I don't know. I was in and out, mostly out. I saw him come in. I saw him leave. He didn't stay long."

I pointed to the bartender, headed our way with a drink. "Was he on duty that night?"

"Yeah." As the bartender put his drink in front of him, Choo-Choo grabbed the report and showed it to him. "Charles, remember this kid? He was in here Thursday."

The bartender studied the photograph. "Can't say I do. He's new to me. They come; they go." He shrugged, handed back the report, took my money for the drink, and started to turn away.

Quickly I showed him Connie's picture. "How about her?"

He gave me a dubious smile. "Come on." He left.

"Charles wouldn't notice his leg was missing until he wound up with one shoe too many," Choo-Choo said. "Take my word for it: He was here." He pointed to the picture of Sims. "The guy in the park steered you right."

"Where would a kid like Sims, new in town, be likely to stay?"

"Kid like that? Ha! I can think of a thousand beds that would open to him like that," he said with a snap of his fingers, "including mine."

I thanked him and left.

Johnny Lee was waiting at the curb for me.

Chapter Seven

"I WAS BEGINNING TO THINK YOU LIKED IT IN THERE," Johnny Lee said, smiling, as I got into the squad car.

"No. But they were telling me such interesting stories about you that I lost track of the time. I never would have guessed, JL, but your secret is safe with me."

He laughed. "Do any good in there?"

"I didn't hit pay dirt, but I struck a vein." I told him what Choo-Choo had said, but before he could react, the police radio crackled with a message that got his complete attention. Next thing I knew, the patrol car's tires were squalling, the siren was blaring, and I was thrown back against the seat as the car shot forward.

"Buckle up, Ben!"

It was impossible to buckle up. I had the strap in my hand, but every time I got the hook near the latch, Johnny Lee swerved or turned or skidded, hitting first the brakes and then the gas, so that I lurched about like a drunk riding a camel. I gave up and resorted to prayer.

Luckily it was a short ride. After laying rubber up Selwyn, Johnny Lee barreled up 10th Street, hooked a right on Peachtree, and screeched to a halt in front of a bar that looked like no more than a hole in the wall. Pink and white letters on its one large window said: The Pink Pussycat — Nude Dancers. Continuous Show. No Cover.

"Better stay here," Johnny Lee barked, jumping from the car. He raced toward the bar, pulling out his nightstick as he ran.

To hell with that, I thought, and jumped out myself. A knot of people stood on the sidewalk, some peering in through the door, others with their faces pressed to the bar's plate-glass window. The crowd at the door parted like the Red Sea before Moses as Johnny Lee pushed through them. I followed before they closed ranks again, stopping just inside the door, a few feet behind Johnny Lee, who had been brought to a halt by a raised, cautionary hand held out by Rick.

"Take the door, JL," Rick said, not looking around.

Johnny Lee moved back a bit and over, so he could watch the door and the action at the same time.

Beyond Rick stood another cop, tall and wiry, who obviously had been fighting. His shirt was ripped open in back and he breathed heavily, audibly. Beyond him, cornered, crouched, looking the worse for wear, stood his opponent, watching, waiting, breathing hard himself. The bar was dark except for some colored lights on a small, crude stage at the rear and a dim light or two on the walls. As I watched, the man moved ever so slightly, and a tiny, cold, blue light flashed near his right hand. He held a knife.

For a long minute all of us stood there like figures in a wax museum. I thought we were the only ones in the place until I saw movement behind the bar. A man, the bartender, I guessed, crouched low there, showing only his head.

Finally Rick spoke to the cornered man. Pointing toward Johnny Lee, he said, "Reinforcements. And there are more where he came from. You can't get away. Give it up."

The man, short but muscular, began to sway from side to side. He looked as menacing as a cobra, "Come and get me, copper; come and get me." It was comical, like dialogue from an old cops'n'robbers film. He had it down pat, I thought, even to the malevolent grin, and the jaunty fuck-you toss of the head and thrust of the chin.

Rick said over his shoulder to Johnny Lee, "A regular Jimmy Cagney we got here." He looked back at the man and sighed hugely. "OK. I tried. Just remember, you asked for it."

That seemed to throw the man. He stopped swaying and lost the grin.

Rick turned to Johnny Lee. "Captain," he said loudly, "you see what we're up against here. Request permission to fire."

"Permission granted," Johnny Lee snapped. "Carry on."

Rick turned to the other cop. "Officer Riley," he commanded, "shoot the bastard."

The cornered man straightened and stood stock still, his eyes darting from one policeman to the next. He looked worried and suddenly uncertain of himself.

Riley, too close to the man, to the knife, to turn away, seemed slow to catch on, but he recovered nicely. "Shoot to kill, sir, or just to maim?"

Rick let the question hang there for one or two beats and then said decisively, "We've wasted enough time on this punk. Blow his ass to kingdom come." Then he turned smartly and walked toward the front door. As he did, Riley shifted the nightstick to his left hand and slapped with his right at his holster.

"Wait!" the man cried. "I surrender."

I heard the knife drop to the floor and felt the tension in the room snap when it hit.

"You wouldn't shoot an unarmed man, would you?" he said. "I give up. Look! See! I give up." He stumbled forward, toward Riley, arms extended, ready for the cuffs, eager for the cuffs. "You got me. Lock me up. I'll go quietly."

In one motion, Riley kicked the knife across the room and cuffed the man's hands behind his back. Seconds later, the guy was leaning over the stage, legs spread wide apart, captive and harmless.

Rick walked over to Johnny Lee and me. He rolled his eyes and said, "Whew!"

Johnny Lee laughed. "Thanks for the promotion. I must be the first cop anywhere to jump from private to captain in one evening."

"You deserve it," Rick said. "It was a standoff until you got here. I thought we really were gonna have to shoot him."

"What was his problem?" I asked as two more cops came in to take the man away. I looked out the door and saw the wagon waiting.

"I don't know," Rick said. "I got here late, tied up on a fender-bender. I was just passing by, saw Tom's car at the curb and a crowd on the side-walk, and thought I'd better have a look. I come through the door, and there's Tom dancing around the room with this goon. The guy sees me and pulls a blade, so there we stand. You know the rest."

"Maybe he thought you wanted to cut in on his dance," Johnny Lee drawled.

Riley walked up. "Speaking of cutting," he said, "take a gander at this." He held the man's knife in front of us, by the point, its six-inch switchblade glinting in the light.

The bartender, a hulking man who looked like muscle gone to flab, came over for a look. "I hope they stick it up his ass in court," he said, and walked away.

The three cops exchanged knowing looks. "Where's he been?" Riley said, nodding toward the bartender. "We don't stick it to criminals anymore. He hasn't been paying attention."

"He believes in the System," Rick said. "Been watching too much television."

"Yeah, I watch it myself," Riley said. "It's the only place left where crime doesn't pay."

A policeman appeared at Riley's side holding open a small, clear plastic bag. Riley dropped the knife into the bag, and the policeman left. Johnny Lee introduced me to Tom Riley as a friend and reporter. "Doing a story on cops and stress," he explained.

"Reporter?" Riley pointed toward the door. "There goes a story for you. He'll be back on the street before I get the paperwork done on this incident. Then he'll come to court next week yellin' police brutality, and then I," he punched himself hard in the chest with an emphatic forefinger, "will probably have to explain why I dared to lay my hands on this pillar of the community. The worst, the worst that will happen to him: The judge will fine him for drunk and disorderly, give him a suspended sentence for carrying the pigsticker, and he'll walk! Me? I'm in court on my own time, right? No time off for that, and no pay. I'll get a lecture on proper arrest procedure and the rights of criminals, and I'll be lucky — lucky! — if I'm not called before the board for hitting the sonofabitch. They'll probably make me polish and sharpen the bastard's knife and give it back to him with an apology."

Rick and Johnny Lee nodded as if to say they'd both been there many times.

"What did happen?" Johnny Lee asked.

"Yeah," Rick said. "I'll be in court with you; I need to know."

"Bartender said the yo-yo was sitting down front there, by the stage, and showing off for his buddies. Got louder and louder, started reaching for the dancers' legs, tryin' to trip 'em or play grab-ass — he couldn't tell which. Bartender called the police. When I got here the guy was up on the stage, had one of the girls pinned, and two or three men were tryin' to pull him off. When I went for him he took a swing, grabbed me, and away we went, do-si-do. Dumb fucker. I never dreamed he was carryin'. I could be layin' here now with a bellyful of steel." He looked at me, eyes wide, chin set. "How's that for stress? Jesus!" He shuddered, then whirled and walked away.

I turned to Rick. "And I thought you were intense."

"He is wound tight, but some of that is an adrenaline high. He'll stay pumped up for a hour or so, and then be okay." Rick moved toward the door, and we followed. "I ain't exactly placid myself," he said, looking around with a disapproving eye. "Let's shake this place, this palace of fun and merriment, this bastion of free enterprise."

"You're more right than you realize," I said, pointing to a blue sticker on the glass of the door. It said: Member, Chamber of Commerce.

Rick looked and snorted. "I'm surprised we don't see them on the asses of whores."

"You don't," said Johnny Lee, laughing, "because that ain't free enterprise."

FIVE MINUTES LATER, THE TWO SQUAD CARS sat side by side, noses facing Peachtree Street, in a darkened parking lot at the lower end of The Strip. It was about half past midnight, and the pace of activity on the street had slowed a bit. Not much, but a bit. We stood between the cars, drinking Cokes from paper cups, and talking.

"So it looks like Sims is gay," Rick said. He had gulped down his Coke and was now chewing on the ice. The heat wave was still with us, and again the night brought little relief. "Where does that leave us with Connie? I've been flashing her picture all night, with no takers."

"Maybe they didn't leave together," Johnny Lee said. "Or maybe they left together but later split up."

"Trouble with that," Rick said, "is you can 'maybe' yourself silly and get nowhere."

Johnny Lee sighed. "You're right. Let's stick with the probable. That's what got us the lead on Sims."

"Yeah," I said, "but what's the probable now?"

"Let's just wing it here for a minute or two," Rick said. "A girl has a crush on a boy. They disappear from the same town on the same day. Conclusion: they lit out together. Six days later the boy shows up on Fag Row. Conclusion: the girl is somewhere nearby."

"But Jane Kimball didn't think that Sims and Connie had a relationship of any kind," I said.

"Right," Rick said. "But you felt she wasn't leveling with you. What was she holding back?"

We all looked at each other and drew blanks.

"Something's missing here," Rick said. "If mama's right about her little girl, what's a girl like Connie doing with a guy who knows his way around Atlanta's gay community?"

"Either mama's wrong," Johnny Lee said, draining the last of his Coke, "or Connie was misled. Hell, maybe the guy goes both ways."

"Either way," I said, "it points to sex. And in Atlanta, sex points to The Strip. Sims has already shown up here, so we must be on the right track."

"Don't be so sure," Johnny Lee said. "Suppose she ran off with him, thinking it was true love, but then found out he was gay. They split up, he heads for Fag Row, she heads for parts unknown."

Rick shook his head. "That's back to the Maybe Game, and that's the second time you've seemed to believe they split up. What's on your mind?"

"Well, I haven't thought it out. But The Peacock and girls just don't go together. Maybe that's it. Sims wasn't out in Piedmont Park selling cock for some quick money — at least as far as we know. Now, that would have made sense to me. But no, he was at The Peacock. Fag Central. He's hardcore."

Rick mulled that over. "He walked in; he walked out. Could've been looking for somebody."

"No. Johnny Lee's got a point," I said. "Even that, somebody would've been hardcore."

"Your friend Choo-Choo had never seen him before," Rick said. "How hardcore could that be?"

That was a good point, too. We stood there stumped.

After a moment, I said, "Maybe you're both coming at the truth, but from opposite directions. Maybe the guy is bisexual. But from what I've read, those who swing both ways actually prefer their own sex. That could explain how he could fool Connie but still gravitate to a place like The Peacock. If he were an out-and-out fag, and Connie did have a crush on him, I figure she would have found out by now that Sims preferred boys, and run back home to mama with a broken heart."

Rick nodded and Johnny Lee said, "Makes sense — if he was her only reason for running off. But where does that leave us?"

"Right where we are," I said, "looking for Connie Phillips and Clifford Sims somewhere around The Strip."

"Then let's saddle up," Rick said, crushing his paper cup. "Catch," he said, flipping it to me.

Reflexively I caught it, and would have thrown it at him, but when I looked up, he was already in his car, starting the engine, window up, a big grin on his face. I shook my head and got into the car with Johnny Lee.

He headed toward Selwyn Street, Fag Row, again.

Chapter Eight

OLD-ENGLISH LETTERING OVER THE DOOR of the No Exit said: "Abandon hope, all ye who enter here." Johnny Lee looked at it, then at me, and then opened the door and entered.

It was like entering a dungeon. The only light in the small lobby came from a tiny shaded lamp atop a cash register behind a counter, and from two pinball machines against the inner wall. The counter, all glass, contained sexual merchandise of every description: dildos, handcuffs, riding crops, whips, harnesses, cock rings, vibrators, pornographic movies.

Behind the counter, on a wooden stool, sat a scruffy-looking man who could have been a young 40 or an old 30. I couldn't tell which, and the poor lighting didn't help me, or him. His eyes widened and his mouth fell open as Johnny Lee walked through the door, but he seemed unable to manage speech.

Johnny Lee put the picture of Sims in front of him, on the counter top. "Ever see this guy before?"

The man started shaking his head no before he even heard the question. Johnny Lee saw it too. In a tone of voice that meant business, Johnny Lee said, "Listen, fellow: That's not the way it works. Look at it first, and *then* answer."

This time the man made a big show of studying the picture and puzzling over it, but finally he said, "No."

"What about this one?" Johnny Lee showed him the picture of Connie. This time the no came more quickly.

"Mind if I ask around?" Johnny Lee said, scooping up the reports.

Confused, the man nodded both no and yes, but Johnny Lee had not waited for an answer. He walked toward an opening into another room, and I went with him.

Black lighting cast an eerie glow in the room, but once my eyes adjusted to it I saw that it was a sort of lounge. It held a Coke machine, two or three video games, a display case filled with more sexual gadgets, another pinball machine, and a couple of straight-back chairs. Posters touting homosexual films decorated the walls, and a curtain closed off the room's only other door.

The room was crowded with young men, but they gave us wide berth and made it clear when we approached them that we might as well be asking for ice water in Hell. Most of them gave the pictures only a cursory glance before nodding and turning away. In fact, our visit was shaping up as a big waste of time until a tall, skinny, young man swept through the curtain, throwing it aside with flair. He stopped dead in his tracks when he spotted Johnny Lee. Suddenly he beamed and clapped his hands.

"Lawsy mercy! Is this a raid?" Holding out his arms, wrists together, hands hanging limply, he pranced up to Johnny Lee and said, "Take me. Beat me. I love police brutality." He looked Johnny Lee up and down. "And ain't you good-lookin'? And so *tall!*" He made a big show of batting his eyelids. "I just love a man in uniform."

Johnny Lee stared at the young man as if he had two heads. Others in the room tittered and gathered around as the young man extended his right hand. "I'm Billy Townsend, but you can call me Scarlett. Call me anything; just call me: 269-6969."

Johnny Lee, still staring, shook the hand, and the comical young man went on, sashaying this way and that as he spoke in a surprisingly rich baritone. "Oh, I see! You, suh, must be a Yankee scout. Is Atlanta burning? God knows, I am. You give me such a fever, ah cain't tell." Dramatically he flung a forearm over his brow, looked up at Johnny Lee and batted his eyes again. "Have your troops reached the old home-place yet? I'd do anything, you know, to save Tara." He faked a semi-swoon and the crowd around him laughed and applauded.

In spite of himself Johnny Lee laughed, too, then showed Townsend the picture of Sims.

A natural clown, Townsend dismissed the picture with a disdainful flick of his fingers. "Oh, that ol' thing," he said. "Why do you need him when you've got me?" He pointed to the photograph. "He's the original good time that was had by all. He's had more pricks than a pincushion." He feigned an exaggerated modesty. "I, on the other hand, am unspoiled goods just waiting to be claimed. Your claim check, please."

It was obvious that he'd never laid eyes on Sims before. Johnny Lee showed him the picture of Connie.

"First a boy, then a girl?" Townsend gave Johnny Lee a broad, dubious look. "Make up your mind, suh." Then, dropping the act, he said, "Runaway?"

"Both of 'em," Johnny Lee said.

Townsend addressed the group around him. "Any of you queens ever seen these two lovely children?" They crowded around for another look, but they still said no.

"Give me those," Townsend said, taking the reports from Johnny Lee. "Come with me." He turned and walked toward the curtained door.

Behind the curtain was a dark, narrow hallway of many doors, and beyond that another hallway of doors, and beyond that still another. Most of the doors were closed, but a few stood open, leading into tiny cubicles. A musty, unpleasant odor hung in the air. The odor seemed strongest at the open doors, and I wondered if it were the smell of semen. The hallways seemed filled with people, some standing, some moving about, but the perception was more sensory than visual. The only illumination came from strobe lights, and often I felt someone near me before the flickering light gave me a fleeting glimpse of him. It was frustrating and a bit spooky. One second the flashing light might reveal somebody in full stride; next second he was gone. It was like watching a worn black-and-white movie lurch from frame to frame.

But Townsend either had better night vision than I or he knew this maze like a blind man knows his bedroom. He kept stopping at figures I hadn't even sensed, let alone seen, and showing them the photographs. Johnny Lee's flashlight flicked on and off so often that it looked as if a giant firefly were lumbering through the maze. But we didn't do any better back there than we had out front. Nobody knew Sims or Connie.

Out front again, we thanked Townsend for his help and left.

When we were rolling again, Johnny Lee said, "Damn strange to me that nobody's seen this Sims kid. You reckon your friend Choo-Choo was leveling with you?"

"I'd bet on it."

"Okay. Then I'm looking at this thing the wrong way. Those little twits back there are just out on a Saturday night having fun: dating, looking for dates, doing whatever those people do when they're footloose and fancy free. Sims is simply not one of 'em."

"I see what you mean. He's also not one of the Piedmont Park element. Question is: What the hell is he?"

Johnny Lee thought for a minute. "He's either so new on the gay scene that he isn't well-known yet. Or, since he lived right here in Metropolitan Atlanta, he's got connections. And if that's the case, there's no reason for him to be out on the street. So he pops up at The Peacock. So what? It's like Rick said: He was looking for somebody. What do you think?"

"Well, you could be wrong, of course, but I think that's a nice piece of deduction. Where else is there to look?"

We were back on Peachtree now, moving north out of The Strip, just cruising.

"Oh, all of that is just the most obvious part of gay Atlanta." Johnny Lee waved a hand to indicate the part of town we were leaving behind. "We haven't, for instance, checked the restaurants. Half the restaurants in this city are owned and operated by gays, and damn near every waiter is gay."

I nodded. You couldn't eat out three times in Atlanta before catching on to that.

"There are more gay bars, too."

"Yippy doo," I said wearily.

Johnny Lee laughed. "How about some coffee? Pep you up, and we can match notes with Rick, too."

"Nothing but sleep's going to pep me up. I've got to go in in the morning and write my story. How 'bout dropping me by my place?"

Minutes later I was home in bed. Nobody had to rock me to sleep.

Chapter Nine

SUNDAY MORNING, I GOT TO THE NEWSROOM around 10 p.m. and phoned the Phillips residence first thing. No answer. Church, I guessed. I went to work on my story. The newsroom was nearly deserted — the Sunday crew wouldn't start drifting in until around noon — so I was able to work with no interruptions, no distractions.

I finished the story in an hour or so and stored it in the computer system, and then I tried calling the Phillips residence again.

Mrs. Phillips answered the phone. Connie was still missing, she said, starting to cry, but she took heart in hearing that the feature story and photograph were scheduled to appear in the next morning's newspaper. "Somebody must have seen my little girl," she sobbed. "Maybe this will make them come forward."

I didn't tell her about Rick and Johnny Lee or about looking for Connie on The Strip — none of that. On one hand, it might raise false hope and, on the other, it might just give her something else to worry about. I assured her I was still looking, and let it go at that. Yes, I told her, I had interviewed Jane Kimball, but hadn't come away with much to go on. I also ran the names of Clifford Sims and Brooks Creighton by her, asking if Connie had ever mentioned them or if she herself knew them. I said they were merely names people had tossed out as possible acquaintances of Connie. I was bending the truth — *but not by much*, I reminded myself wryly.

No, she had never heard of either young man, she said through her sniffles, and soon she thanked me and hung up.

"What was that all about?"

I looked up to see Owens, my boss, hovering over my desk.

"That was the missing girl's mother," I said. "The girl's still missing." I pointed at the computer. "Story's in the system, ready to go."

"Any leads on the girl?"

I told him about Rick and Johnny Lee, and about our efforts so far. "The signs point to Atlanta," I said. "She might have taken off with a young fellow she knew in school. He's missing, too, and there's reason to believe he surfaced in town, on The Strip."

Owens looked pleasantly surprised, "Do tell." He smelled a good story right in his own backyard. Then a cloud darkened his face. "You don't suppose they eloped, do you?"

"We checked," I said. "No license anywhere around here. Besides, they've been gone too long for that, I think. Most elopers can't wait to spread the news after the knot is tied."

"So what do you think?"

I shrugged. "We're operating on the theory — more of a hypothesis, really — that they left together. We could be wrong, but there's not much else to go on."

"I see what you mean. Well, keep looking. And keep me posted."

He turned to walk out into the newsroom, and, as I watched his retreating back, I saw her. She was the first woman who had caught my eye — really caught it — in a long, long time. A tall, slender brunette, she was out in the newsroom, standing by a computer terminal at the copy desk, putting down her purse as if she had just come in to work. I'd never seen her before. She wore a black sleeveless blouse, open at the throat. The blouse and her dark hair set off her face as if it were a cameo. A long, white skirt made her look lithe, but best of all was the way she moved. It was graceful, refined, and yet more athletic than fragile. A curious combination, I thought, but devastatingly feminine. I decided I wasn't in a hurry to leave after all.

I went out into the newsroom and over to the copy desk. The brunette had walked away, but her purse was still there, so I sat down at the computer terminal next to her purse, got my story back on the screen, and pretended I was working. As she returned and sat down at my right, James McGregor, a copy editor just coming in to work, stopped at the terminal to my left. In a teasing voice, he said, "Well, I see it didn't take you two long to get to know each other."

I looked at her, she looked at me, and we both looked at James. "I just got here," the woman said.

I said I had, too, so James, putting down the briefcase he used as a sort of upscale dinner pail, introduced us. Her name was Morgan Matthews and this was her first day on the job. She flashed me a shy but dazzling smile, and soon we were chatting away.

She was married, but separated and getting a divorce. Short marriage. Less than two years. No children. She was from Columbia, South Carolina, but had been working in Atlanta for a couple of years as a reporter for one of the small, community newspapers. All that time, she had been trying to land a job at *The Phoenix*, and had finally succeeded.

"You like being a copy editor?" I asked. She didn't seem the type. In the first place, nearly all our copy editors were male. But beyond that, she seemed too vivacious for such a sedentary job, one that, to me, looked tedious and seemed to attract people who were quiet and retiring.

"It's a foot in the door," she said. "I'm a reporter at heart." There was that dazzling smile again. "I'll just bide my time."

Morgan was easy to talk to, and soon I was telling her about the story I was working on, and the search to find Connie and Sims. It finally dawned on me, though, that I was keeping her from work, so I offered to resume the story over supper that night. She accepted. I left the news building feeling things I hadn't felt in a long time, in places inside me that I hadn't heard from in a long time.

By 6 p.m., when Morgan met me in the lobby of the news building, I was feeling as anxious as a teenager on a first date. We walked over to the Omni, a couple of blocks away, looking for a place to eat, and wound up ordering sandwiches in a delicatessen. I hardly touched mine and she ate only half of hers. Something was going on between us that made food seem unimportant. It also made the supper hour fly by. Still, I learned a little about her and told her a bit about myself.

Her marriage, at 25, to a college sweetheart, had lasted only 18 months, most of it in Atlanta, where he had pursued a master's degree in engineering at Georgia Tech while she worked. He now lived in Savannah, wanted to marry again, and so finally, they were getting a divorce. She lived in Virginia-Highland in a duplex not far from my apartment. Following a recent romance that sounded as if it had just sort of fizzled, she wasn't seeing anyone special.

My story was simpler. Born and raised in Augusta, Georgia, a small city on the Savannah River, I had attended the University of Georgia, married my college sweetheart right after graduation, and gone to work as a reporter for *The Phoenix*. I loved Atlanta, liked my job, loved my wife, and the years had slipped by so quietly I scarcely noticed their coming and going. Then one Friday evening in September, after Joanna and I had been married 18 years, she was killed in an auto accident while on the way to visit her mother in south Georgia. Ever since, for nearly two years, I had felt only half alive, myself.

"No children?" Morgan said.

"Joanna couldn't have children. I got used to the idea, but I don't think she ever did."

"Are you over it yet? Losing her, I mean."

I wasn't. I didn't know if I would ever be. But this wasn't the time or place to go into that. I looked at her and said, "I began to feel much better today around noon." A slight blush bloomed on her cheeks and a smile played around her dark, dark eyes.

She caught me watching her, and blushed more deeply. "I have to get back," she said, sliding out of the booth.

When we reached the news building, I waited with her at the elevators while trying to work up the courage to ask her for a date. Finally I said, "Gee, I never did finish telling you about the search for Connie Phillips."

She smiled. "Tell me later. I am interested."

As I heard the elevator approaching, I blurted out, "Look, I'm a good bit older than you—"

"So?"

"—and it's been more than 20 years since I asked anybody for a date—"

"Yes."

"—but I was wondering if, uh, you might, uh—"

"Yes."

"—like to go out. That is, uh—"

She looked at me and smiled as the elevator doors slid open. "I said yes."

It was my turn to blush. I'd been struggling so hard to phrase a simple request that I hadn't heard her answer. "As you can see, I'm out of practice." I smiled. "Maybe I never was any good at this."

"When?" she said, stepping onto the elevator.

"Years ago. In high school, college."

She laughed and pressed the elevator button. "No. I meant when do you want to go out?"

I groaned. "Sorry." The doors began to close. "Uh, Friday," I said quickly.

"Good," she said. Then, just before the doors hid her from view, she added, "Tell me tomorrow what time."

I said I would, but I found myself talking to steel doors, and knew she hadn't heard me. Not that it mattered; I would see her tomorrow. But I went away shaking my head over my awkward performance and wondering if Morgan thought I was a hopeless case. I felt happy, though, happier than I had felt in a long, long time. I drove home humming and smiling, and went to sleep for the first time in years with a woman on my mind who was not Joanna.

MY STORY IN MONDAY'S *PHOENIX* brought me several compliments and many expressions of concern, but not a single lead on Connie Phillips. That was unusual, almost eerie. There were nearly 2 million readers out there in greater Atlanta, and as a rule everything *The Phoenix* published, be it a classified ad or a one-inch filler buried on page 48-Z, got a rise out of somebody. All I got were the usual kook calls, the kind that plague every newsroom in the country, especially when a mystery is publicized. People think, or at least say, they saw the missing person only recently, and the "sightings" usually range from Raleigh, North Carolina, to Rangoon, Burma. Maybe such people are just trying to be helpful, but most of them sound as if their horizontal hold is on the blink. I put them in the same category as those poor souls who have a tendency to spot flying saucers. One man called to say he had "positively" seen Connie Phillips sitting on a park bench "only last month" in Mexico City.

Read the story again, I told him. That would have been June. She didn't leave home until July.

Another man phoned to say he was "dead certain" that a hitch-hiker he had picked up "Saturday a week ago" on Interstate 20 east, just outside of Atlanta, was Connie Phillips. Dropped her off in Augusta, he said.

But the girl he described, "a tall and skinny redhead with a tattoo of a rose on her left arm," fit Connie's description about as closely as I did — and I was six feet tall, weighed 180, and had blue eyes and brown hair that was turning silver at the temples.

Still another guy called to say, "You can quit looking. Connie Phillips is now my wife. Ran off to marry me. And we don't want nobody to know where we are."

"Look," I lied, "our only concern is that she's diabetic and might not be getting her insulin shots as she should. She has a tendency to forget to take 'em, you know."

"Why, of course, I know. I'm her husband, ain't I? Well, you listen up: I personally give her those shots every day. Got that? Now you leave her alone. She don't want her name splashed all over your newspaper, and I don't either."

Sure, such calls were a waste of time, but they didn't bother me much. What bothered me was the call that hadn't come, the one from somebody who actually knew something, or a call from Connie, herself. If she did no more than call to say she was all right, her mother would be tremendously relieved, and I could call off the search. But no such call came to me, and when I checked with Mrs. Phillips around 5 p.m., none had come to her either.

"She's dead," Mrs. Phillips said, crying again. "I just know it. My little girl is dead. If she was alive she'd call her mother, 'specially after seeing that story."

It was possible, I said, that Connie hadn't seen the story yet, and that was true. But I said it mainly to boost Mrs. Phillips' spirits as she sat at home waiting for Connie to call. No matter what she said, I knew she wouldn't stray far from her phone. Hope for a child dies hard in the mother. She thanked me for the story, and hung up.

I was now alone in the features department. Five o'clock usually emptied the place as if a fire alarm had sounded. I considered leaving, too, but decided to take advantage of the quiet to sit there and mull things over. It just didn't make sense that nobody had come forth with a solid lead. You simply couldn't move around a city of two million people without being seen, noticed, remembered.

Maybe we were looking in the wrong place. Maybe the girl had hit the road to God-only-knew-where. But you couldn't even do that without being seen, could you? Besides, all the escape routes had been checked about as well as it could be done.

Okay, maybe she was dead. Maybe she was right there in Atlanta, but lying in a grave somewhere. She wouldn't be the first person found in a shallow grave right there in the city. In fact, if somebody had murdered her, she'd be lucky to be in any kind of grave. Bodies turned up in Atlanta at about the rate of one a day, and most were left lying where they fell, or dumped like so much rubbish in an alley or in a ditch by the side of a road. I was shaking my head when the phone rang. *Could this be it?* I wondered.

It was Rick. "Good story. Do any good?"

"Not so far."

"Well, it's still early. Say, how about meeting me in City Court tomorrow morning? I've got to be there at 8; the Pink Pussycat case is coming up. You know: Tom Riley's case. Don't know when I can shake loose, but when I do, I'll buy you either a late breakfast or an early lunch. I've got an idea I want to run by you."

"I'll come," I said, "but not for the idea. I want to see with my own eyes a cop pay for a meal, especially somebody else's meal."

He hung up laughing.

Chapter Ten

CITY COURT HAD ALL THE CHARM of a Trailways bus depot. The room, a large one with small, high windows that let in little light, was cheerless, and looked tired and worn. Most of the people there looked tired and worn too, as if life had long ago dealt them one blow too many, and this, being in court, in trouble again, was merely the latest proof that hope was pointless.

The room was filled to overflowing. Most of the people sat wedged in on long, hard, wooden benches, but many stood in back, some leaning against the wall, and more were coming in. Some of them, especially the women, used makeshift fans to stir the air around their faces. The air conditioner, if it was working at all, struggled in vain to overcome so much body heat and a heat wave, too. I hadn't been inside five minutes before I was shedding my sport coat and loosening my tie.

It was 8:30, and court was already in session, but I wasn't in a good position to see or hear much. Still standing near the door, I was hoping to spot Rick so I'd know which way to try to move through the crowd. I spied Johnny Lee first. He was sitting down front on the left with some other cops, all in uniform, and when I worked my way in that direction I saw Rick, too.

Johnny Lee, perched on the end of the front row, saw me coming and stood up. Motioning to me, he leaned against the wall and said softly,

"Recognize that guy?" With a nod of his head, he indicated a short, dark, muscular man standing in front of the judge's bench.

I started to shake my head no, and then realized that it was the man who'd been arrested at the Pink Pussycat, the James Cagney clone with the knife. Standing there in court, head slightly bowed, hands clasped behind him, the man looked so different, so harmless, so meek that I simply hadn't associated him with the menacing, knife-wielding tough I'd seen on Saturday night. I whispered to Johnny Lee, "Sure looks different, doesn't he?"

Johnny Lee nodded. "Like a balloon with half the air let out." Nodding again, this time toward the judge's bench, he added, "That's Tom testifying now. Tom Riley. Rick and I have already been up."

I shook my head in recognition. Riley, standing near the judge's bench, looked about the same as he had on Saturday night in his face-off with the defendant, except that now his uniform was neat and clean. He still looked intense, though, and maybe a bit agitated, as if he might be having trouble getting a point across. I began to pay close attention to the proceedings.

"I'm still unclear as to when you advised the defendant of his rights," said the judge, a round-faced man with jowls and large ears who appeared to be in his fifties. He sat at a bench on a platform, elevated above all others in the room. Riley stood to the judge's right, near the end of the bench.

"Your Honor," Riley said, "the defendant was armed and resisted arrest. I read him his rights as soon as he surrendered and I took him into custody."

"I didn't hear no rights," the defendant said.

"He's lying, Your Honor," Riley said.

The judge looked from the defendant to Riley. "Did you tell him he was under arrest before or after the fight?"

"After, Your Honor. There was no time before."

"Couldn't you have said, 'Stop! You're under arrest,' as soon as you saw him wrestling with the girl?"

The defendant said, "I thought the girl had took my wallet, Your Honor. I just wanted her to give it back."

Riley and the judge ignored the defendant, and Riley said, "Well,

Your Honor, he was on top of the girl, had her pinned down, and my first reaction was to pull him off. She was yelling for help; I figured her life could be in danger."

"But isn't it possible," the judge said, "that a simple 'Stop! You're under arrest,' could have achieved the same end? I ask because I'm concerned here about the use of undue force by heavy-handed police officers. There's a right way and a wrong way to handle these things."

Riley, obviously frustrated, said, "Your Honor, he was attacking the girl."

"That may be true," said the judge, "but this is true as well: He thought you were attacking him. You grabbed him from behind, you say; how was he to know you were a policeman and not simply another brawler?"

"That's right," the defendant said. "He attacked me. I didn't know he was a cop."

"Your Honor," Riley said, "if he didn't know it at first, he certainly knew it as soon as he squared off against me."

"No, I didn't," the defendant said. "Your Honor, it was kinda dark in there, and I'd been drinking. And besides, in all the excitement—"

The judge cut him off. "Let me talk to the officer without interruption. If I see the need for clarification from you, I'll ask." Turning back to Riley, he continued, "Now, about the knife. You say he pulled the weapon when Officer, uh, Casenelli came to your aid."

"Right."

"Weren't you armed with a gun?"

"My service revolver, yes. But I never pulled it."

"And wasn't Officer Casenelli armed with a gun?"

"Yes, Your Honor."

"And you still had not, at that time, told the defendant to cease and desist, that he was under arrest?"

Riley's shoulders slumped and he shook his head as if he couldn't believe how this case was going. Speaking with a show of great patience, he said, "Your Honor, there just isn't time for all that in a brawl. Things happen so fast—"

The judge reared back in his chair and fixed Riley with a dubious look. "Not time for proper procedure?" he asked.

Riley shook his head vigorously. "No, sir, Your Honor, not always. Any police officer can tell you—"

Now the judge was impatient. "Yes, yes, I know. I hear every day what police officers can tell me. What I'm interested in now is this specific case. This defendant, any defendant, has rights, and I mean to see that they are observed in this court. I want to know exactly what happened and when it happened. There are things here that need sorting out."

Riley's face reddened, he jerked a bit in agitation, and his voice rose. "It's a simple case, Your Honor." He pointed to the defendant. "This goon attacks a girl, I go to her aid, he resists arrest, attacks me, and then pulls a knife."

Before Riley got halfway through his account of the incident, the judge, an angry look on his face, began banging his gavel, "Officer Riley! Officer Riley!" Then, when Riley had finished and was quiet, the judge said sharply, "That'll be quite enough, sir. I'll tolerate no such outbursts in my court. For your information, I will decide the points of law in this case, and I'll thank you to control yourself while I try to get to the bottom of this."

Meekly, head bowed, Riley said, "Sorry, Your Honor."

"And now," said the judge, "I think you owe the defendant an apology."

As if he hadn't heard, or couldn't believe what he had heard, Riley stiffened and looked at the judge. "What?"

"You called him a goon. I'll have none of that in this court. Defendants will be accorded the respect due them."

The defendant flashed a big smile and stepped forward, but Riley ignored him. Instead, he looked at the judge for a moment then said softly, almost to himself, "How about cops?"

Now the judge was surprised. "What?"

Riley raised his voice. "I said: How about cops? Don't they deserve respect, too? Don't I have any rights here?"

The cops sitting near me stirred uneasily and a hush settled over the courtroom. The judge pulled back a bit in his seat and gave Riley a look of hard appraisal. "Now, see here—"

"See what?" Riley asked even louder. Raising a hand, he began to move about in front of the bench. "See how you bend the law? Twist it and turn it for the precious rights of the criminal? See how you talk to cops like they were dirt? Is that what I'm supposed to see? Well, that's exactly what I do see."

A collective gasp rose from the spectators, and suddenly the court-room was abuzz with whispers. A few of the cops, Rick and Johnny Lee among them, stood up and tried waving to get Riley's attention, to shut him up for his own good, but it was too late.

"You're in contempt, sir; you're in contempt!" shouted the judge, banging his gavel furiously, face flushed, jowls shaking.

But Riley went on. Whirling and pointing to the defendant, he demanded, "Apologize to shit like that?" The defendant, startled, rocked back on his heels and fell back a few steps. Riley then turned to the judge. "You've already done enough apologizing for both of us." In a saccharin voice, he added, looking at the defendant, "Oh, did we inconvenience you, sir, by bringing you into court for assault with a deadly weapon, for beating up a woman? Did the nasty policemen get rough with you and take your pretty little knife away? We're soooo sorry. Here, let judgie-wudgie kiss your ass and make it all better."

The whole time Riley spoke, the judge was looking around and signaling frantically for help. Soon, two bailiffs burst through a door at the rear of the courtroom and hurried around the bench, each grabbing Riley by an arm.

"Easy! Easy!" the judge shouted. "This man needs help. Take him away and call a doctor. Careful. He's obviously out of control."

Riley went without a struggle, but he didn't go quietly. "Out of control?" he shouted as the bailiffs led him toward the door through which they had come. "It's judges like you that are out of control. Go ahead! Turn the sonofabitch loose. Half the criminals on the street now are people you turned loose with no more than a slap on the wrist. Go ahead. Go ahead!" Now Riley, face crimson and contorted, was screaming. "When he cuts your fuckin' throat one night in a parking lot or in your own bed, you'll have nobody to blame but yourself. And you'll wish a crazy, good-for-nothing, heavy-handed cop like me was around to save your sorry ass. You hear me! Somebody better listen to me! Something's not right here! I'm not the one out of control. It's the god-damn system! You hear me? You hear me, motherfuckers?"

The bailiffs finally got Riley out the door and closed it, but it soon became obvious that order in the court could not be restored. Everyone was standing, many milling about, and the commotion drowned out the judge's repeated calls for order. Finally, giving up, he signaled one of the cops and ordered him to enlist the other policemen to clear the court-room. Defendants and others with business there were herded into the hallways outside. The rest were told to go home, and bailiffs took up sta-tions at the doors to the courtroom, with orders to admit only those who were called by the clerk. I fell in behind Rick as he worked with the other cops to clear the room. When that was done, we found Johnny Lee and left.

WE WENT TO A COFFEE SHOP UP THE STREET from the courthouse, ordered breakfast, and sat there glumly until it came. We had walked to the shop in silence, and now ate in silence, not knowing quite how to break it. When we finished eating, and the waitress refilled our coffee cups, Rick finally just plunged in.

"Jesus!" he said, "I knew Tom was having his problems, but I never dreamed he'd come apart like that. Christ! He snapped like a towline. And right in court!"

"If you ask me," Johnny Lee said, "court's the right place for it. Every word he said was the mother-lovin' truth, and there's not a cop any-where who doesn't know it."

"Yeah," said Rick, who looked a bit dazed, "but think of Tom. Next stop for him, a rubber room. What'cha wanna bet he's in a straitjacket right now? And what comes next? Two to one, they fricassee his brain with shock treatment. And what good'll that do? Even if they find all his pieces and get 'em back together, he'll still be The Cop Who Came Unglued in Court. He'll be lucky to work as a crosswalk guard at some grammar school."

"Maybe not," said Johnny Lee, sipping his coffee. "They have pro-grams for this sort of thing now."

"Police chaplain. Ha!"

"He's just where you start," Johnny Lee said. "You know that."

"Yeah, and it's a laugh — you know that." Rick stirred his coffee vigorously and then looked at me. "The brass finally figured out that, hey, being a cop is stressful. What did your study say? Second only to air traffic control? To which I say, 'Bullshit.' No air traffic controller has to take a knife away from some punk to do his job. Right? Anyhow, the brass want to be modern, up to date, and build a bigger bureaucracy, so they put in a few programs. Got a problem? Come tell us about it; we understand. Well, there ain't a cop alive who hasn't got a problem. Look at the divorce rate among cops. Look at the suicide rate. Look at the courts — hell, the whole criminal justice system. But what happens if you go for help? Right away it's reported to your supervisor. The damn chaplain, your father confessor, is a fuckin' stoolie, a stooge for the brass. Next thing you know, you've been reassigned. You're pushing paper all day for the desk sergeant or you're a file clerk in records. Result? You've got an even bigger problem: a rep as a guy who can't hack it anymore — to say nothing of terminal boredom. Thanks, but no thanks." He turned to Johnny Lee. "Hey, I notice you didn't go to the chaplain when your marriage headed for the rocks."

Johnny Lee eyed Rick coolly. "Well, maybe I should have. What I did, which was nothing, certainly didn't help."

Rick looked hard at his friend a moment, and then clasped his forearm. "Sorry. You did all you could do."

"Thanks. But, no, I didn't. In fact, I did all the wrong things." Johnny Lee looked away. "If you don't mind, I don't want to talk about it."

"Sure. I shouldn't have brought it up. Change of subject." Rick turned back to me. "I been thinkin' about our girl, the runaway. Heard anything yet?"

I shook my head.

"Well," he said, "there's still nothing to indicate she left the area, right? So let's go from there. It's odd, I grant you, that nothing's turned up." He pointed a finger at his head. "But let's use a little ratiocination here." He smiled. "Didn't know I knew a big word like that, did you?" Indicating Johnny Lee, he said, "I'll explain it to country boy here soon as I can find some crayons."

Johnny Lee laughed and said, "Up yours."

Rick went on. "There are groups of people who just don't run to the phone to tell Establishment types anything, unless maybe there's a reward attached, which in this case there isn't. I'm talkin' criminals, prostitutes, pimps, gays — get the picture?"

I nodded.

"Now, we've already checked out the gays; we have no reason to think she's involved in a crime; and she's certainly not a pimp. That leaves the prostitutes, which, as I think about it, makes some sense. She must be underground somewhere—"

"Maybe literally," I said.

"True," Rick said. "But that's the worst-case scenario, and there's no evidence of that either. Now, as I was saying, looking among prostitutes makes sense. Our runaway has to eat, and sooner or later most people out on their own have to work. If she had a legitimate job, somebody would've tipped us off by now. Besides, she wouldn't be the first young girl to hit the big city, need money, and find out in a hurry that she had been sitting on a gold mine the whole damn time."

I didn't like hearing it, but it made sense, and I was just about to say so, when Johnny Lee jerked violently and said, "Shit! You mean to tell me we been wasting our time looking for a whore?" He glared first at Rick and then at me.

"Hey, wait a minute," Rick said. "That's just a guess."

"Yeah? Well, I ain't wasting my time looking for no whore. I got better things to do." Johnny Lee pointed a finger at his chest and jabbed several times. "I got a little girl, you know. And I'd help anybody look for their lost child, even if she is 18 or whatever and legally an adult — as long as she's worth finding. But I'll be damned if I'll bust my ass to look for human trash." He looked from me to Rick again, and then at his empty coffee cup. Snatching it up and holding it aloft, he snapped, "Waitress! Fill 'er up."

Rick sighed heavily. "Again, it was only a guess. Even if I'm right, let's not jump to conclusions. Plenty of young girls get forced into that kind of thing. The most predatory SOB in the concrete jungle is your average pimp. And those bastards look for the naive, the lost, the innocent like a snake hunts birds." He tapped Johnny Lee on the arm. "Hey, what am I tellin' you for? You've seen the pimps hangin' 'round the bus station down on Spring Street." Then, to me, he said, "Let a sweet young thing step off a bus by her lonesome, strands of hay still in her hair, and before you can say 'Welcome to Atlanta' the pimps are on her like ticks on a blue hound." He caught himself and laughed. "Listen to me," he said: "'ticks on a blue hound'." Jerking a thumb toward Johnny Lee, he added, "Country boy here's got me talking like he does."

"'Bout damn time," Johnny Lee said, his anger apparently gone. "You've been in the South for, what, how long now?"

"Eight years last month." Then hamming it up, Rick added, "Cain't ya'll tell how ah've changed? Pass the grits, Bubba. And you, Verona Jean, fetch me anotha mint julep, honey chile."

I laughed, but Johnny Lee just shook his head. "Listen to that damn Yankee throwin' off on his betters. You can't find a dago anywhere whose name isn't Rick or Nick or Vinnie, or Angie or Maria, but he makes fun of us. And they all make that voodoo sign on themselves" — he flicked his fingers about his chest, indicating the sign of the cross — "for everything from a foul shot in basketball to a period that's a day late. As if God gave a damn whether East Jesus High won the game or if another little wop got knocked up."

Rick laughed. "We are a fertile race, m' boy. No argument there. It's a sign of God's favor. You WASPs, especially of the benighted Southern strain, would do well to study our example."

Johnny Lee hooted. "Gettin' deep in here, ain't it, Ben?"

Rick raised his hands. "But back to business. What do you think of my idea?"

"Well," Johnny Lee said, "I hope to God you're wrong, but you just might have something there."

"Couldn't have put it better myself," I said.

"Fine." Then, pausing dramatically, Rick added: "Now what do we do about it?"

I looked at him, obviously puzzled.

He went on, "We could pound the pavement until Peachtree Street became a gravel path, but those hookers would never open up to us. C-o-p spells trouble any way they look at it."

"They might open up to me, a reporter."

"They'd tell you more than they would us," Rick said, "but they still won't rat on a girl to a man."

"Do we know any female cops who could help us?" Johnny Lee asked.

"In plain clothes, of course."

"Too risky," Rick said. "We're working this case freelance, remember? We need to keep quiet about it, especially to other cops. And there's no way I'd go through channels for something like this. One, they wouldn't approve it — and I wouldn't blame 'em. It's only a runaway, and we've got nothing to go on. Two, for even bringing it up, I'd get yanked out of squad cars forever by the brass. Forget it."

I broke into a big smile. "You can both relax; I think I know just the woman for the job."

Chapter Eleven

THERE STILL WAS NO WORD ON CONNIE PHILLIPS when I got to the news-room around 11 a.m. and checked my messages. Rick's deduction was making more and more sense to me, and besides it was all I had. Even if he were wrong, I figured, we'd be doing something, a strategy that had never failed me in the past. *Keep moving, keep stirring, and you're bound to flush out something.*

I still had some time to kill before Morgan was due in to work, so I typed up a note to the city desk, with a copy for the police reporters, tipping them off to Riley's breakdown in court. Shortly before noon, I saw Morgan out in the newsroom, and went out to tell her what I had in mind.

She jumped at the idea. "Sure, Ben, I'd be glad to help out. When?"

"Not so fast," I said. "This is something you ought to think about. It could be dangerous — and all for nothing. And you'd have to do it at night, either after you got off work or on your days off."

"I'll do it."

"And it won't be easy. Pimps are careful and they watch the street like hawks. Know The Hamburger Joint at Peachtree and Alden? That's where a lot of 'em hang out. Through those big plate-glass windows, they can see the street in three directions. I used the same vantage point in a story on street people awhile back. If the pimps think you're a cop, or anybody official, they'll give their girls a sign that'll leave you feeling like a leper. They might do that anyhow. One glance and they'll peg you as straight. And when they see you asking questions and flashing Connie's picture, they're gonna want to know what's going down. Your best bet is to come up with a pitch that gets you in and out quickly with each girl. Maybe you could be a naive tourist asking directions. Or Connie's big sister. I'll leave that to you. But I repeat: It ain't gonna be easy. And it might be dangerous. Pimps are mean SOBs."

"I can take care of myself."

"On the other hand, I'll be close by, and my cop friends, Rick and Johnny Lee, will try to keep an eye on you, too. And you just might get a hell of a story out of this that could spring you from the copy desk. No reason you couldn't do a sidebar to my story on the search for Connie Phillips or share a byline on the main story — if there is a main story. And, mind you, that's a big if. For all we know, our runaway could be working in a dime store in Denver."

None of that lessened her enthusiasm. "Say when. Better still, take me to supper and fill me in. I know nothing about the two policemen who are helping you."

The invitation was tempting, but I planned to be on The Strip around suppertime. Rick had been right: It wouldn't do me much good to talk to the prostitutes. But there were males down there, too. I wanted to try my luck.

"I've got a better idea," I said. "Ride with me for an hour after work. The Strip will be busy then, and you can see what you're up against. You can get an idea, too, how to dress for the job. You don't want to go down there looking too straight." I noticed then for the first time what she was wearing: an outfit with red and white stripes that looked like a dress but was actually two matching pieces. It fit her well and showed off some curves I hadn't noticed before. "For example," I said, indicating her outfit, "that's nice, but much too tasteful for The Strip. Think flashy. Think red-hot mama. You'll see."

She laughed. "Gotcha."

"I'll be out front at nine."

After work, I went home to my small apartment — bedroom, sitting room, kitchen, breakfast area — all I needed, really. I showered, ran an electric razor over my face, and changed clothes while a TV dinner warmed in the oven. Eating in front of the TV set, I caught the evening news and scanned the newspaper for the first time that day.

Somewhere around the comics page, I realized that I was humming, had in fact been humming for some time. Not a recognizable song, just one of those bouncy little tunes that the mind sometimes makes up when it's feeling pretty good about things. Euphoria set to music? Well, I did feel good, and I didn't have to search my mind to find out why. I was going to see Morgan again, be alone with her, away from the newspaper, for the first time, except for that hurried supper hour. That was it, of course. Nothing extraordinary there.

Still, it was revealing. It had been months and months since I had felt a sense of well-being when alone at home. Joanna was the reason, of course. For that was when I missed her most, when I'd come home in the evening to an empty house, one in which she was everywhere, but nowhere, one in which she was a presence, but not a reality. That she had never even lived in my apartment changed nothing. After her death, I sold our house and moved, only to find that she had moved with me. The most heart-rending legacy of the dead was that their absence somehow became their presence, which made their absence all the more bereaving.

But now I was humming. And it was all because of Morgan. I glanced guiltily at Joanna's photograph, smiling at me from a table at the end of the couch. It was a smile framed by dark tumbling hair and lit by dark brown eyes, a smile that seemed to poise precariously between innocence and mischief. I picked up the photograph and kissed it, then put it away in a drawer of the table. No matter how painful the surrender, I could not go on living in the one-dimensional world of photographic love. Neither, came the unbidden thought, could Mrs. Phillips. I hurried to brush my teeth, and left the apartment, headed for The Strip, glad to have something to do while waiting to see Morgan.

Chapter Twelve

THE MIDTOWN MANOR HOTEL, located in the heart of The Strip, had given up all pretense of being a real hotel. The carpeting had been ripped up, rolled up, and stacked here and there against the walls. A cigarette machine was the lobby's only piece of decor, its only furnishing. People in need of a place to sit sat out front on the steps or simply went on needing a place to sit. No doorman guarded the entrance, no bellboys hustled about, no fleet of registration clerks stood uniformed and ready to be of service. But the Midtown Manor was open for business and obviously getting some. People milled around out front, and came and went in the lobby. I could tell from the noise of the elevators that they stayed busy.

"Oh, this p-p-place m-m-makes m-money," the night clerk said, smiling. Tall and black, he sat in a small cubicle about halfway down the narrow lobby, near the elevators. He stuttered worse than anybody I'd ever heard. "You'll have t-to excuse m-m-me," he said. "I have this s-s-silly s-s-s-speech im-im-pediment. It'll g-get b-better once I g-g-get u-u-used to you."

A buzzer sounded and a red light lit up on the switchboard. He put down the book he had been reading, plugged into the switchboard and said, "D-d-desk."

I stood at the front counter and could easily see the title of the book, a paperback. It was Bertrand Russell's *Wisdom of the West.* When he pulled the plug on the switchboard, I said with raised eyebrows, "A hotel desk clerk who reads Bertrand Russell?"

He smiled sheepishly. "You'll r-read anything on a j-j-job like this."

I introduced myself, told him why I was there, and we chatted a few more minutes. His name was Jerry Chatham, he was 30, lived there in the hotel with his wife and little girl — and had a college degree in mathematics.

"Pretty far from your field, aren't you?" I didn't want to throw off on his line of work, but surely a man with a college degree could do better than he appeared to be doing.

He tried to act matter-of-fact, but sadness lurked behind his eyes. "M-my d-d-dream was to be a t-t-teacher. But have you ever s-seen a s-s-s-stuttering t-teacher?"

I hadn't. Had never even thought of it. I shook my head. "I'm sorry."

He raised his hands, palms up. "I th-thought I c-could l-l-lick this th-thing, b-but I haven't. N-n-no-b-body else w-wants a s-stuttering m-m-mathematician either. I g-got this job 'c-cause I work cheap." He waved a hand to indicate his surroundings.

It seemed a good time to change the subject, so I showed him the pictures of Connie and Sims. "My main interest is the girl. The guy seems to like boys."

Jerry nodded and studied the pictures, then shook his head. "No. N-never s-seen either one." He added, however, that if Connie were anywhere on The Strip he might be able to help me. "Th-this hotel is f-full of p-prostitutes and p-pimps, and if s-she's out th-there, there's a g-good ch-chance they've s-seen her."

Just then, a short brunette wearing a skirt and blouse easily a size too small for her passed the desk on her way out. Jerry hailed her and she sauntered over to the desk.

"Ever s-seen this g-girl, S-Sherri?" He showed her Connie's picture.

The girl, about 20, looked at the picture then at me, and finally at Jerry. "No. Kinda young, ain't she? Big boobs, though." She looked up at me, giving me the once-over. "You looking for young stuff?"

"No," I said. I almost added a ridiculous "thank-you," but caught myself before saying it.

"He's n-n-not a j-john," Jerry said.

She looked me up and down again. "Too bad," she said. She glanced again at the photo. "Nice tits, though. Like to have a pair like that, myself." She strolled on out the door.

Jerry turned to me. "S-stay here awhile and I'll ask a f-few m-more. B-but your b-best bet would be a p-pimp."

"Can you direct me to one?"

He laughed. "They ain't exactly l-listed in the y-y-yellow p-pages, you know. Besides, n-no pimp gonna g-give you the t-time of day."

"Surely, there are some around here, some you know."

He nodded.

"Would you mind asking for me?" I heard the lobby doors swing open and turned to see a short, wiry young man coming toward us. He sported a Little-Richard hairdo and wore clothes that looked flashy but cheap. "How about him? He a pimp?"

Jerry watched the man as he stopped at the cigarette machine, just out of hearing range. "He's n-no pimp; he's a shrimp." He laughed and explained, "A s-shrimp is someb-body tryin' to be a p-pimp." He turned thoughtful for a moment, and when the young man got his cigarettes and left, he said, "L-look, p-pimps wouldn't give m-me the time of day, either. B-but there are a couple here in th-the hotel who owe me a f-favor. Hold on."

He went to the switchboard and rang one of the rooms. I moved away to a discreet distance so he could make his pitch in private. Soon he came back to the desk front. "He d-didn't like it much, b-but he said to s-send you up. Room 412."

"Name?"

"J-just call him Ray — and d-don't ask for a last n-name to g-go with it."

I thanked him and went to the elevators.

When I knocked on the door of 412, a surly male voice came from within. "It's open."

I entered the room and saw a tall, thin man standing at the window, looking out through blinds onto Peachtree Street. "Jerry sent me," I said.

He went on peering out the window for a minute and then turned to face me. "You a cop?"

"Reporter."

"Got any I.D.?"

I took out my billfold and showed him my *Phoenix* identification card. My picture was on it. He looked at it carefully and handed it back. "I don't like this," he said, obviously meaning the situation.

"I'm just trying to help somebody."

"Ain't nobody ever help me." He eased down into a chair and lifted his feet onto the bed, crossing them at the ankles. "What she look like, this chick you lookin' for?"

I took out Connie's picture and handed it to him.

He looked at it. "They a reward out for her?"

"No. Her parents are just plain, everyday people."

"I ain't seen her." He leaned over to peer through the blinds again. "How long she been gone?"

"Eleven days."

Still looking out the window, he said, "What make you think she 'round here?"

"Just a guess. We've looked everywhere else. Figured we'd try here."

He looked quickly around at me. "Who's we?"

To cover my slip-up, I said, "Other reporters."

He looked at the picture of Connie again, still in his hand, and then gave me a scrutinizing look. "This chick must be somethin' special."

"Only to her mother and father. And to me, I guess."

"What she to you?"

I squirmed a bit. "I lost somebody special one time. I know how it feels.

He looked at me for a long moment, his face flat and expressionless, and looked at the picture of Connie again. Then he called out, "Maxine, get in here!"

Through a door I hadn't noticed, a door into another room, a short, very curvaceous, peroxide blonde entered. "You call, Ray?"

He snorted. "If I didn't call, what you doin' here?"

She dropped her gaze to the floor and said nothing.

"Come over here," he said.

She walked by me and around the foot of the bed. He handed her the picture of Connie and pointed at me. "This man's lookin' for that chick. Tell him did you ever see her before."

Maxine looked at the picture and then at Ray. He said pointedly, "Tell him the truth."

She glanced at the picture again, then at me. "I've never seen her before."

"Give him back the picture and get out," Ray said.

She handed it to me as she started back to the other room. When she got near the door, the pimp snapped, "That ain't out. *Out* is on the street. And this time you better put yo' money-maker to makin' money. I catch you sittin' on it again, you be one sorry little mama."

Looking flustered, she motioned toward the door. "I need my lipstick."

"You need what I say you need, and you *need* to get yo' ass out on the street."

She went.

When she closed the door, the pimp yawned and stretched. "She good, but lazy," he said.

I folded Connie's picture, put it away and started to leave, but I had a question I couldn't resist asking. It might help me find Connie. "What makes a girl become a prostitute?"

He looked at me as if he could not believe I didn't know. "Money," he said. "M-o-n-e-y."

"No offense, but Maxine didn't seem all that eager to get out there and make money."

He eased his feet off the bed and began to slip on shoes. "Maxine think small. She done made $300 today and she think that enough. He stood up and smoothed his pants. "When she was waitressin', she done good to turn $150 a week. Maxine got a million-dollar ass and a five-dollar brain. She need me to tell her what's enough."

He turned to look out the window again. I thanked him and left.

Jerry was away from the desk when I got back to the lobby. When he hadn't returned in a couple of minutes, I scribbled a note saying, "No luck, but thanks," and left it where he'd see it.

Chapter Thirteen

BACK OUT ON THE STRIP, I checked the time: nearly 8 p.m. There was a lot of traffic in the street, especially for a Tuesday night, but the action seemed slower than usual. Lots of shoppers, but few buyers, it seemed — but it was still early.

I walked down a block to another hotel, showed the desk clerk the pictures and came up empty. Crossing the street, I worked a liquor store, a drug store, a porn movie theater, a couple of seedy bars, even a parking lot where a night attendant was on duty. No luck. It was then 8:30, so I headed back to my car, parked just around the corner from a massage parlor. I had passed it up before because I saw only women there, three of them, sitting on a raised platform that held a red velvet couch and chair in the display window. They were still there, but as I passed this time, I also noticed a man standing in the doorway. I stopped.

The man, about 35, short and stocky, grinned when he saw me. "Welcome to The Velvet Touch," he said. "What'll it be this evening? Blonde, brunette or redhead?" He stepped back, into the building, and with a wave of his hand invited me to come in and look over the merchandise.

I stepped inside. "Thanks, but I was wondering if you could help me find another girl." I took out Connie's picture and handed it to him. No use asking about Sims here.

"You're not a cop," he said, looking me up and down. I could tell he didn't think I was. Just checking.

"Reporter. The girl's a runaway."

He looked at the picture, and next thing I knew the girls in the window were clustered at the edge of the platform, peering over to see, too.

"Geez, look at those boobs. How old is she?" said the redhead, who was tall and thin, and dressed in sheer purple pajamas that looked like something Frederick's of Hollywood might call Arabian Nights.

"18."

"Gee," she said wistfully, "I was 18 once, and only three years ago."

"Six," the brunette said dryly. "And you never had boobs like that." The brunette was as tall as the redhead, but with bigger bones and more curves. She wore a navy-blue see-through chemise.

The redhead fixed her with a disdainful look. "I'm still younger than you, dearie. And I'll have you know I've never had any complaints about my boobs." She stuck out her chin, her lips, and her chest.

"Now, girls," the man chided. Then, looking at me, he said, "Sorry," and started to hand back the picture.

"Let me see that," the blonde said. She took the picture and studied it. At length she said, "I'd almost swear I've seen this girl. Where's she from?"

My pulse quickened. "Avondale Estates."

The blonde shook her head. "It wasn't there. I grew up in north Atlanta, North Springs."

She studied the picture some more, and I studied her as she did. She was about five feet two inches and a few pounds overweight, but she filled out a pair of white short-shorts nicely and had a pretty face. I figured her for 21.

She handed back the picture. "Gee, I can't place her, but she does look familiar. How old did you say?"

"18."

"She looks younger, but, heck, I've seen 'em out here 14." She nodded toward the street.

A phone rang somewhere in back, and the man went to answer it. Two men came in, and the redhead and the brunette began talking to them.

"You thought you recognized her," I said to the blonde. "From how long ago?"

"Not long at all. Last few days, I'd say. But it was just a glimpse, and I'm not sure it was that girl. Just something about her face rings a bell, you know. Maybe she just looks like somebody I know. Maybe I simply saw her in passing. I just can't say. Sorry." She managed a little smile that looked sincere.

"Well, look," I said, "let me leave you my name and number. If it does come to you, give me a call, day or night. Okay?"

She said, "Sure," and I got out my reporter's pad and scrawled the information on a sheet of paper.

"The top one's my office phone and the other's my home phone. Remember: day or night. And if I'm not in, please leave a name and number where I can reach you."

"You really want to find her, don't you?"

"Yeah."

"How long you been lookin'?"

"Forever, it seems."

She caught my eyes with her big blue ones and smiled shyly. "Well, why don't you stay awhile, relax?"

The invitation was unmistakable, and she was nice, not hard-looking like the other two.

She took my hand. "Come on. It's on the house. Can't beat a deal like that."

It was tempting. I wavered. I hadn't been with a woman, not even interested in being with a woman, in two years. But I pointed to my watch. "Thanks, but I've got to run. Got to pick up my girlfriend in 15 minutes."

"Bring her back with you," she said softly, reasonably, still giving me the shy smile. "I go both ways."

That really threw me. I began fumbling for words, and wound up telling a polite lie. "Uh, well, I'll tell her. And, uh, if she's interested, we, uh, just might do that."

Then I got out of there fast.

MORGAN WAS COMING OUT THE FRONT ENTRANCE of the news building when I pulled up to the curb. I leaned across the seat, rolled down the window, and signaled to her.

"Still wanna do it?" I asked when she got in.

She smiled and feigned shock. "Why, what a question, sir! And I only just got here." I laughed, and then she said soberly, "I said I did, and I do." She smiled again. "Now show me The Strip."

It was my turn to feign shock. "Why, ma'am, I just got here, myself!"

She laughed, and I headed back over to Peachtree, telling her about Rick and Johnny Lee as we went.

THE PACE ON THE STRIP had picked up a bit, but it was still nothing compared to a Friday or Saturday night, when the uninitiated might mistake all the commotion for a street carnival. That thought gave me an idea.

"Look," I said as we crept along in traffic, "a Friday or Saturday might be the best time for you to do this thing. The sidewalks will be thronged and you won't be nearly as conspicuous."

"Uh huh." She was distracted, caught up in watching the hookers work the street.

"But there's a down side to that too: it won't be as easy for us to keep an eye on you, either."

"Uh huh."

"You listening?"

"Sure, Friday's fine," she said. "Why don't you and I go to supper early, say, 7, 7:30, and after that you can drop me off here?"

"You mean this Friday? No way. We've got a date."

She turned to look at me. "Ben, we can date before and after we do this. It can't take more than an hour, can it? And if I don't come up with anything Friday, then we'll still have Saturday to try again. All right?"

I didn't like it, but I said all right. The sooner we checked this out, the better.

"Besides," she added with a sly look, "there'll be other weekends."

"Now *that* I like," I said, feeling even better when she smiled.

A few minutes later, I pointed out the Midtown Manor Hotel and told her about going there, then showed her The Hamburger Joint, where the pimps hung out. I also drove down Selwyn Street, so she could see the homosexual hangouts, told her about Piedmont Park at night, and finally took her past the massage parlor while telling her about the blonde who thought she recognized Connie's picture.

"What will you do between now and Friday?" she asked.

"Keep looking. By Friday, I will have canvassed most of the places along The Strip. By the time you work the prostitutes, we'll have a pretty good idea whether she's out here or not."

"What if she's not? What then?"

I sighed. "God only knows. Go back to square one, maybe. Or give up. I can't make a career of finding Connie Phillips, you know. Besides, the paper will pull me off the story, and ought to, if I don't come up with something soon. I'm beginning to doubt, myself, that she's out here. She could be anywhere. She could be dead."

I drove Morgan to the newspaper's parking lot and pulled up beside her car, a maroon Toyota Corolla that had seen better years. The lot, dimly lit, was below street level, and above us the taller buildings on Marietta Street seemed to crowd in, blocking out the eastern sky. Mostly office buildings, they were dark except for a lighted window here and there or an occasional glint of moonlight on marble or glass. The impression was that here, in the heart of a great metropolis, we were completely alone. Only the whine of an occasional bus along Marietta or the hiss of tires from a passing car broke the silence around us. Otherwise, the city seemed deserted and still, closed down for the night, sleeping. In a cold and austere way, it was beautiful, a great city resting from its mammoth labors. But I pitied anybody who was out there in it with no place to go.

"I hope Connie Phillips is in a warm bed and not a cold grave." I meant it, of course, but I said it mainly to have something to say. The silence between us had grown awkward.

Morgan stirred on the seat beside me. "Don't give up yet; something will break."

"Yeah," I said wearily. "I just hope it isn't Mrs. Phillips' heart."

"Me, too." She reached for the door handle.

I put my hand on her arm to stop her from getting out. "Speaking of hearts . . ."

She moved her hand from the door handle and sat very still. "Yes."

"I think my own may be in some danger here."

She looked at me and smiled. "Better be careful, then."

"Yeah, I keep telling myself that."

She looked away. "And do you listen to your own counsel?"

"Not a bit. How 'bout you?"

"Same here," she said, as I pulled her to me, smearing the words on her lips with my own, kissing her before I had even made up my mind consciously to try.

After that, I watched until she was safely out of the parking lot, on her way home, then I drove home myself, as dizzy as if I had been drinking.

PART TWO

Chapter Fourteen

THE PHONE RANG JUST AT DAYBREAK, rousing me from a deep sleep of fewer than six hours. It was Rick. "Get dressed and be out front in three minutes. Hurry!"

It takes me awhile to wake up even after a good night's rest, but somehow I managed, while still semi-conscious, to throw my clothes on and find my way out to the street. I came wide awake, though, when Rick picked me up with a California rolling stop. I barely got into the car before he stomped on the gas and sped off. "Jesus, Casenelli!" I shouted. "You trying to kill me?" Quickly I slammed the still-open door and buckled my seat belt.

"You can thank me later," he said, blowing through a stop sign at the end of my street, barreling onto Monroe, tires squealing, and speeding toward Piedmont. Soon he was roaring down a ramp onto the Northeast Expressway, blue light licking over the hood as he let the engine unwind. Now on a straightaway, he continued, "Sims turned up just before daybreak, say six. Somebody punched his ticket. Johnny Lee's there now, and I thought we ought to be too. But if I don't get you there before the Homicide boys take over, you won't be able to go in."

"You mean he's dead?"

"As in stone cold."

"Murdered?"

"You got it."

"But—" I was going to say that Sims was just a kid, who would want to murder him? But it was a silly question. Anymore, bodies turned up in Atlanta like toadstools after a rain, and somebody somewhere was always asking why, as if murder could ever make sense. "Any sign of Connie?" I was almost afraid to ask.

"No. But it's Sims, all right. Johnny Lee made the I.D. He got the call and radioed me. That's when I called you. And that's about all I know."

Rick peeled off the freeway and turned west. Not much later we were pulling into a part of North Atlanta called Brookhaven, an area of small odds-and-ends shops and slightly seedy apartment complexes strung out along one of Peachtree Street's less prosperous stretches. In Brookhaven, he turned off on a narrow road that ran downhill to a small and poor black neighborhood perched on a wooded ridge. Then he turned onto a wider road that seemed to cut through a forest that developers had somehow overlooked. I even saw a farm or two.

"Farms in Atlanta," I said. "I know they're here; still it always surprises me to see them."

"Horses, mostly," Rick said. "But if we had the time, I could show you a couple of corn fields, and even a watermelon patch — not backyard gardens either. But we're getting close, so listen up. One, I didn't call you. Got that? Two, you were at work and heard the call on the newsroom's police scanner. Three, you flagged me down as I came through Brookhaven. Car trouble. OK?"

"Yeah."

"Letting you ride with me on patrol is one thing; tipping you off to a homicide and bringing you to the scene, that's another thing entirely. I'm in enough trouble with the brass already. *Comprende?*"

"Gotcha."

"There it is," he said, pointing just ahead to a squad car parked in some trees along the side of the road.

As we got closer, I saw two more squad cars. "We too late?" I asked.

"Naw. They're patrol cars. Probably heard the call and came out of curiosity."

Johnny Lee was waiting in his car, but as soon as he saw us he got out and started into the woods, signaling us to follow.

Well before I saw the body, I smelled it. The odor, like no other in the world, sour, rank, was nauseating, nearly overwhelming when it rode full force downwind. I steeled myself and walked on through the waist-high weeds.

"It's not far now," Johnny Lee said, "just down this gully a ways."

We followed in silence. The morning was warm and still except for an occasional stirring of air, and I noticed for the first time that the sky was dark and low, threatening rain and holding back the dawn. Shadows still clung in the thickets around us, like remnants of night snagged in the trees.

We came out of the weeds into a forest of tall pines and under-growth. Through the brush I saw two cops moving around and heard voices. Stronger now, the smell at times made me gag. I swallowed hard and held my breath.

"How far you make it from the road?" Rick asked Johnny Lee.

"Hundred yards, I'd say. They came in on down the road, around the curve, but it's about the same either way."

"Any car tracks?" Rick said.

"No. That old red clay's hard as concrete," Johnny Lee said. "No foot-prints either, far as I could tell, but you see what the light is like. Tell you the truth; I didn't want to look too good. Homicide would wind up saying I tramped all over a murder scene."

"Homicide couldn't find a killer on Death Row," Rick said.

"All the more reason not to give 'em my ass as an excuse," Johnny Lee said.

"They on their way?" Rick said.

"Yeah, but you know them. I talked to Jonesie again just a minute ago. He said the victim ain't going anywhere anyhow."

Over his shoulder, Rick said to me, "A real sleuth, our Jonesie. Figured that out all by himself."

"Yeah," said Johnny Lee, "and he's the smart one in Homicide."

"You tell him it looked like rain out here, and that rain has been known to wash away tracks, footprints, blood — little things like that?" Rick asked.

"Yeah, and you know what he said? He said, and I quote, 'If it rains, it rains'"

"He figured that out, too?" Rick said. "The man's a mental giant."

Johnny Lee added, "'Rain is an Act of God,' he said."

"He said that, too?" Rick asked. "Gee, JL, I hope you took notes on these pearls of wisdom. We could put 'em in a book: *Homilies from Homicide*. Better still: *Homilies that Triggered Homicide*."

Johnny Lee brought us up short. The odor was very strong now, but I was getting used to it. "He's just ahead," Johnny Lee said. "Stay below his feet, and you won't trample anything that hasn't already been trampled."

We moved forward a few paces, and there on the ground, in a small clearing and wearing only underpants, lay Clifford Sims. Face down, body bent, arms and legs sprawled at odd angles, he looked at first like a life-size doll discarded by some petulant giant. Up close, though, the grisly handiwork of death was all too real. One side of his face was exposed and the flesh was bloated, discolored. The mouth, slightly agape, was caked with dried blood, and the eye was open in a glazed and vacant stare, a lens focused on eternity.

Most telling, though, at least to me, was the eerie stillness of the dead. Over the years, I had seen several bodies under similar circumstances — a suicide, a drowning, a car wreck, a shooting, a few others — and always I was struck hardest by the utter stillness of the corpse. Life was motion, however slight, and I had never seen a corpse that seemed to be somebody merely asleep. Death wasn't the Big Sleep; it was the Big Stillness. I didn't even know the boy, this crumpled form clad only in Jockey shorts, but a wave of pity welled up in me as I watched black ants move in and out his ear, down his neck, scouting, exploring. Nobody, least of all a kid, should have to die like that, murdered and left out in the open to rot.

"How'd he get it?" Rick said.

"Bullet. Back of the head," Johnny Lee said. "Not much left of the other side of his face. I turned him enough to look."

"Find any shells?" Rick asked.

"No, but like I said: The light was bad, and I didn't look all that good anyhow." He pointed to the two other cops, who were searching the woods about thirty yards beyond us. "I've got them looking over there." He then pointed to our right, where we could see the weeds beaten down, forming a makeshift path. "I just don't want anybody in *that* area."

"How long's he been dead, JL?" I asked.

"I'd say a couple of days; wouldn't you, Rick?"

Rick nodded. "Who found him?"

"Harmless old drunk. Lives up the road near that little black community you came through. He was gonna sleep it off in the woods, but I think the smell sobered him up. If it didn't, stumbling over the body did. He wouldn't come back in here. Brought me to the edge of the woods and pointed. I sent him on back home."

"Is that something on his arm, JL?" I pointed to the right arm, half hidden beneath him. "There on the wrist?"

Johnny Lee squatted and leaned in close. "Damned if it ain't," he said, leaning closer. "Looks like twine." He shook his head. "I missed that."

All thinking the same thought, we turned our eyes to the other wrist. A faint, barely visible line encircled it.

"His hands were tied, all right," Johnny Lee said.

"Damn," Rick said. "That's like an execution."

"Can you get a closer look at the twine?" Something about it was trying to connect up deep in my mind. "I've seen twine like that a thousand times, but can't remember where." Are there different kinds of twine? I wondered.

Johnny Lee plucked at a loop on the ground, and pulled. A piece of twine about eight inches long slid from beneath the body. It was thin and golden, the color of ripe hay. I strained to remember where I'd seen that kind of twine so often, but the memory wouldn't come. Probably wasn't important anyhow, I thought; twine like that must be used for a thousand different things.

Rick was scratching his chin. "Who'd want to execute a teenager? Doesn't make sense."

I was about to say we'd better figure it out in a hurry, because the same fate might be in store for Connie — if she were still alive — when one of the two cops searching the woods called out, "Fresh grave over here. Least, that's what it looks like."

"Uh, oh," said Johnny Lee, standing up and looking toward the cop, who was now about forty yards away. Rick and I looked at each other, sharing the same fear. "This way," Johnny Lee said, moving in a wide arc around Sims's body. "Come on."

We followed him through more tall weeds and into a smaller clearing, where the cop, a stocky redhead, stood looking at freshly turned earth. Holding his cap and mopping his brow with his shirtsleeve, he said, "Is that a grave or is that a grave?"

"I'd bet my pension," Johnny Lee said.

The other cop, balding and beefy, had come over. "Not very wide, is it?"

"Wide enough," Rick said. "Long enough too. We'll know soon; Homicide is here." To me he whispered, "That's Jonesie leading the way. C. L. Jones." He nodded toward two men in plainclothes coming through the woods. Behind them were three or four more men, one carrying a camera, another toting a big black case.

"Good. The lab boys are with them," Johnny Lee said.

"Over here," the balding cop called out, "I think we got you two for the price of one."

"Jesus," said Jones, who stopped in front of us and looked from one uniformed cop to another, "who's minding the store?" Jones was a thin man with white hair, watery-blue eyes, and the weary air of a man who had seen much and liked little.

"I just dropped by for tea," said the redhead. He started backing away and soon was leaving. The balding cop followed him.

Jones looked at me, and then at Rick and Johnny Lee. "Who's he?" Rick told him I was a reporter for *The Phoenix*, and Jones shook his head. "No press."

I spoke up. "I gotta know who's in this grave."

Jones looked surprised, puzzled. "Why?"

"It's very important to the mother of a runaway girl," I said. "I believe she ran away with that boy back there." I pointed in the direction of Sims' body.

"I know the story," Johnny Lee said to Jones. "I'll fill you in later."

Jones looked at me, then up at the trees, and then down at the ground. He turned to one of the men with him, apparently a lab man, and pointed to the grave, "Open that up." He looked at me again. "After that . . ." He made a jerking motion with his thumb, the meaning clear.

"Thanks," I said. I walked over to sit on a tree stump and wait. Rick and Johnny Lee wandered off, but didn't go far.

The sky was still overcast, but the light was much better now. I could tell it was going to another hot August day, clouds or no clouds. I was too far away to see into the grave, but I watched as the man zipped opened a big case and took out a small shovel in two pieces. He screwed the pieces together, surveyed the shallow grave for a moment or two, and began to dig.

Actually, he did more probing and scraping than digging. Whoever was in the grave wasn't covered by more than a foot of dirt, maybe not that much. Holding my breath much of the time, I watched the man work. It was a hell of a way to make a living, I thought, digging up bodies in various stages of decay. But then, all of the work in Homicide struck me as ghastly.

Dealing with death by natural causes was gruesome enough. The human body, once it stopped breathing, was more perishable than tomatoes. So who in his right mind would choose to toil every day in the slaughterhouse of murder? It required a stomach, a stoicism, a detachment, maybe even an indifference — *something* — that I knew was utterly beyond me. Even if I could steel myself against the blood and gore of human savagery, the rest of the job would warp my mind. I knew I simply could not immerse myself day in and day out in the dark machinations of the murderous mind — the motive, the means, the method, and all the twisted circuitry of the act of murder. "I'd rather punch a time clock in Hell," I said under my breath.

Several minutes later, I saw that the man had found something. He paused, poked the ground gingerly with the pointed blade of the shovel then started to scrape the soil in a tight little pattern. "Jonesie!" he shouted, still scraping.

By this time I was standing, and Rick and Johnny Lee were hurrying over, with Jones right behind them. I braced myself and walked to the grave, afraid to look, but knowing I had to. What would I say — what *could* I say — to that poor girl's mother? I closed my eyes as I got close enough to see into the grave, and my heart stopped when I opened them and saw a foot: a female foot, with toenails painted red showing through a white, open-toe shoe.

Rick, Johnny Lee and I exchanged looks of dejection as the man with the shovel scraped more dirt from around the foot, revealing the shoe to have a high heel and a strap around the ankle. When he began to probe for the other foot, though, something in me snapped. "The other end, for Christ's sake, work on the other end!"

Surprised, the man looked up at me, a scowl on his face, as if to say,

"Feet, head, what difference does it make now?" But he moved to the other end of the grave, laid the shovel aside, and began feeling in the loose dirt with his hands.

"Careful now," Jones told him.

Soon the man stopped probing and began to scrape dirt aside with his hand, a little at a time. As though in a trance, I stared at the spot he was working on and realized that sweat was seeping through my eyebrows, leaking into my eyes, burning them.

The man stopped scraping and began brushing away dirt with his fingers. Slowly, ever so slowly, white patches of skin began to show through the soil, and then, as if by magic, as if the man had somehow conjured it from the ground with voodoo, the outline of a feminine face appeared in the dirt.

My blood ran cold and nausea gripped me as I stooped for a closer look. With so little of the face showing, it was difficult to make a positive identification and, after all, I had never actually seen Connie Phillips. Then it hit me: I *still* hadn't seen Connie Phillips. It wasn't her. It was a young woman. But it wasn't her.

A great rush of air flew out of my lungs, and I stood up. Rick and Johnny Lee had seen, too, that it wasn't Connie, and looked at each other with expressions of enormous relief. I felt so giddy I almost laughed, and I thought I saw Rick's lips moving in a silent prayer.

It was awful, of course, to be glad that the poor girl, whoever she was, was there. After all, she too had a mother, or *some*body who loved her. But that was life — or, in this case, death — I told myself. I hoped only that Connie Phillips, wherever she was, was worthy of such emotion.

They were still scraping dirt off the girl in the grave when Rick and I left, and a slow, steady rain began just as we got to the car. The heat wave had broken like a high fever, and all around us the trees sighed and swayed in a slight, wet breeze as if delirious with gratitude. Any other time, I would have celebrated, too, but my mind was still on those two bodies back in the woods. I felt drained, and no ordinary rain was going to replenish me. Death in a mature adult was bad. In a youngster it was hideous, a perversion of nature and a mocking of heaven. Rick must have felt pretty much the same way. We rode in silence back to town.

Chapter Fifteen

AROUND NOON, RICK CALLED ME AT WORK with the autopsy report. "This is only preliminary," he said. "They're still working on the bodies. But get this: It wasn't a bullet that killed Sims. That was just for insurance. He was strangled."

"Strangled?"

"The girl, too, but in a different way. She was choked by somebody with powerful hands. With Sims, it was a garrote of some kind. They're still trying to figure out what."

"When was it done?"

"Probably Sunday night. Maybe Monday. Both about the same time. Somewhere else, too; not there."

"Any I.D. on the girl?"

"Bonita Catledge, 16. Runaway. Left home — Charlotte, North Carolina — about six months ago. She was nude, except for the shoes."

"She shot, too?"

"Chest. Close range. Close range on Sims too. Same gun. Ruger .38."

"What do you make of all this?"

"I make this much: We better find Connie Phillips in a hurry."

"Are you that sure she left with Sims?"

"No. But I told you: I'm not a strong believer in coincidence. We've been looking for two runaways; well, we found one of 'em ~ dead. And

I sure as hell thought the other was in that grave."

A chilling thought stabbed into my mind. "Maybe there's another grave out there."

"No. I thought of that, too, and planted the idea with Homicide. There was only one."

"I still don't know what to make of it. Why was only the girl buried? Why not both? Why no clothes? Why Sims and a girl? Hell, we've been assuming he was gay. I just don't get it."

"Let's wait for the full report. They'll have it by the end of the day, if not before, but I'm headed home for some sack time. I'll call you after I go on duty at eight. Home or office?"

"Home. I'm dragging too."

I hung up the phone and walked out into the newsroom. Stopping by the city desk, I told one of the assistant city editors about the two bodies. He said they already knew about them and had a reporter working on it, but thanks anyhow. I went over to where Morgan was sitting, and told her.

Her eyes got wide. "Ben, we'd better not wait until Friday. Let's start tonight. Okay?"

That surprised me. I had expected her to back out altogether. "Morgan, it's not a simple runaway case anymore; it's murder."

"All the more reason to find Connie Phillips and find her quickly."

I couldn't argue with that. It was too reasonable. I tried another tack. "Yeah, but that doesn't mean you have to do the finding. It's too risky."

"Look," she said, "Connie might not even be connected to Sims, right?"

"Right."

"But if she is — or was — then you're on the right track." She pointed a finger at me. "But you still need a woman to talk to the prostitutes. Here I am, ready and willing."

I looked into her eyes. They were ablaze with determination. "All right. It's against my better judgment, but all right. I'll be out front at nine."

"No. Pick me up at my apartment at ten: 629 Orme Circle, just off Monroe. That'll still give us plenty of time, and I won't have to come back here for my car."

"Okay. But we're gonna lay down some ground rules before I let you go out there. I want some hard and fast boundaries. And I want to be able to see you at all times."

She smiled. "Why, sir, even working girls have to go to the ladies' room."

"Funny, Morgan," I said dryly. "Very funny."

I left work early to beat the rush-hour traffic, showered as soon as I got home, and then slept for a few hours. I got up at 8, put a TV dinner in the oven, and went into the bathroom to shave, expecting Rick to call any minute. I needed to tell him that Morgan and I would be on The Strip shortly after 10, so that he and Johnny Lee could help me keep an eye on her.

When he still hadn't called by 9, I got a little worried, and by 9:40 I was a lot worried. Ten minutes later, I left for Morgan's apartment ready to call the whole thing off. When she came to the door, I knew damn good and well I was going to call it off. She was dressed up like a hooker.

"Well," she said, stepping back and turning, "how do I look?"

For a moment I just stared, stunned, but when I could finally manage speech, it spilled out. "Uh, uh." I shook my head. "Nix, *nein, nada*, no. No, no, no. It's too dangerous. No way."

"But Ben," she said, "It's the *best* way. You were right. If I go out there as a reporter or some kind of social worker, those girls won't tell me anything. This way, they'll tell me everything."

"Yeah, and the pimps will spot you in two minutes as fresh meat — new to the street and greener than grass. What do I do if one hits on you, blow my cover?"

"No. You keep calm — that's what you do. Guys have been hittin' on me since I was 16. I can take care of myself."

I was only half listening. "Besides, I've been unable to reach Rick or Johnny Lee. We'll be out there on our own."

"You said we might not be able to count on them anyhow, so what's the difference?"

"There's a *lot* of difference. No. It's just too great a risk."

"Why?" she said. "Don't I look the part?"

I started to say that that had nothing to do with it, but she stepped back into her living room a pace or two and pirouetted, derailing my train of thought. Her short, pleated, white skirt swirled around the best-looking legs I had ever seen, and the fringe around the collar of her red, low-cut blouse added a touch that made her look bewitching.

When she had completed the turn, she stood there, hands clasped demurely in front of her. "Well?"

"Dammit, you look like a million bucks, and you know it."

"What about the makeup?"

I moved forward for a closer look and peered at her face, her fragrance enveloping me. "Good," I said, feeling a bit giddy. "Very good."

"Here." She leaned closer. "I forgot to blot my lipstick. Think you can help me out?" She closed her eyes and moved her lips close to mine. I kissed her softly.

"You don't fight fair," I said.

"Don't think of it as a fight; think of it as a pact, sealed with a kiss." She picked up her purse from a chair near the door. "Let's go. We've got a runaway girl to find."

Chapter Sixteen

AT PEACHTREE AND FOURTEENTH, NEAR COLONY SQUARE, I pulled over to the curb. "You'd better get out here. Any closer to The Strip, somebody might see us and later put two and two together. I've never seen the hookers come up Peachtree this far, but only one block down, you'll run into some."

She nodded.

"Walk down Peachtree, on the other side of the street, till you're opposite The Hamburger Joint I showed you. Work your way on down to the end of the block. Right across that side street is the Midtown Manor Hotel. Don't cross that street. The hotel is full of pimps and they'll be watching right out front. Let the girls come to you as they troll up and down the block."

"Yes, Daddy," Morgan said in a simpering voice.

"When you've done all you can do there, cross Peachtree and work your way back up this side of the street, toward The Hamburger Joint. I'll have you in sight the whole time, and as soon as you walk by I'll head for the car and pick you up either here or along the way here. Got it?"

She nodded.

"Now, if you hit pay dirt before you've come full circle or if you want to call it off for any reason — bend down as if you were having a problem with a shoe and then start walking back to this spot. I'll pick you up here if not before."

"What about a signal for trouble? I might not be in a position to fiddle with my shoe."

"Signal? Trouble?" I said archly. "But you're the big girl who can take care of herself, remember? Guys have been hitting on you since you were 16."

She rolled her eyes and said wearily, "Ben."

"Okay," I said. "A signal for trouble: scream."

"Scream?"

"As loud as you can. I'll come running. And who knows? Somebody nearer might come to your aid, too. Chivalry can't be completely dead, not even on The Strip."

"'Scream,' the man says."

"Sorry, but that's the best I can do."

She opened the car door and started to get out.

I whipped out the picture of Connie and said, "Wait. You'll need this."

She looked at the picture and closed the door again. "Hold it a minute," she said. She opened her purse and took out a roll of Scotch tape. "Give me that." She took the picture.

Seconds later she had the picture taped inside the flap of her shoulder bag. Practicing, she lifted the flap a few times as if going into her bag for something, and each time she did, Connie's picture popped up. She could flash it all night without being conspicuous about it.

"Smart girl. What else you got in there?"

"Tape recorder." She opened the door again. "Voice activated and very sensitive. Any other questions?" Smiling prettily, she got out, closed the door, crossed the street, and began walking down Peachtree.

"Good-lookin', too," I said to myself.

The Strip seemed busier than usual for a weekday night. Ordinarily, the street had a predictable pattern of heavy activity — weekends, government paydays, conventions — but except for weekends I hadn't kept track of it lately. Whatever the cause, it was a break for us.

Inside The Hamburger Joint, I ordered a cup of coffee at the counter then took up a position at the front, where a long, high shelf ran the length of the room and overlooked Peachtree. A few stools were provided, but most people stood, sipping coffee or Coke, and watching the action on The Strip.

Only seconds later, Morgan appeared out of the shadows and stopped on the corner to talk to a short, young brunette wearing tight blue jeans and high-heels. Two men, both tall, muscular blacks standing to my immediate right, noticed her too, but they went back to their conversation when it appeared that Morgan and the girl were merely chatting. I saw Morgan open the flap of her purse, and the girl shake her head, but they continued talking until a blue Dodge van turned off Peachtree Street and stopped at the corner. The girl walked over to the passenger side and soon beckoned Morgan to join her, but after a moment or two Morgan backed away from the van as the girl climbed in.

Thirteen minutes later, when the blue van pulled up to the same corner again, and the girl got out, Morgan was about halfway down the block. The hookers were talking to her, all right, but they were all shaking their heads. Men were talking to her, too. Three stopped her on the sidewalk, and one, driving a Gran Prix, pulled out of traffic and got out of his car to speak to her. But she kept moving.

A man to my left, a tall, lean black with a ring in his ear, said to his companion, "That chick in red harder to pick up than a watermelon seed. Must be savin' it fo' Christmas."

His companion laughed and sang, "Here come Santy Claus, here come Santy Claus . . ." They both laughed, shuffling about and nudging each other, before turning their attention in another direction.

As Morgan got near the Midtown Manor Hotel, I sometimes lost her in the crowd. There must have been 30 hookers on the two corners at the end of that block, with seven or eight more in the street. It was hard to count them, they came and went so frequently, but after several anxious minutes I saw Morgan emerge from the throng and cross Peachtree.

On my side of the street, she stopped to talk to a tall redhead. Two other girls, then a third, joined them. Soon all the hookers were pointing to the other side of Peachtree, and I felt a rush of apprehension as Morgan recrossed the street and headed straight for the Midtown Manor Hotel.

Keeping my eye on her as she walked up to a short blonde in front of the hotel and began talking, I eased out the front door of The Hamburger Joint and headed in her direction, walking slowly, watching.

Morgan opened the flap of her bag, and the girl peered at Connie's picture. So far, so good, I thought — and then somebody yelled "Thief! Thief!" and all hell broke loose.

The guy doing the yelling was a fat man of about 50 wearing a suit and glasses. He stood in the middle of Peachtree Street by the open door of a Ford Thunderbird, waving wildly. Pointing first one way and then another, he shouted, "They took my wallet! They stole my money! Stop them! Stop them!"

It was impossible to know whom he meant. Hookers were fleeing in all directions. But not all got away. Four rushed into a coffee shop near the Midtown Manor Hotel and ran right into the arms of two policemen running out of the place to see what was going on. While one of the cops stayed behind to hold the girls, his partner ran toward the robbery victim.

It was then I noticed that Morgan was still standing there on the sidewalk — and I knew with a sudden sick feeling what was coming next. The cop grabbed her, placing her under arrest, and hustled her toward the man in the street, who was still yelling and waving wildly.

Still half a block away, I ran toward Morgan and got there in time to hear the robbery victim, a bit calmer now, say he couldn't identify Morgan as the thief. "She was a brunette, but I think she was dressed different. Younger, too. It all happened so fast."

The cop, a beefy guy with a beer belly whom I'd never seen before, saw me pressing in and told me to move back, but while I had his attention, I blurted out, "She didn't do it. She's with me. I'm a reporter for *The Phoenix*. She is, too."

"Sure," he said slowly, looking Morgan up and down.

I whipped out my billfold and showed him my press card.

He turned to Morgan. "And where's yours?"

Calmly, she said, "They haven't issued me one yet. I'm a new employee."

With a look that said, "Yeah? Now tell me another," the cop said, "Um, huh."

"It's true," I said. "We're out here to do a story on prostitution. That's why she's dressed the way she is."

"Hey, what about my wallet?" the robbery victim said.

Other motorists, blocked by the victim's Thunderbird, had begun to honk their horns.

"Hold your horses," the cop told the victim. "For the time being, pull your car over to the side there so the rest of these people can get through." He turned to Morgan and me. "You two stay put."

The man moved his car, and the cop signaled for motorists to come on through. Turning back to Morgan and me, he said to Morgan, "I don't know, little lady. You don't look like any reporter I ever saw. But," He pointed toward the coffee shop, "I got four over there that I *know* are hookers. So I'm letting you go."

"Thanks, officer," I said, enormously relieved.

But Morgan said, "And what will you do with them?" She indicated the girls in the coffee shop. "I was interviewing the little blonde when the robbery occurred, so I know she didn't do it."

I looked toward the coffee shop, and sure enough the short blonde was one of the four under arrest. "It's likely none of 'em did it," the cop said. "But all the same I'm gonna take 'em in."

"On what charge?" Morgan demanded.

"Loitering," the cop said in a superior tone.

"Then take me, too," she told him flatly, jaw set. "If *they* were loitering, then I was loitering."

"What!" I said. But she kept her eyes locked on his. I turned to him. "She didn't mean it, officer; she didn't mean it."

"I meant every word," she said with a determined toss of her head.

The cop studied her for a minute. "You sure you ain't got a press pass?"

"I'm sure."

"Then you talked me into it," he said. "Go over to the coffee shop and tell my partner I sent you. There's always room for one more." He turned to me with a sharp look and raised a hand, palm up. "I tried, pal."

I groaned as Morgan marched smartly toward the coffee shop. I started to follow, but the cop stopped me. "My partner ain't as nice as I am," he said. "You go over there, *you* might wind up in the pokey, too. Better to cool your heels awhile. You can pick her up in a couple of hours."

"Where?"

"City jail."

Chapter Seventeen

I ARRIVED AT THE JAIL AT 1:45 A.M., paid the jailer $50 bail, and sat down in the waiting room, a dreary place with dirty windows, walls of institutional gray, a dull, black linoleum floor, and cheap metal-frame chairs and tables, all of them beat up or bent. A waiting room in Hell would have more charm, I thought.

A few other people waited, too — an elderly woman, two middle-aged men, and a couple whose age I guessed as late 20s, early 30s.

Except for the couple, we all sat apart, looking, I imagined, like subjects in an Edward Hopper painting, figures caught in the various attitudes of the tedium of life in forlorn settings. I thanked God that I was only temporarily one of these people. In my role as a reporter, I had seen their kind many times before, most notably in courtrooms and jailhouses all over the South. They were people whose whole lives seemed to be spent on standby, waiting to bail others out of jams. The eternally disappointed waiting for the eternally disappointing. They looked careworn and poor, defeated and despairing, and they all wore the same expression: stricken but resigned, human rabbits caught in the headlights of misfortune again.

Fortunately, I didn't have to wait long. Around two o'clock a buzzer sounded, a heavy green metal door swung open, and Morgan, looking none the worse for wear, walked into the waiting room.

"You OK?" I asked, getting to my feet.

She smiled and came to me. "Well, fine — for somebody who's been fingerprinted, strip-searched, and held in a two-man cell with four other women for an hour."

"You did ask for it," I reminded her.

She gave me a look of surprise. "You don't blame me, do you?"

I tried to smile, but a yawn overtook it. "Not at all. It'll make a hell of a story — speaking of which, did you get any leads on Connie?"

She frowned. "Nothing, Ben. If she's a prostitute here in Atlanta, she's not working The Strip, at least not as a streetwalker. I talked to enough of them to be convinced of that."

"Strike three," I said wearily. "Let's get out of here. This place is depressing."

Just as we got to the exit, the door opened and Rick and Johnny Lee, looking tired and disgusted, came in with a prisoner in tow, a lean, muscular black male who appeared to be about 19 or 20, and whose clothes, jeans and tee shirt, were blacker than he was.

Rick saw us first and brightened. "Hey, Reporter! Just the man I want to see. Hold up till we get rid of this yardbird and I'll buy you a cup of coffee. Looks like you could use it." He gave Morgan an appraising look. "No. Plan B: Meet you at Pete's. No. Make it the Majestic. It's closer. Ten minutes max — if the radio cooperates, of course." He waved and went on.

THE MAJESTIC, AN ALL-NIGHT DINER on Ponce de Leon Avenue, was an Atlanta landmark that had seen better days, back when Ponce was a fashionable address. Old Atlantans still spoke of it fondly, but few of them went there anymore. A reversal of fortune that began in the 1960s had reduced Ponce de Leon to a street of broken dreams, seedy and in places only a notch or two above skid row. The Majestic, caught in the street's undertow, had gone down with it.

It still served good, strong coffee, though, and a cup of it gave me my second wind. Morgan drank hot tea, and soon Johnny Lee and Rick came in. After the introductions and ordering coffee, they explained

that they had been tied up all night in a search for their prisoner, a burglar they finally found hiding in a chimney on the roof of a house off
Piedmont Avenue.

We then told them about our evening. Rick, smiling, said, "That
confirms it: all reporters are nuts." He looked at Morgan. "See, the idea
is to stay *out* of jail, not to get *in*."

She laughed. "Believe me, once was enough."

Rick turned to me. "Now, about the autopsy." He glanced at Morgan.
"This ain't nice, but you look like a big girl to me."

"I'm a big girl. Go ahead."

"Both Sims and the girl had been bound and both had had sexual
intercourse. They found semen in the girl's vagina—" Rick hesitated
before adding, "-and in Sims' anus."

"Rape," Morgan said.

Rick shook his head slowly. "They don't think so. There were no
signs of struggle — bruises, scrapes, scratches — and the girl had a record,
been picked up twice for soliciting. It wasn't Sims' first time for that
kind of thing, either. I don't know how they can tell, but they can."

"So he *was* a fag," Johnny Lee said, looking disgusted. "Or at least bi."

I looked from Johnny Lee to Rick. "I'm drawing a blank on all this;
how about you two?"

"Doesn't add up," Johnny Lee said. "Fags and hookers don't usually
run around together."

"Beats me, too," Rick said.

"And where does Connie fit in?" I asked. "None of this sounds like
the girl described to me."

"Yeah," said Johnny Lee, "but it was her *mother* who did the describing."

"True. Still . . ."

"Wait," Rick said. "Johnny Lee's right. You're trying to make the
Connie you know fit in here. She doesn't. But the *real* Connie Phillips
might, and I'd still bet my badge she left home with Sims. Keep in mind
that we didn't expect to find Sims mixed up in anything like this, either."

I nodded, but my thoughts had snagged on something Rick had said,
and were trying to get untangled. I had read somewhere — how did it
go? — that if you asked the right question, the answer was inherent in
the question. Okay. Fine. But what was the right question?

I started with the most obvious: why had we been unable to find Connie Phillips? That much now seemed simple: We had been looking in the wrong places. Okay, what was the *right* place to look? No, I thought; that was putting the question too broadly. But for the life of me I couldn't think how to frame it.

I went back to the beginning: Jane Kimball was not only lying, or at least hiding something, she also seemed — what? — scornful of anybody Connie seemed interested in. Scornful? Or jealous? But if jealous, why? She was probably everything Connie wanted to be: trim, pretty, poised, confident. Why would Jane Kimball be jealous of Connie Phillips?

I knew there was something there, but it wouldn't come into focus, so I left it alone for the moment and moved on to other thoughts, recalling every aspect of our search, hearing again a solid chorus of "No" and seeing again all those shaking heads. All but one, anyhow: the little blonde in the massage parlor, the one who thought she recognized Connie's picture.

But *where*, I asked myself, would a massage-parlor hooker have crossed paths with Connie, especially if Connie were nowhere around The Strip?

And that's when it hit me: In my mind's eye, I saw the little massage-parlor blonde smiling and I heard her say again, "Bring your girlfriend, too; I go both ways."

I jerked straight up in the booth, startling the others, and blurted, "I got it! At least, I think I've got it." I was so excited that I had trouble telling them how I had put it together. But when I finally got it all out, they saw it too, or at least found it mighty interesting.

"She's gay, for Christ's sake!" I said. "Jane Kimball *knows* that. That's what she was hiding. And that's where the blonde in the massage parlor saw her — not on The Strip or anywhere else prostitutes hang out, but where women who like women socialize." I raised my hands as if to say, "There it is: the missing piece; what do you think?"

"I don't know, but it fits," Rick said. "It's right out of the textbooks, too. Most detectives screw up by overlooking the obvious."

Johnny Lee looked impressed, but he also looked more disgusted than ever. "Christ Almighty, Blake! The deeper we go, the worse it gets." He cursed under his breath.

"Sorry. I had no idea — and I still might be wrong."

"Hell," he said; "we start out looking for a little Miss Homebody — a *virgin*, you said — and next thing you know we're hip-deep in murder and perversion, and running our asses off — Pardon me, Miss Matthews — looking for a dyke. A dyke! No damn wonder she's still a virgin."

Rick said, "Hey, JL, you gotta admit it's interesting."

"Yeah?" Johnny Lee said, bristling. "So is a freeway pile-up." He slumped back into the booth and tapped on the plate-glass window. "Just once I'd like to run into somebody out there who's normal. Whole damn city's full of people with dark, stinking secrets."

"You been on the job too long," Rick said. "People are just people."

"Yeah, and they're no damn good." Johnny Lee caught himself and added: "Present company excepted."

Rick laughed, clutched Johnny Lee's arms with both hands and said in a lisp, "Don't exthept me, John-John; I've juth been dying to tell you my little thecret."

Johnny Lee looked at Rick and laughed in spite of himself. "Creep," he said.

In his normal voice, Rick continued, "And if you think I don't know about those red satin high-heels and that off-the-shoulder cocktail dress in your locker, you're sadly mistaken."

Johnny Lee blushed. "You *ought* to know. You asked if you could stash them there."

We all laughed, but when the laughter died, the question that was on all our minds hung in the air before us, waiting for an answer. "OK," I said. "What next?"

"I know a couple of lesbian bars on Cheshire Bridge Road," Rick said, "Sisters and Garland's. But dykes'll be even harder than prostitutes to get anything out of."

"Try the message-parlor blonde again," Johnny Lee said. "What you've figured out might jog her memory."

"Yeah," I said, "but first let's make sure we're on the right track this time. Is there a pay phone in here?" I looked around, but didn't see one.

"Just outside," Rick said, pointing. I got up out of the booth. "But who are you gonna call? It's nearly 3 in the morning."

"Know a better time to catch somebody at home?" I headed toward the door.

Chapter Eighteen

I GOT LUCKY. Jane Kimball, instead of her mother, answered the phone. "Hello." She spoke softly, but sounded surprisingly alert for that time of night.

I didn't even tell her who I was. She'd know soon enough. "I've got some quick questions for you, and I want straight answers. You hear?"

She knew who it was, all right. After a short silence she said, "Yes."

"Here's the first: Was Connie Phillips gay?"

I waited for an answer, and when none came, I thought she had simply put down the phone. But then I heard her breathing. "If you'd prefer," I added, "I can come by tomorrow and discuss your relationship with Connie more fully — with your mother present."

"No!" she whispered fiercely, frightened. "Don't do that."

"Then, was Connie Phillips gay?"

Still she hesitated. "Is this for the paper?" Her tone of voice was pained, incredulous.

"I won't use your name — if you cooperate. But if you don't . . ." I let it hang there. There was no way I could use her name in such a connection without proof, and probably not even then. But she didn't know that.

Finally, wearily, she said, "Yes. Now can I hang up?"

"In one more minute. Did she have any gay contacts in Atlanta?

Females, I mean."

"I don't know."

That sounded like the truth. "Ever mention any gay hangouts?"

"I don't—"

"Think!" I snapped. "Connie's life might depend on it."

"Is she—"

"Answer the question."

"She did mention a place once, a place where women go. But I don't remem—"

"Was it Sisters?"

"I don't—"

"Was it Garland's?"

"Yes. That's it."

"She mention any names?"

"Only that Miss Curry, our gym teacher in high school, took her there. This was about a year ago."

"This Miss Curry—"

"She's gone. Moved away. She got fired, I heard."

I could guess why. I was ready to hang up. "Thanks," I said.

"Wait. There's something you have to understand. I'm not that way."

"Gay, you mean."

"Yes."

I couldn't resist. "She raped you, you mean."

"Well, no—"

"Oh, I see: you just lay back and enjoyed it."

She hesitated. "Well, yes. We started spending the night together, and one thing just led to another. You have to understand that."

"I understand," I said, meaning more than the words conveyed. I had a life-sized picture in my mind of an imperious Jane Kimball, this Goody Two-Shoes teenager, lolling in bed while Connie's head bobbed dutifully between her thighs. Jane Kimball was one of life's takers. No giving or even sharing in that girl. "Pleasant dreams," I said, and hung up.

BACK INSIDE THE DINER, we didn't know whether to celebrate or hold a wake. At last we had a solid lead, but it was leading straight to heartbreak, if not worse, for two very worried parents.

"I knew it," said Johnny Lee, scowling. "It was too awful not to be true."

"She's still very young," Morgan said. "Maybe she's just confused."

"They're *all* confused," Johnny Lee said. "I never met a hooker who wasn't going to quit next week and go straight, or a fag who wasn't in therapy and looking for somebody else to blame, or—"

"Let's worry about her sex life later," Rick said. "That was one nasty customer who chilled Sims and the girl, and Connie just might be mixed up in it too. Let's concentrate on finding her."

I looked at my watch. "It'll have to be tomorrow. Too late tonight."

Johnny Lee waved a hand. "Forget it. Rick's right; those dykes won't tell you squat."

"They might tell me," Morgan said. "Ben can go with me. It might help if they think we're just a kinky couple looking for kicks."

I looked at her. "You don't have to do this, you know."

"We have to if we're going to find Connie Phillips," she said.

"It's our only shot," Rick said, raising his eyebrows.

"Aren't you three overlooking something?" Johnny Lee said. "We could be stepping on Homicide's toes on this one, and you know where that'll land us."

"Play dumb," Rick said simply. "We're just helping a friend look for a runaway girl. If she was involved with Sims, we certainly didn't *know* it. Besides, if we went to Homicide with our hunches — and that's all they are — they wouldn't lift a finger to find Connie."

Johnny Lee thought that over. Finally he shrugged and said, "Hell, I don't have to *play* dumb. I *am* dumb."

"Tomorrow," Morgan said.

Chapter Nineteen

GARLAND'S TURNED OUT TO BE A NICER PLACE than I had expected. Cheshire Bridge Road, just off Piedmont, was littered with strip joints and cheap retail stores, but here and there a nice restaurant or bar had elbowed its way in, giving the neighborhood a touch of class. Garland's was one of these establishments. It sat way back on a wooded lot, all but hidden from the street, and was approached by a narrow horseshoe drive that curved beneath a canopy of pine and oak branches. Going there was like leaving the city for a hideaway in the forest.

A forest hideaway seemed to be what the designer of the place had in mind, too, for the bar was built like a log cabin, and its only concession to commercialism was a small sign over the door in blue neon script. I pulled into a crowded parking lot on the side of the building and parked.

"Do I look OK?" Morgan asked. "Not too working-girlish?"

She had come straight from work, and wore a white linen sundress with a navy-blue jacket. From a paper sack, she pulled dark high-heels and slipped them on.

"You look great," I said. And she did.

Inside, Garland's looked more like a club than a bar. To the right of the entrance was a sitting room, nicely furnished, and to the left was a game room with a billiards table. Straight ahead was the bar, a cozy place softly lit by low lights and candles, and beyond was a dance floor.

The place was crowded, but the hostess found us a table, and soon a pixy-ish waitress took our order, a vodka tonic for Morgan, a Michelob for me.

As the waitress left, I asked Morgan, "How do we do this? If you start right in asking questions, they might get suspicious and clam up."

"We'll just have to take that chance," she said. "We'll know soon enough whether this is a waste of time."

"Not soon enough for me. Do you realize I'm the only man in this place?"

Morgan looked around. The dance floor was crowded with women dancing to music played by a deejay, and the bar was lined with women too. Even the bartender was a woman, though the only clue to her sex was big breasts under a white T-shirt; otherwise she looked like a male, a tough male. Nor was she the only one there with short hair, and mannish looks and mannerisms. About half the patrons looked that way, as if male and female genes had somehow collided, causing an accident of nature. *Hello, police? I want to report a gender-bender.*

"Just my luck," I said, "to be surrounded by women — and they're all queer."

Morgan gave me a pointed look. "Not all, my good sir."

"Do you suppose they even have a men's room here?"

Before she could answer, the waitress arrived with our drinks, and Morgan struck up a conversation with her. "Nice place you have here" — that sort of thing, and soon Morgan was showing her Connie's picture. "My little sister," she explained.

The waitress nodded no and left, but when she got back to the bar she said something to the mannish bartender that made her look our way. Morgan saw it, too, and said, "Be back in a minute." Seconds later, she was showing Connie's picture to the bartender, as well as to some women sitting nearby at the bar. None of them showed a sign of recognition, but when Morgan walked away, heading for the hostess, they leaned together and talked it over with the bartender, or so it seemed to me.

Soon Morgan was back at our table. "No luck," she said, sitting down.

"Don't be so sure." I directed her attention to the bartender, who was now on the phone. "Give it some time."

A few minutes passed, and then our waitress showed up with fresh drinks. "On the house," she said. "Courtesy of the management."

"Yeah?" I said, surprised. "Who's that?"

Before the waitress could answer, a tall, red-haired woman walked up, dismissed her, and said, "I'm Eve Garland. The house, so to speak. The drinks are on me. May I sit?"

She was a good-looking woman of about thirty-five with an air of authority that was enhanced by the expensive gray pinstripe business suit she wore. I stood and made the introductions, and then we both sat down.

"Morgan," Eve said. "What a pretty name." Suddenly, as if by magic, a drink appeared in front of her. She tested it with a sip and nodded. The waitress went away again. Then, taking her time, she lit a cigarette and looked first at me and then at Morgan. "My employees tell me you're looking for someone, a girl."

We both nodded and Morgan said, "My kid sister."

The woman gave her a measured look and then said pleasantly, "Why here?"

I was about to say, "Because we've looked everywhere else," but Morgan said first, "I know my sister."

"I believe you have a picture of her," the woman said. "May I see it?"

Morgan raised the flap of her handbag and pushed the handbag toward the woman. The woman looked at it and took another drink. Turning to me she said, "Are you a relative, too?"

Something told me to play it straight, that under her polished exterior this woman was one tough cookie, and smart too. "I'm a reporter for *The Phoenix*." I took out my wallet and showed her my press card. She nodded, and I added, "The girl's mother asked me to try to find her."

I thought I saw the woman's interest quicken. But she remained cool, poised. "And what happens if you do?" she asked.

"I tell her mother where she is."

Her eyebrows went up and she looked at me. "No story about finding her?"

"Well, yes, I'd do a story, too."

"What if she doesn't want to be found? She's 18, I believe you said."

I thought that one over. "Then I wouldn't reveal her whereabouts. I'd assure her mother that her daughter was well, if in fact she were, and I'd try to persuade Connie to call home and tell her mother so. But beyond that, nothing. It would be out of my hands."

"Would you like another drink?" she asked.

Both Morgan and I said no, thanks. We still hadn't touched the second ones. Besides, I thought the woman knew something, was feeling us out, thinking things over, and I didn't want her distracted. When she didn't speak for several moments, I said, "Look, Miss Garland—"

"Please, call me Eve."

"Eve," I said, "the girl we're looking for may be in danger."

Eve looked at me, measuring again, and then drained her glass. Almost before she put it down again it was whisked away, and a new one put in its place. She lit another cigarette and said, "I read your story about this girl, and no sister was mentioned. I believe, in fact, that you said she was an only child." She turned to look at Morgan.

Morgan didn't bat any eye. "I'm a reporter, too," she confessed. "Some people don't like to talk to reporters; we thought we'd get farther saying I was the sister."

Eve turned to me again. "I also saw the story in this morning's paper. The one about the two bodies being found."

"We believe Connie left home with that boy, Sims, the one who was murdered. If she did . . ." I didn't go on, my meaning obvious.

For a moment, Eve sipped her drink and smoked. I had the impression that she was tempted to reveal something, but at length she smiled and said, "Wish I could help you." She rose.

I had one more gambit to try. "We were told that the girl used to come here with a woman named Curry, a high school gym teacher at Crosskeys High School."

Eve gave me a long, long look, but finally said, "Sorry." She snapped her fingers and a waitress hurried to her side. Pointing to us, Eve said, "These people are my guests." The waitress nodded and Eve left, saying, "Stay as long as you like."

A few minutes later, we left. Outside we found Rick waiting for us. Cap pushed back on his head, he stood leaning against a front fender of his squad car, parked right at the front entrance next to a no-parking sign. When he saw us he stood and stretched. "'Bout time," he said. "I've been here so long, I must have scared off 30 or more customers. They see the squad car and just keep going."

I pointed back toward Garland's as we walked over to him. "Buddy, there are some women in there who wouldn't be scared of you and two more like you."

He laughed. "Find out anything?"

I shook my head. "Mum's the word in there — but I think they know something." I turned to Morgan. "Don't you?"

Morgan thought so, too, and we told Rick about our meeting with Eve Garland.

"Maybe if I came back alone . . ." Morgan said.

"She's a hard woman," I said. "If she knows anything, she won't tell us until she gets good 'n' ready to tell. Let's give her time to think it over."

We all looked at each other. Time was one thing we felt we didn't have.

"We have no choice," Rick said. "The string's run out."

Looking glum, Morgan and I nodded our heads.

"Waiting's the toughest part of any case," Rick said.

I knew he was trying to sound optimistic, but I knew also that most things moved in their own good time, and it was rare when they moved fast enough to suit most of us.

"Tell you what," Rick said. "Let's sleep on it and then put our heads together tomorrow night. JL and I have some comp time off — a Friday night, for a change — and we're getting together with some other cops at The Blue Lantern. Know it?"

I nodded. It was a tavern on Ponce. Then I looked at Morgan. We had a date, but we could visit the tavern awhile, I figured. She said OK.

"Eight o'clock," Rick said. Looking at me, he added, "You want to know about cops and stress? You'll get an earful at The Blue Tavern. Riley might drop by, too."

My interest quickened. Riley's breakdown in court, sad as it was, would make a good story, bring home to the reader just how frustrating and destructive police work could be. I looked forward to a first-hand account of his ordeal. "What did they do to him?" I asked Rick.

"He's in counseling, on a paid leave of absence — pending an in-house review."

"What'll be the outcome?"

Rick looked at the sky, as if consulting the stars. "Well, he'll never be a real cop again." Then he lowered his gaze and gave me a look that said,

"It's not fair, but this is the way it is." Counting on his fingers, he said, "One, you don't get a second chance after losing it in the line of duty. Too risky for all concerned. Two, you don't break down in public. Bad for the department's and the uniform's image. And, three, you don't talk to a judge like that and get away with it — ever. Bad politics. They'll find Riley a desk somewhere, out of the way, and give him some meaningless records that need to be moved from one side of the desk to the other today, and then back again tomorrow. It's the department's version of cutting out paper dolls."

"So the counseling is a charade. There's no such thing as rehabilitation." *Jesus*, I thought. The average person had no idea what it was like to work in law enforcement.

"Oh, they might put Humpty together again," Rick said. "But it won't be as a cop." He raised a cautionary finger. "But that's not as cynical as it sounds. The higher-ups *do* see the counseling procedure as a way to ferret out the weak links — but the average cop does, too. Knowing what you know about Riley, would *you* want him as your partner? Would you like to get in a jam and call for back-up, and hear that Riley was on his way to help?"

He knew my answer already. No prudent person would say yes. Still, I found it hard to accept. As a newspaperman, I wanted to expose problems to which there were remedies. What good could it do to report on wrongs that couldn't be righted? I knew I'd have to come to grips with that sooner or later. Now wasn't the time. I changed the subject. "Where's JL tonight?"

"On duty somewhere," Rick said. "I didn't tell him I was coming over here. He's still getting used to the idea that Connie's gay."

"What is it with him and gays, anyhow?" I asked.

"Yes," Morgan said. "Any mention of sexual deviation seems to set him off."

Rick glanced at Morgan and then at me. "Well, in the first place, JL's so straight you could use him as a plumb bob." He hesitated. "But there's something else. You know that blues song: 'I'm in love with a woman; she's in love with a woman, too'?"

I knew the song, but I didn't see the connection.

"JL's wife left him for another woman," Rick said.

"Oh," Morgan said.

"Ouch," I said.

Rick continued, "But I think it goes deeper than that. JL's just a simple country boy at heart. Good as gold, truly decent, and expects everybody else to be, too. Well, they aren't, and that's the first thing you learn as a cop. This job doesn't just show you the worst side of your fellow man; it rubs your nose in it. And you either adjust or you don't. And for some reason a lot of cops don't. Can't, I guess. Me, I just roll with the punches. But JL seems unable to do that. The Big City shattered his rose-colored glasses, then his wife left him, and now everything looks black to him."

"So why — a guy with that many problems — is he helping to find Connie, especially if she's gay?" I asked.

Rick shrugged his shoulders and leaned against the fender of his squad car again. "Why am I helping? Why are *you* helping?" He looked at Morgan. "Why is *she* helping?" He grinned. "Me? I love a mystery."

I didn't know what to say. I was helping, I thought, because a decent and helpless woman had appealed to me for help, and of course because there might be a good story in it.

Morgan cleared her throat. "Well," she said, as if unsure whether to speak, "Johnny Lee may be looking, without realizing it, for his own little girl. We're not always as rational as we might like to think."

She had a point, I thought. I hadn't agreed to help until Mrs. Phillips mentioned Joanna. And Morgan had lost her husband, her marriage. Maybe life's losses left holes in us that we felt compelled, in whatever way, to try to fill. But if that were the case, what had Rick's loss been? Innocence? I was about to ask, but just then he spoke and I got distracted.

"You may have something there," he said to Morgan. "JL really loved his wife — Sue Ann's her name — and he's crazy about their little girl. But I worry about losing JL. Sue Ann's leaving him was just more proof that people are no damn good. So JL's caught in a bind and can't break out. He loves her, but she's no damn good, so *why* does he love her? I keep tellin' him to quit the force while there's still time." He held up a hand, showing the thumb and index finger nearly touching. "Sometimes I think he's *that* close to a flameout."

"I'm sorry to hear that. " I thought of the high suicide rate among cops, one of the highest in the land. "I really like Johnny Lee."

"There's not a better partner on the force," Rick said. "I'd hate to see him crash and burn." Then, as if to shake off an idea he found too horrible to contemplate, he straightened up, grabbed my arm, and smiled. "But, hey, let's lighten up here; I'm gettin' depressed." He opened his car door, gave us a salute, and started to get in the car. "Eight o'clock. Blue Lantern. Sometime in the evening—" He grinned. "—before we get wasted, the four of us can huddle in a corner and plan our next move."

We waved goodbye, but a second later he was climbing back out of the car, the grin gone.

"Forgot to tell you," he said, standing with the car door open. "Our GI bleeder didn't make it. Died around 7 this evening."

He looked dejected. I felt like a tire slowly deflating. "You did all you could."

"I'm sorry," Morgan said.

Rick sighed heavily and looked up at the night sky.

"He waited too late," I said.

He sighed again and made a sour face. "Yeah. Win some, lose some," he said. He got back into the car and drove off.

Morgan and I gave each other a consoling look, and walked in silence to the car. Before we left, though, I stopped the car in front of the club, tempted to go back inside, to talk to Eve Garland again.

"You're thinking what I'm thinking," Morgan said.

"Right."

She put her hand on my thigh and smiled at me. "Let her sleep on it. That's the only way with some people."

"Right," I said and drove off. "What are you doing tomorrow night?"

Chapter Twenty

THE NEWSROOM WAS A BUSY PLACE ON FRIDAYS. Reporters and editors were hard at work on both the Saturday and Sunday papers, hoping to wind up as much as they could as early as they could, and get a head start on the weekend. Most reporters who had been on the road during the week were back in the office, looking forward to a weekend at home.

I sat quietly at my desk, the activity swirling around me as if I were a rock in a river. Where the hell was Connie Phillips? *Did* Eve Garland know something? Or was that my imagination? And if she did know something, was it important? Would it matter? I'd have to go back to see her, but it would be nice to have some leverage when I did.

I took the elevator down to the newspaper's morgue and searched the files for something on Eve Garland. I found nothing but a yellowing news clip in which the opening of her new club was announced in September 1976. There was nothing in the files on a teacher named Curry, either. Or, for that matter, Clifford Sims, except for the story of his murder.

I went back to my desk and called the Sims' residence. I hated to do it. Telephone calls to the bereaved were, in my book of journalistic ethics, beyond the pale. *The Phoenix*, in the interest of aggressive journalism, often required reporters to make such calls, but I didn't know any reporter who thought it was an acceptable thing to do. Yet there I was, calling.

"I'm sorry, but Mrs. Sims is unable to come to the phone." The voice, a woman's, had turned cold as soon as I identified myself as a reporter.

"I know it's an awful time to call," I said, "but this could be terribly important. Please. Just ask her if her son knew or ever mentioned a girl named Connie Phillips."

The voice remained cold. "The missing girl? One moment, please."

I held my breath, but soon the woman was back on the line. "He never mentioned her," she said.

I thanked her and hung up just as Owens approached my desk.

"How's it coming on the missing girl?" he asked.

I shook my head.

"Hang in there," he said. "How about cops and stress?"

"That's coming along fine. In fact, I'm meeting some cops at a tavern tonight for more information."

"Good," he said. "A few beers ought to loosen their tongues." He laughed and walked away.

Just then, I noticed that Morgan had come in. I picked up the phone to call her.

When she answered, I said, "This is an obscene phone call, long distance, collect; will you accept the charges?"

She laughed. "Well, that depends."

"On what?"

"The distance. I don't want to get all worked up if you're too far away."

"I *am* too far away. But maybe I can remedy that tonight. Do we still have a date?"

"We'd better have. I've invested a week's pay in the meal I'm serving you. And I'm getting off at 6 instead of 10."

"We're going to your place?"

"Any objections?"

"Well, you *did* just get out of jail for prostitution."

"Get your facts straight, Mr. Reporter; it was loitering."

"Oh. Well, I can loiter with the best of 'em."

"Good. How does 7:30 sound? We can go to the Blue Lantern for awhile, and then come back to my place for a late dinner."

"Good," I said. "Till then." I hung up.

Chapter Twenty-One

THE BLUE LANTERN MIGHT MORE FITTINGLY have been named the Blue Collar. Policemen, I had noticed, favored working-class establishments as hangout places, though they probably would have been just as welcome in the city's tonier restaurants and watering holes. I had seen it often: The presence of a cop seemed to reassure both patrons and management, which was one reason they were treated to free coffee and food most anywhere they went. "It's good economics," one restaurateur told me. "Cops in, riffraff out."

This was true of the Blue Lantern, too, a typical down-at-the-heels neighborhood pub, with neon beer signs glowing in the window, a row of high-back wooden booths along a wall, a few tables scattered here and there, a couple of video games over in a corner, their lurid light-boards flashing and beckoning, and a television set, the sound turned down, flickering on a shelf behind and above the bar. Any other time, a tavern on Ponce would be loud and rowdy, especially on a Friday night, but tonight in the Blue Lantern a cloister of nuns could have drunk in perfect peace. In fact, the five or six men sitting at the bar looked as solemn as parishioners at a prayer railing, and the other people there, fifteen or twenty, talked quietly at their tables or in their booths. Even the jukebox was throbbing at a sedate volume.

Five policemen were there, three of them with dates, huddled in a booth and spilling out along a table that had been pushed up to the booth to make room for everybody. None of the cops was in uniform, but other patrons in the tavern probably knew they were cops. The bartender would make sure of that, although it might be unnecessary; some people swore they could spot a cop in plain clothes at fifty paces.

Morgan and I sat down at the end of the table as Rick made the introductions. He had come with Johnny Lee, who sat across from me, and neither had brought a date.

"I'm meeting somebody later," Rick explained. Then he sang out, "Bartender! Another pitcher, if you please." Two full ones sat on the extended table already.

"You got a late date, too, Johnny Lee?" I said. I was hoping he'd break into a big smile and say yes.

"Naaa," he said. "Sleep is what I need. I'm gonna turn in early."

After the third pitcher of beer arrived, Rick announced somewhat grandly that I was a "fearless reporter" doing "fieldwork" on cops and stress, and that he wanted them to give me "an earful before the night was over."

I had planned a less formal approach to the subject, but Rick's way got results. As if the men had been waiting eagerly for an opportunity to unburden themselves, they pulled into a tighter circle and launched, all talking at once, into a chorus of complaint.

Much of what they said was beside the point, amounting to no more than occupational bitching – what the U.S. Marine Corps dubiously called a sign of good morale. Rick, knowing that I needed more than grousing and griping, soon channeled the talk into deeper waters.

"How many divorces here?" he asked.

"Two for me," said a young cop named Patrick, a handsome redhead who didn't look old enough for one divorce, let alone two. He smiled sheepishly at his date, a striking honey blonde named Shirley who looked 10 years older than he.

"I'm a three-time loser," said the cop sitting directly across from Patrick in the booth, against the wall. "Working on number four." His name was Buckner and he appeared to be about 45. His date, Nell, holding onto his arm, gave it a reassuring hug. Apparently she hoped to be wife number five. She looked about 40 and was an attractive brunette showing flecks of gray.

"Once for me," said a cop named Terry, "but no more." He flashed a mischievous smile. "I'm 33, and I finally figured out what causes divorce."

Somebody bit. "What?"

"Marriage," he said, laughing. Hoisting his glass, he said, "Let's hear it for bachelorhood."

"You rat!" said his date, a voluptuous blonde named Audrey, about 25. But she had the last laugh. She raised her left hand and passed it under the noses of all, flashing an engagement ring.

Everybody laughed and razzed Terry, then congratulated him and his fiancée.

Rick glanced at his watch and nudged me. "Wait'll Riley gets here," he said loudly, more for the group's benefit than mine, "then you'll get some real scoop on stress."

He said it to goad them good-naturedly, but at the mention of Riley's name they fell silent. It was as if what had happened to Riley reminded them of things better left unsaid, ghosts that only the foolhardy would disturb. After an awkward moment, Terry spoke.

"Riley blew it, no question," he said, lighting a cigarette, the smoke curling upward into a plume of light like a genie let out of a bottle. "But he didn't say a goddamn thing that every cop here hasn't felt, and wished he had the balls to say. In public like that, I mean. And if you ask me, he picked the perfect place to say it: the courtroom."

"Yeah," the other cops muttered.

"It had to happen sooner or later," Patrick said. "I'm sorry it had to be Riley who took the fall. He's a good cop, a good guy. But this has been building a long time." He leaned out over the booth's table as if signaling all of us to draw closer and pay attention. "Think back. It's 1976, right? What's the first thing the new mayor — our new, *black* mayor, the city's first — does. He bounces the white police chief and puts in a black."

"Right," somebody said.

"Next thing you know, we're all guilty of police brutality — and who are the victims? Hizzoner's constituents, the black community."

"Which happens to be damn near two-thirds of Atlanta," Buckner said, glancing around for approval.

Patrick went on. "Who's committing the crime?" His voice and eyebrows rose, prompting.

"Same people: Hizzoner's constituents," Terry said.

"Fuckin' A — pardon my French," Patrick said. "By actual count, 95 percent of the crime in Atlanta is committed by—" He raised his hands, as if directing a chorus "—all together now:"

The group knew their cue. "Blacks," they sang out.

"Right on, brother," Buckner added, draining his glass and then pouring it full again.

"And who are the victims of all this crime?" Patrick asked in a singsong voice.

"Same people: Hizzoner's constituents," Terry said.

"Right, again," Patrick said. "By actual count, 90 percent of the victims of crime in little ol' Atlanta are black."

"You wouldn't think the black leaders — and they are powerful enough to do something about it — would put up with it, would you?" Buckner said.

"They're caught in a bind," said Johnny Lee, elbows on the table, chin cupped in his hands, muffling his words. He raised his head. "If they blame their own people for their problems, there goes their political base *and* the most effective thing they've got going for them: this myth that all their troubles are caused by the white man."

"You got that right," Terry said, putting out his cigarette. "They might debate what color Jesus was, but to them the devil is white."

"Talk about racism," Buckner muttered, rolling his eyes toward the ceiling. "Have you taken a stroll through City Hall lately? All the faces are black. White folks don't work there anymore."

"My aunt, who's sixty-one, lost her job there," Nell said softly, glancing about furtively, as if unsure whether her comments were welcome in this male forum. "She was a clerk in the tax assessor's office. She'd been there fifteen years, too."

"Did she vote for Hizzoner?" Patrick asked.

Nell shook her head slowly and said no.

"Then, there's your answer," Terry said. "Spoils of war."

Buckner put on a smile of innocence. "I wouldn't have bet on the dark horse, either."

Everybody groaned.

"Well, let's keep things in perspective," Rick said. "Only a few years ago, City Hall was all white, except for the maids and janitors. There were very few blacks on the police force back then, either, and none of them held any rank. And, lest we forget, police brutality was a problem in this city."

"I grant you, that's true," Patrick said. "But look what you got now. Is it any improvement? The city's up to its ass in crime, and the courts let 'em out faster than we can haul 'em in."

"Yeah," Buckner said, "and we're the murder capital of these United States, ain't we? I know we were only a couple of years ago, and if the pace has let up any, I haven't noticed."

"I think we're in a hot race for the pennant with Houston," Johnny Lee said.

"Yeah," Buckner added. "What has the Book of the Month Club got on us? Here in Atlanta you got the *Body of the Day* Club. Have you been down to the morgue lately? They're booked fuller than Holiday Inn."

"Crime's bad all over," Rick said, waving a hand.

"Not like here, it ain't," Buckner said. "New York City's got 8 million people. So how come Atlanta, with only about a half million in the city limits, is stacking up bodies like cordwood?"

"Say what you will," Patrick said, "it all started five years ago with the new regime, and you know I'm tellin' it like it is. What was the first thing Hizzoner's new, black chief did? Took the second man out of the patrol cars, right?"

The cops nodded.

"Well," Patrick said, "how do you like it out there all by your lonesome, hopin' that when you need backup, the other guy's not tied up on the other side of town on some fender-bender?"

As if by magic, two more pitchers of beer appeared, and three empty ones were whisked away. As the bartender left, another man joined us, pulling a chair up to the end of the table. Rick introduced him to Morgan and me as Buddy Rentz, "another of the APD's boys in blue." Although balding, Rentz appeared to be about Rick's age. Rick grabbed him by the scruff of the neck and squeezed. "No offense, ol' buddy," he said, "but I was hoping you were Riley. He said he'd try to drop by."

Rentz laughed and spoke expansively in a drawl straight out of South Georgia, "Well, I'm sure as hell glad I ain't Riley. My mama didn't raise no fools." He caught himself and made a funny, apologetic face. "Oops. I shouldn'a said that. I like ol' Riley. He's okay in my book. But he's gone and done it now, an' that's a fact, ain't it?"

All nodded sadly. Then Rick got up and looked about. "I think I'll call Riley," he said. "I'm sure he could use some R and R." He walked away.

Rentz edged his chair closer to the table. "Gimme that glass there," he said, pointing, "and pass that pitcher. I heard what ya'll was talkin' about as I walked up, and I want to get my two cents worth in." The group waited as he poured himself a glass of beer. "I miss my ol' partner, Donnie Youngblood, that's true. Ya'll know him." He waved his glass around to indicate whom he was addressing. "But what I really miss is my shotgun." His voice was a comical wail, his face a picture of incalculable loss, as if the shotgun had been a favorite, trusty dog or a girlfriend he had really liked.

"Hear, hear," Patrick said, raising his glass in a solemn salute. "I was just coming to that."

"I don't know which was worse," Terry said, "taking the shotguns out of the cars or giving us those damn play bullets."

I knew about both moves by the new chief. Controversial, they had been aired thoroughly in *The Phoenix*. Police officers now had to get special permission to check out shotguns, and permission was granted only in emergencies. Before that, a shotgun had been standard equipment in each patrol car, locked upright in a special rack located between the driver and his partner. A short while later, all the officers were required to turn in their regular bullets, round-nose ball ammo. These bullets were replaced by wadcutter, lighter weight, low-velocity bullets used mainly for target practice, more likely to maim than kill. The policemen complained bitterly about the change, saying that wadcutter wouldn't stop a runny nose, let alone a charging adversary.

"I put *two* of those damn things into a turkey last year — this was in a free-for-all down in south Atlanta, a drunk and disorderly," Buckner said, "and that sucker all but laughed at me. Just kept comin.' He didn't drop till I went up 'side his head with my nightstick."

"Yeah," Terry said, "they shouldn't've taken the bullets *and* the shot-gun. Next thing you know, they'll be issuing cap pistols and lassoes."

"You know why, don't you?" Buckner said. "They don't want us to *hurt* any of the little darlings."

"Yeah," Patrick said. "You're supposed to *counsel* them." In a mincing, prissy voice, he added: "Now, Leroy, you *know* it ain't nice to knock lit-tle ol' ladies down and take their purses. I know you didn't *mean* to hurt poor Mrs. Jones with that tire iron. It's just that you come from a bro-ken home 'n' all. But this is naughty, naughty and you're going to have to be punished. Here, hold out your wrist."

"Talk about hurtin'," Rentz said. "I never hurt *anybody* when I had the shotgun. All I ever had to do, anybody give me any shit, was let 'em look down that barrel of doom. Man, you draw down a shotgun on a bad-actin' dude, and all of a sudden he's got Sunday-school manners. Ain't that right, Rick?"

"They'd rather get caught in a McCormick reaper," Rick said, sitting down. "So would I." Rick turned to me. "No answer at Riley's. Maybe he's on his way."

"How 'bout the latest?" Terry said. "No more stakeouts. Can you believe it?"

"Yeah, I can believe it," Rentz said, nodding solemnly. "Too many black brothers gettin' blown away."

"Well, goddamn," Patrick said. "Serves 'em right. There's not a con-venience-store clerk in all of Atlanta who isn't scared shitless—" He caught himself and said, "Sorry, ladies," and continued. "—and who doesn't shake in his boots at the thought of working nights."

"You mean *her* boots," Audrey said. "Most of those clerks are female."

"Right," Buckner said. "But what is it with blacks and convenience stores, anyhow? They can't pass by one without gettin' this overwhelm-ing urge to rob it?"

"*And* shoot the clerk — don't forget that," Patrick said. "Even when the clerk cooperates and offers no resistance." He shook his head in wonder and poured another glass of beer.

"Must be something in the genes," Buckner said.

"It is," Terry said, a deadpan expression on his face. "It's called the 7-11 gene. It was discovered — by accident — just recently by this scientist out in California. He stumbled onto it while he was tryin' to find out what makes blacks steal television sets. I mean, show 'em a broken window in a pawn shop. Do they grab a Rolex? Do they go for the diamonds? Hell, no. Like ducks to water, they grab a Sony, and haul ass. It's in the genes. Right, Rick?"

I could tell that Rick felt uncomfortable. If he had such feelings toward blacks, he had kept them to himself around me, and yet these were his buddies, his fellow officers. He didn't want to alienate them. At length he said slowly, seriously, "Tell you the truth, I haven't noticed that blacks are any worse than whites when it comes to crime. We see more black criminals because Atlanta is a black city. Becoming that, if it isn't already. I think every race has its share of rotten people, and, to me, rotten is rotten, no matter what color it comes in."

To my surprise, the other cops nodded in sage approval, even Terry, who raised his glass and said, "I'll drink to that."

"So will I," Rentz said emphatically.

"Hell," Patrick said. "Even black cops don't like black criminals. Ya'll know Detective Green. Black as the ace of spades, right? Well, he was interrogatin' this ol' boy, black, too, the other day — I brought him in for shopliftin' at Rich's. The boy started in on this brother stuff, thinkin' Green might go light on 'im if he laid on some of that racist crap. Well, Green looked 'im straight in the eye and said, 'Blow it out yo' ass, Jack; you ain't no brother of mine.' "

"Ain't *that* the truth?" Rentz said. "Black cops don't like black scum any better than we like white scum. Still, in all, there may be somethin' to this genes business, though it sure ain't limited to blacks. I've known some white folks I wouldn't let into Hell, let alone Heaven, if I was the gatekeeper, and sometimes it runs slap dab through a whole family."

He grinned and edged forward in his chair. "They's a family of Spiveys down home — big clan — an' they ain't a damn one of 'em, male or female, that's worth two hoots in Hell. Sorriest bunch of people you ever saw — and not white trash, either, mind you. Daddy's a big landowner. But they'll steal the pennies off a dead man's eyes. Tell you a lie right to your face, even if the truth would serve better. They get more fun out of cheatin' than you do out of a parade and a fireworks display. They just won't do right — no way, no time, no how. But everybody in the county knows 'em and don't expect no better out of 'em. 'That's just a Spivey, for you,' they say, 'n' go on about their business."

Rentz' story, as colorful as it was, sent the conversation down new paths, away from cops and stress, so Rick said, "Wait a minute. All this talk about guns and ammo makes us sound like a bunch of little boys, angry because the brass took away our toys. This newspaperman wants to know how being a cop affects you as a *person*, what it does to your psyche."

"Your what?" Audrey said.

"The spirit," Nell said. "The soul." She looked around as if to apologize for her knowledge. "I'm a nurse," she offered.

"Well," Rentz said, "I think the guns and stuff are a big part of that. I want every edge I can get when I hit the streets. Man, it's a jungle out there."

"Kid you not," Buckner said. "I was in Vietnam. They wouldn't let us win over there, and now they don't want us to win here. Hell, in some of the places I have to go into in south Atlanta, I'd call in artillery and air cover if I could."

"So fear is one of the job's pitfalls," I said, hoping to encourage them to speak more directly about it.

Nobody spoke for a moment, but then Buckner said, "Well, I ain't afraid to admit it. I was scared the whole time I was in Vietnam, and there are times when I'm just as scared here on the streets of Atlanta."

"Me, too," Rick said. "Every time I stop a car on a dark street, and have to get out and walk up to it, I'm so scared I could wet my pants." He turned to me. "You wonder why I'm hyper? *That's* why — stuff like that. My whole damn nervous system's in overdrive."

"Amen," Patrick said. "You don't know *what's* waitin' for you in that car, and there you are, out in the open, a sitting duck."

"Doors are my thing," Johnny Lee said, "closed doors. There are times when I feel like I just can't knock on another damn one. I feel like — I don't know — like something horrible, maybe Death, is hiding behind it. I'll knock and it'll slowly swing open, and Death will be standing there smiling, saying, "Ah, so *there* you are." He shuddered. "Gives me the willies just to think about it."

"Hell, you can't help it," Buckner said. "Everybody here has had a friend on the force who got his ticket punched just that way, or some way similar. Remember ol' Ray Roundtree?"

Others nodded. Roundtree, I knew, had been killed in the line of duty a few years back, stabbed in broad daylight at Five Points by a crazed street preacher, one of a tribe of would-be evangelists who ranted and raved in and around Central City Park. They were considered harmless nuisances, but some of them carried on as if the flames of religious zealotry had burned through the firewall of sanity. Pedestrians gave them wide berth whenever they could.

Buckner went on. "Him and me had been battin' the breeze over a cup of coffee maybe two minutes before he bought the farm. Fact, I saw it happen. All Ray was doing was telling this yo-yo to move on. He was harassing people there at the bus stop, Peachtree and Marietta – you know how these street preachers do. I looked around to see what the commotion was, and *wham!* Guy planted a butcher knife right in Ray's chest. *Thunk!* Clear down to the handle. Went right through his heart. He was dead before he hit the pavement. Damndest thing I ever saw. Like lightning, too. But that's just how quick you can get it out there."

"Jesus!" Patrick said. "'Repent or *sayonara*, baby' – the Gospel according to Saint Wacko." He took a sip of beer. "Catch the guy?"

"Sure," said Buckner. "Not me – I was busy with Ray." A far away look crept into his eyes, and I could tell that he was reliving the incident in his mind, as he must have done a thousand times since that day. "Not that it did any good. Like I say, he was here one minute and gone the next." Buckner lifted his glass for a drink. "He went from a coffee to a coffin," he snapped his fingers, "just like that. Had a wife and two kids, too. The crazy? He's in the loony bin. Unfit to stand trial, they said. So he's gettin' three squares a day and sittin' in the rec room watchin' the soaps, all at state expense. Tell me crime doesn't pay."

Nell patted his arm as if to ward off demons, and Audrey, a solemn look on her face, stared at her engagement ring as if it were a crystal ball in which she was seeing for the first time the shadow of an uncertain future.

"I'm scared, too," Terry said, "scared of just that sort of thing – the unpredictable. But what gets me most is what I see. I mean, behind the most average-looking doors, you can find – do find – the damndest meanness. I'm talkin' out-'n'-out cruelty – man to man, man to woman, woman to man, parent to child, child to parent - every combination you can think of. I've got to where I don't trust anybody to be what they seem."

"You trust me, don't you?" Audrey asked.

"Ah, you know what I mean," he said, lighting another cigarette. "But, seriously, The average John Q. Public drives down the average residential street believing that each house contains this average American family doing average American things, living average American lives — and for the most part, he's right. But he's not right near as much as he thinks he is. I'm surprised that some of the hatefulness he's driving past doesn't blow some of those doors off their hinges. Man, I've opened *some* doors that should have been manhole covers; there was such a human sewer behind them. And I *know* that contributed to my divorce. I simply knew things about people, how people really are, or can be, that Marilyn didn't know, couldn't know - and couldn't have accepted if she had known. After awhile we just lived in two different worlds." He turned to Audrey. "Fair warning," he told her, meaning it.

She nodded and smiled.

"I know what you mean," Johnny Lee said, "about being suspicious of everybody. I mean, I can leave my gun and my uniform behind in my locker when I go off duty, but my policeman's *mind* goes with me wherever I go. I can't eat out in a restaurant unless they can seat me facing the door. I'll either wait or go somewhere else."

"Same here," Patrick said.

"Here, too," Rick said.

Johnny Lee continued: "Even on vacation, usually down home, to Claxton, I catch myself driving through towns late at night, on the way there, checking doors, windows, movement of any kind, just as if I were back on my beat. I just can't help it. Wish I could."

"Well, at least you ain't as bad as this ol' boy," Rentz said, grinning, meaning himself. "Two years ago, I was down home in Hawkinsville for a family reunion, and my grandmother, bless pat, admitted to stealing a scarf from a general store when she was nothing but a teenager. I had my cuffs out and was reading 'er her rights before I caught myself."

For a second or two, nobody knew whether to believe Rentz or not, but then Nell scoffed and said, "Oh, you," and everyone burst into laughter.

"You sure that was the Spiveys who'd rather lie than tell the truth?" Johnny Lee asked.

Rentz grinned sheepishly. "Well, they may *be* some Spivey in me. I *did* say they was rounders, so you never know."

The pitchers were getting low again, so Rentz hailed the bartender. While he was doing that, Morgan, Rick, Johnny Lee and I gave each other inquiring looks and agreed silently to leave. It was already past 9 p.m., and Morgan and I still had not eaten.

"Tell you what," Rick said, "Let's all run by Riley's place." He meant the four of us. "Looks like he's not going to show here, and I'm worried about him. He lives alone, and the last thing he needs to do now is withdraw. Could be he's home, just not answering the phone. I get that way sometime." He looked at Morgan and me. "You could follow in your car. It's not out of your way; he lives in a duplex just off North Highland."

Chapter Twenty-Two

RILEY'S DUPLEX WAS ON BELVIEW, in a neighborhood on the east side of North Highland that I seldom went into, though it was less than a mile from where I lived. No main thoroughfare or shortcut ran through it, so there was little reason for most nonresidents to go into it. It was like the rest of Virginia-Highland, though: a hilly network of residential streets and small bungalows, mostly of brick, set close together.

Lights were on in Riley's apartment — one half of a small brick house — and a car was in the driveway, so we all stopped and got out.

Rick ran a few steps ahead to the front door, which stood ajar, as if somebody had just come in. He pushed on the doorbell and called through the screen door, "Hey, Riley. Company!"

Nobody answered, but we could hear a radio playing softly somewhere within, so Rick opened the screen door and sang out again. "Hey, Riley, it's Rick. You decent?"

When there was still no answer, Rick said, "Maybe he's in the shower. Let's go on in and surprise him."

He stepped into the living room and we followed. The room was lit by table lamps at each end of a couch, and, beyond a small, bare dining room, the kitchen was lit, too, but there was no sign of Riley. No sound of water running, either.

"Maybe he stepped out for minute," Johnny Lee said.

"Could be," Rick said. "Wait here."

He started off down a hallway that ran to the right, following, I figured, the sound of the radio. It was turned down low, but I could make out the nasal twang of a country music song.

Suddenly Rick's voice shot down the hall, startling us. "Oh, no!" he cried, the two words dragged out in an unearthly wail of pain. Then the voice turned both piteous and angry. "Oh, Riley, you poor dumb fuck. Jesus H. Christ. Why? Why?"

Johnny Lee, Morgan, and I rushed toward the sound of Rick's voice, and a split second later stood in the doorway of a small, dimly lit den. Inside, hanging from a rope running into the attic, was Riley, a thick brown belt looped under his chin. He had opened the door to the attic, thrown the rope over a rafter, slipped the belt over his head, and kicked away a wooden chair. It lay on its side near his dangling feet, like a last chance discarded with disdain.

"Holy Jesus!" Johnny Lee said, gaping at the horrible sight.

Morgan, in front of me, gasped and whirled to bury her face in my chest. Rick sat on the floor, slumped near Riley's feet. His handsome face was warped with anguish, and he was crying and looking up at the body.

"Do something!" Morgan said, her words muffled against my shirt. She had pulled herself into a small, tight huddle, as if to make a smaller target for the shocks of life.

"Too late," Johnny Lee told her. "Look at him." Realizing what he had said, he quickly amended it. "I mean, he's dead."

I looked at him anyhow; in fact I had not taken my eyes off him. The sight was so horrible that I felt transfixed. As a reporter, I had seen many of death's faces before — on victims of drowning, burning, shooting, suffocation, electrocution, name it — but this was the first hanging victim I had ever seen, and hanging, I realized with a new respect for both life *and* death, was easily the ugliest. Riley's neck was stretched to twice its normal length, maybe more, and his head was a grotesquely swollen bruise, engorged with blood, the face lavender, and the lips puffed and purple. His whole body, in fact, appeared stretched, as if muscles, cartilage, and ligaments had simply slipped their bonds, collapsed. Even his feet looked macabre, the toes pointing down at the floor in an angle I did not know the human foot could assume. A man broken on the rack must have looked like that, I thought — sprung in every joint, long and limp like a spring pulled beyond its limits. The human body reduced to a sagging tube of loose bones. The eyes were the worst, though. The lids were pulled half-way down, like tiny window shades in a doll house, and the pupils, two-thirds exposed, had rolled down, not up, like two dark moons sinking beneath a horizon.

"I'll call it in," Johnny Lee said. He left the room.

"Why don't you go with Johnny Lee?" I said to Morgan. She nodded and followed him down the hall, not looking back. I went over to Rick and knelt on one knee in front of him. "You all right?" I asked.

He sighed and shook his head, first yes and then no. Then, glancing up at Riley's body, he pointed at it, his face still full of hurt, and said — no, demanded, "Why do people *do* that? What, in God's name, is so terrible that anybody would want to do *that* to himself? Jesus Christ!" He winced. "Don't they know it'll pass? That whatever it was, they'd get over it?" He shook his head again, this time as if to clear it. "What a waste! What a big fucking waste."

"Stay angry," I said, remembering what had pulled me through after Joanna died. "It'll help more than anything else."

He blinked and looked at me. "You're right," he said. "It's the only way to deal with this." He rubbed his eyes and got to his feet. But when he looked at Riley again, his resolve seemed to give way. "Oh, Riley," he said. It was the voice of a man wounded to the quick, a man who had not known that pain could drive so deep.

I got right in his face to get his full attention. "Hey! Some people just don't cherish life the way most of us do," I said, biting off my words. "They don't recoil from the thought of suicide, the way others do." I pointed toward the body and snapped, "You have to *think* about something like that to pull it off. Riley *knew* what he was doing."

I was saying only part of what I felt. To me, suicide was one of the saddest, most wrenching events in life, a tragedy of incalculable proportions. But Rick didn't need to hear that. Not now. What he needed to hear was what he was already feeling: that suicide was one of the most stupid acts of man — an unconditional surrender to despair, a head-long rush into oblivion with no turning back, no thought of the healing balm of time. I could not fathom such hopelessness. What candle snuffed out its own flame? Even in the tightest clutches of grief after Joanna died, I had never once thought of suicide. I loved life too much. "He knew what he was doing," I repeated. "People like that do it sooner or later, no matter what. It's a sickness. They love death, not life."

Rick lifted his eyes toward the ceiling and seemed to study it. The small rectangular hole there yawned like the trap door of a gallows, and the rope seemed to tremble under the weight of its deadly burden. Then he looked at the wooden chair, lying on its side near the dangling feet. A rafter, a chair, a rope, a belt — ordinary objects pressed into gruesome service, tools in the knotty problem of self-destruction, a final exam in physics. Botch it and you fail; pass it and you die.

Rick shook his head in disbelief and left the room. I took one more look around and detected for the first time the odor of excrement. I wondered glumly how many people knew that evacuation of the bowels, and even seminal emission, was a common occurrence at death. It was especially true of hanging, I had read somewhere. As you launched yourself into the Great Beyond, you wafted to the hereafter with shitty britches. I wondered how many suicides knew they were inviting such an ignominious end. "Shit," I said, and then I got out of there, too.

"Took 'em six minutes," Johnny Lee said, glancing at his watch, impressed, as the police arrived. "And here comes the meat wagon," he added a minute later as an ambulance pulled up outside.

We sat in the living room and waited for them to come in, Morgan and I on the couch, Rick and Johnny Lee in chairs. Morgan sat close to me, seeking the comfort of the living, I imagined, but she was quiet, her thoughts apparently turned inward.

"Back there," Rick told the two cops as they came in the door. He pointed down the hallway, but didn't follow them, didn't even get up.

Seconds later, I heard the familiar rattle of a gurney, and soon two medics pushed through the door. The rattle of the gurney was oddly unsettling to me until I realized that I now associated it with death.

Every time I heard it rattling, the Grim Reaper was hovering nearby. First, the GI bleeder — one Randolph Tillman, I had learned in reading his obit, and now Riley. I was glad I didn't live in this environment of violence and death every day. Like being a coroner or even a funeral director, it simply wouldn't be worth it, paycheck or no paycheck. Sure, somebody had to do these things. But it would have to be somebody besides me, a different kind of man. Same went for Rick's job — or Johnny Lee's or any cop's job. No. Not even on a dare. No thanks.

We sat and waited, four frail souls holding an early wake, disinclined to talk. Somewhere a clock ticked audibly, counting off Riley's first minutes and hours in eternity. Every now and then the refrigerator's compressor kicked on and off back in the kitchen, but both inside and outside the house a growing hush settled in, broken only by an occasional thump or shuffle or muffled word from down the hall. When somebody finally did speak, I jumped as if a firecracker had exploded in the room.

"Did you call his wife?" Rick asked Johnny Lee. "I mean his ex-wife — Annie."

"No. I didn't want her to come running over here. I'll call her soon as they leave." He nodded toward the hall.

"He had three kids, didn't he?" Rick asked.

"Two or three," Johnny Lee said. "I forget which."

"Well, at least he didn't eat his weapon," Rick said, a disgusted look on his face. He looked at Morgan and me. "I can't tell you how many policemen never fire their service revolver at a living target until they turn it on themselves. I've known three who checked out that way. Ever seen what a .38 slug can do to the human head?"

"No," I said. I had seen what a twelve-gauge shotgun blast could do to it, but I didn't want to talk about it.

He made a face and groaned. "Umm."

I didn't encourage him to talk about such things, either. We'd all had enough death for one evening, I thought, especially him — but the subject wouldn't go away.

"How long do you think he'd been dead?" Morgan asked.

Johnny Lee looked at Rick. "Couple hours?"

"I figure," Rick said. "I wonder if he was rigging up that damn contraption the whole time I was trying to get him on the phone, going merrily about the task of killing himself." Angrily, he lashed himself with bitter thoughts, saying in a nasty, biting voice: "Sorry. Can't come to the phone. I'm hung up."

It wasn't pretty. It wasn't Rick. But I knew then that he'd be all right. Not himself — not for a while. But all right. I looked at my watch. It was after 10. "Any reason for us to stay?" I asked.

"Naa," Johnny Lee said wearily.

"No," Rick said. "Sorry the evening turned out this way, but there'll be other times."

"Call if you need me," I said as Morgan and I got up to leave.

Just as we were about to pull away from the curb, the medics brought Riley's body out the door and down the steps. I drove away hearing again the death rattle of that damn gurney.

Chapter Twenty-Three

WE HAD GONE ABOUT A MILE IN SILENCE when Morgan suddenly threw both hands to her face and said, "Omigod! The pork chops! I left them cooking in the oven." She looked apprehensively at me, then anxiously at her watch, tilting her wrist to catch some streetlight on its face.

"I'll eat 'em," I said. "I'm so hungry, I don't care *what* condition they're in."

The pork chops were delicious. They had been cooking for more than three hours, but at a low temperature, about 250 degrees, and were tender and succulent. Rarely had either of us eaten dinner so late, 11 p.m., but we made the most of it, dining by candlelight and treating the late meal as a romantic novelty, a flirtation with decadence. We also avoided the subject of Riley's suicide. Such talk had its limits; to push beyond was masochism. Still, our mood was somber – or, if not somber, pensive. One's thoughts just naturally turned inward when chilled by the winds of death.

Hunger sated, we soon were seated in the living room, on Morgan's couch, sipping a nice Bordeaux. She had changed into more casual clothing and was now wearing a black top and pants. Out of nowhere she asked, "Why did you become a reporter? What attracted you to it?"

It was an interesting question, interesting to me because I didn't really think of myself as a reporter. "I think of myself more as a writer," I said.

"I'm not all that interested in reporting as such. What I *am* interested in is people and life — the human condition, if you will — and I don't know anything that covers the whole spectrum of that the way a newspaper does, especially a big-city newspaper."

"Is that why you're not behind a desk after 20 years?"

"Exactly. Editors simply *read* the paper, like everyone else. Earlier than the average reader, of course, but still their focus is the paper, not life itself, not life first-hand. I write what they read, or at least I help write it. Reporters are the eyes and ears of editors. I'd rather be my own eyes and ears." I took a drink of wine. "No. I've tried editing, and I know it's not for me. I want to be out there on the front-line, out where it's all happening."

"For the excitement?" She lifted her glass and sipped again.

"No. I do find it stimulating, but I'm not like Rick; I'm no excitement junkie. I simply want the closest observation post I can get, front row center, if possible. Even onstage, if that's what it takes." I looked at her pointedly and said in a teasing voice, "Though, unlike *some* reporters I know, I'd as soon stay out of jail."

She laughed.

"You've had quite a baptism in your first few days on *The Phoenix,* haven't you? Trolling on The Strip—"

"I was not trolling." She threw me a pout and sipped her wine.

"—jail," I continued. "Cruising in gay bars. Carousing in taverns."

"Blame it on the company I keep," she said.

We turned solemn again, both having the same thought. "And then tonight," I said.

"A night I'll *never* forget," she said, shuddering. Then she did something that would endear her to me forever. She raised her wine glass, extended it toward me and said softly, "To Riley."

I clinked her glass with mine and added, "To *all* the Rileys of this world."

We drank.

"So what's next for Ben Blake?" she asked. "More stories, more bylines, more awards?"

I took my time answering. She might have had an ulterior motive in asking, I figured, and I didn't want her to think that I was a man with no ambition.

"I want to write," I said. "I've always wanted to be a writer — never even thought about a *career* in journalism. Journalism was a means to an end, one of the few available to an aspiring writer. Heck, I see college campuses and newsrooms as virtual refugee camps for the country's would-be writers. Where else can they go?"

She nodded thoughtfully.

"But I'm not complaining. Journalism is excellent training for a writer. Reporters, after they've been around awhile, have seen everything. In fact, I know of no other occupation that exposes you to so many facets of life, life in the raw. Police work, I guess, would be a close second — and that's one reason I'm so interested in their problems. I think I know now why they find the work so stressful."

Morgan raised her eyebrows. "You do?"

"If I don't, I think I'm very, very close. I believe it's rooted in alienation — that and naivety."

"Cops, naive?" she asked.

"Yes. Day in and day out, they see man at his worst, human nature about as base as it gets. They weren't prepared for that, not trained for it, either, and most of them have little more than a high-school education, so they really don't know how to deal with it. Mistaking the part for the whole, they go from disillusionment to cynicism, and become dysfunctional. Dysfunction sooner or later leads to breakdown — breakdown of all kinds: personal, interpersonal, social. Fail often enough, and you give up hope. Give up hope, and you lose the will to go on. That's what I think."

Morgan seemed impressed. "That's going to be a good story, Ben."

"*If* I ever get to it," I said, draining my glass.

"More?" she asked, reaching for the bottle. It sat on the end table beside her.

"Please."

When she had poured more wine, she settled back again and asked, "Why did you take on the search for Connie Phillips? You could have written about her disappearance and then dropped it, couldn't you?"

The question caught me off guard. Her nearness while pouring the wine had derailed my thoughts. I searched her face for a clue. "You mean besides thinking there might be a good story in it?"

"Yes." Raising her glass to her lips, she kept my eyes locked with hers and sipped, bright red lipstick meeting dark red wine.

A lamp behind her cast a halo around her dark hair, making her face, framed in shadows, faintly luminous, a living cameo. For a moment I got lost in the beauty of it, but finally I said, "She seemed so helpless – Mrs. Phillips, I mean. And the bureaucracy can be – *is* – so damned bloodless." I paused. Sensing a deeper reason, I groped for words to express it, but finally said simply, "Besides, I know what it's like to lose someone."

Wine and lips met again, and still her eyes held mine. "You loved her very much, didn't you?"

I looked away, fixing upon a ghostly white wicker chair across the room, but not really seeing it. Images of Joanna, scenes from our lives together, spun through my mind in a carousel of memory. "Yes. Very much." Then, afraid that Morgan might read too much of the past into the present, I turned back to her and said, "But I hope you won't be— That is, I hope you won't let— I mean, I wouldn't want—"

She leaned forward and put a finger to my lips, sealing them. "I'd be disappointed," she said, "if you *hadn't* loved her so much." She leaned closer and replaced her finger with her lips in a kiss that held as much balm as heat. "Come on," she said rising, putting down her glass. "That's enough talk for one evening." She took my hand and led me down the hall to her bedroom.

We were so hungry for each other that undressing was difficult. Somehow we managed, fumbling for buttons, tugging and twisting and shrugging to shed clothing without breaking our feverish embrace. Moments later we tumbled into bed nude, still kissing, still locked in each other's arms.

I kissed her like a man slaking a long thirst, but it was the feel of her skin, her body pressing mine, that brought the greater pleasure. I had gone so long without feeling the body of a woman, her rose-petal softness, the dizzying configuration of curves and planes. My skin drank in the sensations as if they were raindrops falling on a parched earth.

All that, however satisfying, was mere prelude to the joy of entering her. When I finally moved on top and found her open and wet, and thrust, a deeper thirst was quenched. Soon, our need, naked and urgent, hit like a sudden thunderstorm, a squall on the sea of passion.

We surged against each other as if no depth of penetration could be too much. Moments later, she shuddered in the momentary paralysis of orgasm, moaning. Clutched in the grasping, quivering, velvet deep of her, I came, too.

After catching our breath, we cuddled and talked for a long time, until around 2 in the morning, in the middle of some anecdote I was telling, purring sounds of slumber told me I had lost my audience.

Not much later I drifted to sleep, myself, but it was a troubled sleep, plagued by dreams of corpses, of funerals and wailing loved ones, and of shadowy, sinister figures lurking just out of sight, waiting. Watching and waiting.

Chapter Twenty-Four

SOMETIME BEFORE DAWN, I SLIPPED OUT OF BED, got dressed and went home. It was tough to leave Morgan's bed. I had forgotten how reassuring it could be to wake up and find a woman I cared for sleeping next to me. But I was sleeping fitfully anyhow and would want fresh clothes to put on in the morning, to say nothing of needing a razor and toothbrush, so I went on home — but not before leaving a note on the kitchen table that said: "You were terrific. Will call later today." I signed it "Phantom Lover" and left.

When I got home, there was a message on my answering machine, but I ignored it for the moment. A shave seemed more urgent, and I needed a shower to bring me fully awake.

I was just about to step into the shower when the phone rang. What the hell? I thought; it wasn't 6 a.m. yet. Naked, grumbling, I went to answer it.

The voice was that of a woman — fairly young, I figured, but not Southern — and the voice had both an edge and a slight slur to it. Had she been drinking? "So you finally got home," she said. No salutation, no preamble; just that.

"Who is this?"

She didn't answer. For a long moment, she didn't say anything. I was about to hang up, figuring it was a wrong number, when she spoke again. "She knows more than she told you." The intonation was matter-of-fact, but slightly taunting.

I held my breath. "Who?" I said. "Who's 'she'?"

For another long moment the caller said nothing, just breathed audibly into the phone. I repeated my question.

"Eve Garland," she said. "The Divine Ms. Eve," she added with a sarcastic spin.

Not drunk, I concluded. Drinking, but not drunk. Again I heard the breathing. "Tell me more," I said.

"You're looking for Connie Phillips, right?"

"How did you know?"

"Word travels fast," she said nonchalantly. "Travels very fast in some circles."

"What circles are those?"

"Don't play coy. You know what circles."

"Did you know Connie? You a friend of hers."

She laughed. It was a seductive, teasing laugh. "You might say that."

"What do *you* say?"

"It was I who introduced her to Eve."

For a moment I was more puzzled than ever. Then it hit me. *The fired school teacher!* I thought with growing excitement, the one Jane Kimball told me about.

"Is your name Curry?"

I heard a small gasp, but she recovered nicely. "Well. I see that you truly are looking for Connie."

"Are you in town?"

"Never mind where I am. I've already told you all you need to know."

I corrected her. "You didn't tell me why you think Eve Garland knows Connie or anything about her."

A scornful laugh sounded in my ear. "You ever hear that old song, 'The Tennessee Waltz?'"

I heard a tinkling sound. Ice in a glass? "The pop hit by Patti Page?" I said. "Nineteen-fifty-something."

"That's the one," she said. "Well, *that's* what happened to me. To me and Connie." She began singing in a soft, sad voice: "'...my friend stole my sweetheart from me.'"

"You and Connie were lovers?" I asked.

"I've told you all you need to know – and all that I'm going to tell you. Go back to Eve Garland."

The line went dead. The woman had hung up.

I hung up, too, and started back into the bathroom. But then, on a hunch, I went back to the phone and pushed the button for messages. It was the same voice, same message. Three of them: "Go back to Eve Garland." I pushed the "Save" button.

After showering and shaving, I put on a pot of coffee and dressed while playing the messages over and over. I pegged the voice as Midwestern and the tone as perhaps vindictive, but that was all I could divine. Didn't matter anyhow. I would have bet the farm that it was the Curry woman, but the important thing was that her tip and my instincts pointed in the same direction.

I got out the phone book and looked under G. There weren't that many Garlands, and only one E. Garland, 1310 Lafayette Drive. I thought I knew the street, but I got out a city map to make sure. I was right. It was in Ansley Park, an upscale neighborhood of rolling hills, serpentine streets, and small parks between Peachtree Street and Piedmont Avenue, and not far from Colony Square, a complex of hotels, shops and restaurants between downtown Atlanta and Buckhead.

Ten minutes later, I was on my way to Ansley Park.

THE HOUSE WAS A ONE-STORY BUNGALOW of wood and stone, gray trimmed in white, which sat close to the street. A screened porch, entered from the driveway, was on the front, shaded by awnings. There was no sign of life in the house — it was only 7:10 — but that was in my favor, I figured: the element of surprise. I got out of the car and walked to the door.

Eve Garland was surprised to see me, all right. Her eyes grew wide when she opened the door, and she seemed taken aback. She recovered quickly, though. She wasn't one to lose her poise for long. Dressed in pajamas and a robe, she said wryly, "I figured you'd be back, but I didn't count on your coming at the crack of dawn."

"Oh, is it that early?" I said, glancing at my watch, pretending I hadn't known the time.

I didn't fool her. She looked knowingly at me and said, "Never mind. I'm an early riser. Come in."

I followed her through the living room, dining room and kitchen to a sun porch on the back of the house.

"Have a seat," she said. "Coffee? I just brewed a pot."

I said yes, thanks, and a few minutes later she was back from the kitchen, carrying a silver tray. She put the tray on a low table in front of a couch and sat down. Pouring cream into one of the two cups, she stirred it in, sipped from the cup, and sat back on the couch. "Now," she said, lighting a cigarette.

I sat across from her in an easy chair and sipped my coffee, too, looking at her over the rim of the cup. In the light of day, I saw that she was even more attractive than I had thought at the club. A firm jaw line, shaped like a horseshoe, lent her facial features a sort of purposeful balance, and her green eyes, alert and with a hint of cunning, radiated self-confidence. There would be no way to outflank a woman like that. You engaged her head-on or not at all. "I've got to find Connie Phillips," I said, "and I think you know something about her, something that might help me find her."

"Oh?" she said. "Why? I mean, why do you think I know something?"

"Instinct."

She blew smoke and gave me a level look. "That's not much to go on, is it?"

"And a little birdie."

She gave me a raised eyebrow. "What kind of birdie?"

"A jealous one."

"Oh." She blew smoke toward the ceiling and said, "Elaine Curry.

"She didn't give her name."

She smiled. "No, but I see her signature in this. She's banned from my club, you know." She took another long drag on her cigarette. "But I probably should send her a thank-you note and let her back in; she first introduced me to Connie. Brought her to the club one night a few months ago. But she's *sooo* possessive."

"Look," I said, wondering why she was telling me all this, "my only interest is in finding Connie."

Eve lifted her coffee cup to her lips and smiled again. "Look behind you then," she said.

At first I didn't know what she meant. But then I turned. Standing in the doorway was Connie. I nearly spilled my coffee.

"Come on in," Eve told her. "This gentleman is a reporter, and he has been looking high and low for you." Eve patted the cushion beside her. "Here," she said. "Come sit by me."

Wearing a pink terry-cloth robe, Connie came on into the room and sat down beside Eve. She looked as if she had just come from the shower. Her hair was still slightly damp.

"Say hello," Eve prompted.

"Hello," Connie said shyly, avoiding eye contact.

I realized suddenly that I was staring. My mouth was probably agape, too. I was glad to see her, but it all seemed so anticlimactic: all that worry about her welfare and safety, all those mother's tears and prayers, when apparently the whole time she had been languishing in the lap of luxury. Anger flew all over me, but I suppressed it.

"Now don't be afraid, Connie," Eve said. "He just wants to talk to you."

I hardly knew where to begin, so I just launched in. "I won't tell you how worried your mother has been. You already know that. Or how much trouble you've put a lot of people to. I won't even ask why you ran away; I think I've figured that out. But I *will* ask if you and Clifford Sims ran away together."

Her face crinkled up and I thought she was going to cry. She nodded yes and reached out for Eve's hand.

"He's dead, you know."

She nodded again and fought back tears.

"Do you know who killed him?"

She shook her head no. "But I saw who might have."

"You saw?" I said.

She sniffed. "There was this man — actually two men, but I didn't see but one — his face, I mean. The other one's back was turned. Anyhow,

I caught only a glimpse of the face. I had left and—"

"Hold on," I said. "Left where?"

Eve patted her hand. "Just be calm and take your time."

"Yes," I said. "And start at the beginning."

Her story still came out disconnected and with a few holes in it, but this much was clear: She left with Sims because he seemed to know his way around Atlanta and even knew a place where they could stay awhile, the Midtown apartment of a friend who was out of town. But a few days later, when Sims tried to talk her into appearing in a pornographic movie with him, she got angry and stormed out. At nightfall, she went back to get her suitcase and to move out, but she left without it when she saw Sims and two other men engaged in sex in the bedroom.

"She came here that night, Thursday a week ago," Eve said, "and has been with me since."

"Did the men see you?" I asked.

"I don't think so. But I can't be sure," Connie said.

"Any idea why they were there — other than for sex?" I asked.

"Well," Connie said, "Cliff had said that two men were coming over that night to talk about this film, to make a deal."

"And even if they didn't see Connie, Sims might have told them about her, might have given them her name," Eve said. "In fact, it stands to reason he did."

I looked at Eve and then at Connie. "What makes you so sure these two men were involved in Sims' murder?"

Connie frowned. "Well, I'm *not* sure."

"We're just not taking any chances," Eve said.

"Nobody else knew where we were," Connie said.

"Nobody?" I said. "How'd you get there?"

"This guy we knew. Cliff told him we were running away together. He gave us a lift into town."

"Brooks Creighton?"

Connie gave me a look of surprise. "Yes."

"So at least one other person knew where you were."

"Yes."

"Is Creighton gay?"

Connie laughed, the first time I had seen her laugh. "No way."

"Of course," I continued, "Clifford could have met dozens of people after you left and before you went back for your suitcase."

"Yes," Eve said solemnly, "but look at the circumstances: Sims' body was found with a girl's. Connie's replacement? They were both nude and both had had sex. Sims was gay. And all this came only a few days after Connie had seen Sims with two men who wanted to do a porn movie."

"We don't know they were the same men," I said.

"It's safer to assume they were," Eve said.

I had to agree, but while the circumstances called for caution, they didn't make a case for murder. I looked at Connie. "Was Sims gay — or bisexual?"

Connie looked at her lap. "I thought he was straight. But he was gay."

Eve gave Connie's hand a little squeeze. "Thinking he was straight — that was another reason Connie left with him." She smiled and looked at Connie. "She was having a bit of a problem sorting out what *she* was." She reached over and patted Connie's knee. "But that's all over now. Isn't it, sweetheart?"

Connie nodded, but still did not look up. Seeing the opening, I took it. "You sure this is what you want, Connie? I'll have to tell your mother something—"

"No!" she said, suddenly alert, alarmed.

" unless *you* prefer to tell her. She's been worried out of her mind."

Haltingly, Connie said, "I'll call her." She looked at Eve, who nodded. That wasn't good enough for me, but I let it go for the moment.

"Whom do *you* have to tell?" Eve asked.

"I have to write a story saying she's been found. We owe the readers that. But I don't have to say exactly where she is, or who she's with or why. The only people I have to tell that are my bosses and two cops who've been helping me look for Connie."

Eve looked worried. "The police are looking for Connie?"

"Not the police — just two friends. They've been helping me on their own. They can be trusted," I said. Then I got an idea. "Connie, if these friends of mine could arrange it, would you be willing to look through the police mug file? The guy you saw may be in there."

Connie looked at Eve who, with a shrug, indicated that they had nothing to lose by trying it.

"Let's say today at noon, police headquarters, front steps." I said. "If I can't set it up that quickly, I'll call."

Connie nodded. I looked at Eve. "She wouldn't take off again, would she?" I wanted her word more than Connie's.

"She'll be either here or at my club," Eve said.

I got up to leave, but I couldn't resist one last question. "Are you happy, Connie? With your decision, I mean?" I was still wondering what I could say to Mrs. Phillips. Sooner or later I'd have to talk to her.

Connie gave me a darting look and then looked at Eve. Convincingly she said, "Yes."

Eve said, "She just had to come to terms with herself, Mr. Blake. Is it so hard to believe that a lesbian could be happy?"

I knew a loaded question when I heard one. Whatever gets you through the night, is my philosophy – and sooner or later life brings some long, long nights – but I said nothing.

She continued, "I went through the same thing at about her age. I was miserable, too, until I faced up to the truth about myself." She lit another cigarette, and Connie handed her an ashtray. "Believe it or not, I want Connie to be happy, too. But I know her, and you don't — her parents don't either. I'm taking good care of her, too. Look at her: clean, well-fed, fit. Why, she's shed seven pounds just since moving in with me."

I had to admit that Connie looked a lot better than she did in the photograph I'd been carrying around. In the picture, she looked sort of like a young girl gone to seed. Sitting there on the couch, she looked well groomed and even attractive. But I kept my thoughts to myself — except for one.

Looking at Eve, I said, "And what's in it for you? I mean, why Connie? There's a roomful of young girls in your bar every night."

She gave me a thin smile. "Well, it's a bit early in the day for candor, but you asked, so I'll tell you. Connie is a special girl. She's big and strong and, shall we say, eager to please?"

"And that's where you fit in," I said dryly.

She smiled coyly. "Let's just say that I'm somewhat demanding and that a big, strong girl like Connie is just what the doctor ordered." She flicked ashes from her cigarette and looked at Connie appreciatively. "She never tires. Just look at those shoulders." She leaned back, completely at ease. "Show the nice man your shoulders, my pet."

In the wink of an eye, instantly obedient, Connie slid the robe off her shoulders, holding it closed over her chest, and turned this way and that. Her shoulders did indeed look big and strong, but hell; she didn't have to show me. I glanced at Eve, who looked downright smug, and then back at Connie.

Very composed, Eve said, "Now show him your nice, strong back, dear. Drop the robe to your waist."

Connie, bare under the robe, did as she was told, unveiling a pair of spectacular breasts, globular and taut. I noticed, too, as she turned that the large nipples were extended.

"Now stand," Eve said casually, supremely confident. And when Connie rose to her feet, she added, "Now drop the robe altogether and turn slowly. I want this man to see what a prize you are."

Before I could speak, Connie stood there naked, the pink robe puddled at her feet. In spite of myself, I stared. About five feet five, Connie was an odd combination of muscles and curves, solid and powerfully built, but unmistakably female — and not just for the obvious reasons. If her muscles were those that a man might envy, so might any woman envy her curves. It was as if nature, in a capricious mood, had given her the physique of a muscular male and then added the features of an Amazon. Peter Paul Rubens would have declared her a great beauty, and I could easily see that somebody like Eve could put that powerful, opulent body to good use.

I looked at Eve. "I get the picture: She's yours — and you want it to stay that way."

She nodded, reaching out languidly to run an appreciative hand over Connie's ass. "It's going to stay that way; isn't it, Connie?"

Connie dropped her eyes and answered softly, "Yes."

Eve gave me a pointed look. "So you might bear that in mind when you talk to your friends, the policemen, and to her parents. It's her decision. And she *is* of age."

I couldn't argue with that. I said nothing.

Eve stood up, and Connie got her robe and began slipping it back on. "See you at noon," Eve said.

I started to leave but couldn't — not just yet. "One more thing," I said.

"I want you to call your mother before I leave."

I thought she was going to refuse, but after a moment she looked at Eve. "Call her," Eve said. "Use the phone in the kitchen."

Eve walked me to the door as Connie stood at the phone and dialed. I lingered at the front door until I heard Connie say, "Mother. It's me, Connie." She then began crying into the phone, and I left.

Chapter Twenty-Five

RICK LIVED IN A HIGH-RISE ON PEACHTREE, near Collier Hills. I drove straight there, and got him out of bed by leaning on his doorbell and banging on the door until I woke him up. He looked like death warmed over when he first opened the door, but he came wide awake when I told him I had found Connie Phillips.

"Hot damn!" he said, pulling me inside. "When? Where?" He held up his hands, palms out. "No. Wait." He looked down at himself. He was wearing only pajama bottoms. "Make some coffee while I throw on some clothes." He pointed toward the kitchen and disappeared into his bedroom. "Tell me about it while I dress," he shouted through the open door. "I can hear you."

Moments later he was back, dressed and standing in the doorway, running an electric razor over his face. He turned it off and stared at me. "Naked?" he said.

"As a jaybird."

He smiled. "Sonofagun. Some guys have all the luck."

A moment later he was back at the door. Turning off the razor again, he said, "So this Creighton guy was how they got into town, huh? No wonder we couldn't find anybody who'd seen them leave. That's running away in style, though, isn't it? Guy in a Corvette provides taxi service."

Then he turned serious. "I've got a flash for you, though: We aren't out of the woods on this case yet. That girl could be in real danger, worse than we thought. If the guys she saw with Sims saw her, and if they are the ones who bumped Sims off, you can bet they've been look- ing for her as hard as we have. And if you can find her, they can too."

"That's why I'm here, Sherlock."

"Five'll get you 10, Miss Garfield figured that out, too, and that's why she let *you* find Connie."

"Right, again. But she was taking her own sweet time about doing it. Thank God for anonymous tips."

"They solve more crimes than all the detectives and crime labs put together. And the best tips come from those with an old score to settle." Rick clicked the razor back on and stood for a moment as if absorbed in thought. "Well, the mug file's as good a place as any to start, I guess. I can set it up; I used to work in Records."

"Good."

"Tell you something, though," he said, moving the razor around his chin. "We can't tell JL that last part — who Connie's with and why. And certainly not about that little display you witnessed. You know: the Eve Garland version of drop-the-hankie. He'd split a gut."

"He'll never hear it from me."

Rick poured two cups of coffee and then called his friend in Records. When he got off the phone, I called Morgan to give her the news and ask when her story could be ready.

Sunday, she said.

Good, I said.

I finished my coffee. "I'm headed for the newsroom to get to work on the story," I told Rick. "See you at APD at noon."

CONNIE'S SEARCH THROUGH THE MUG FILE turned up nothing, and after she and Eve left police headquarters, Rick and I stood around out front, on the sidewalk, giving each other helpless looks and wondering what to do next.

"Dead end," I said, watching people hurry in and out of the building, and up and down the street. APD was located within a stone's throw of Five Points, the heart of downtown Atlanta, and the city's hustle and bustle all around us made me all the more aware that we were stuck, stalled, becalmed.

"Not so fast," Rick said. "Let's think about it. He's not in the mug file. All that means is that he has no record. Is he an amateur? Amateurs make porn movies every day without having two of the actors wind up with their tickets punched. What could have gone *that* wrong?"

"Got any informants with connections to porn movies?"

"No. JL wouldn't have, either. Can you picture him giving two minutes to anybody connected with porn?"

I moved closer to the building and leaned against it, angling for a bit of shade from the afternoon sun. The heat wave was gone, but the summer burned on. "Maybe Homicide'll turn up something," I said.

Rick, seeking shade too, sat down on the steps, feet on the sidewalk. "Don't hold your breath. They don't have any more today than they had after the autopsy. Tell you something else, too: They checked the place Sims was staying. Clean. And the guy who loaned him the place is in Key West and hasn't left there since he got there. This is interesting, though: They didn't find Connie's suitcase."

"How do you know?" I was sure he hadn't asked. He wasn't supposed to know anything about the suitcase.

He smiled. "I have my ways." Then, looking sheepish, he added, "I read the reports."

"Jesus!" I said. "What if the killers got it?"

"Yeah, what if? Still want to wait on Homicide?"

"Do we have a choice?"

He frowned. "I'm thinkin', I'm thinkin'. But forget Homicide. They couldn't find a train depot if you showed 'em the railroad tracks." He looked at me as if wondering whether to tell me something else. "Besides, I want us to crack this case. I want to make detective." He laughed self-consciously. "Didn't know that, did you?"

"You'd make a good one."

"Fat chance. To the Brass, I'm just a loudmouthed troublemaker. I'll be on their shit list forever — unless I can pull a rabbit out of my hat. But crack this case, and they'd have to promote me. And Connie is the key. I feel it in my bones."

"You don't think she's holding out?"

"No, but I think she knows more than she knows she knows, and that's why she's afraid." He got up and began pacing, moving back and forth on the sidewalk in front of me.

"But we don't even know if the men she saw had anything to do with the murders — and she doesn't either."

"No," he said, still pacing, "but sometimes we sense more than we know, more than we can explain. At any rate, I sure would like to have a chat with the two men; they're all we've got. Or at least all we *had*. With no I.D., we're up a stump."

"You think she's in any real danger?"

"Well, *she* thinks so. And she doesn't even know the suitcase is missing." He gave me a penetrating look. "Don't take this wrong, but I almost hope she *is* in danger. Our only chance, as I see it, is for somebody to make a move."

I didn't like the sound of that. "Now *you've* been on the job too long. It's one thing to know *who* might make a move; it's another to have no idea who. Or when."

A devious smile crept over his face. "Well, why don't we try to determine the *when*? Then, if Connie's instincts are right — and mine too — we just might bag a *who*."

I peered into his eyes. "You lost me on the first turn."

He laughed. "We gotta go fishing, m' boy, and to catch a fish, you need bait. B-a-i-t."

I began to see what he was getting at — and didn't like it one bit. "If b-a-i-t means C-o-n-n-i-e, forget it. Here, read my lips: Forget it!"

He shrugged and held out both hands, palms up. "It's our only shot. She can't hide forever. Remember: You found her; they can too. I'm *suggesting* a way we can be there when they do. Sure, it's risky. But it beats doing nothing."

Grudgingly I said, "You've got a point. But have you got a plan?"

He smiled and moved closer. "I'm glad you asked that. When will your story run — the one about finding Connie?"

"Monday." Nobody at *The Phoenix* even knew yet that the girl had been found — but I knew newspapers. The story would run just as soon as the editors could get it. I also knew Owens, my boss. They would get it in time for Monday's paper, not before.

"Good. Perfect! JL and I have Monday and Tuesday off. Now all you have to do is tell the world on Monday morning where Connie Phillips is. Killers read the papers, too. Then we stake out Connie's place — and wait."

It was a brilliant idea, I thought — if it worked. And potentially disastrous if it didn't. "What's to keep the killer from waiting till Wednesday? Or Friday? Or Sunday?"

"Look at it this way; if *she's* in danger, then *he's* in danger. And if he's in danger, he can't afford to wait. Besides, you can say more in your story than simply where she is; give him a *reason* to move."

I still had my doubts, but I knew I was going to do it. Or at least try. "I'll have to get Connie's permission. Eve's too."

Rick grinned. "Now you're talkin'. Let's call 'em now. There's a pay phone just inside here." He jumped to his feet and bounded up the steps; I followed.

I made the call, catching Eve in her office, but I put Rick on the phone to tell her the plan.

Moments later, he hung up. "Smart woman," he said. "She'll do it. Connie will too."

I nodded, thinking about Eve's house. It was close to the street, the street was a quiet one, not a thoroughfare, and Lafayette was dark at night, too. Perfect.

"I'll go by there sometime this evening and check it out," Rick said. "She said the back is secure. No back door, high fence, storm windows, burglar alarm. Both doors, front and side, can be seen from the street. That's a break. We'll use your car and mine. Johnny Lee'll be with you, and Eve will stay home to cover inside. We'll start just before nightfall, say eight."

"And what if he decides to come at noon?"

"Not likely. Criminals are like Dracula: The nighttime is the right time. Besides, that Eve is a tough broad. 'I've got a .32 revolver and I know how to use it,' she said."

"Will I need a gun?" I said.

Rick laughed. "No. Didn't they tell you: The pen is mightier than the sword?"

PART THREE

Chapter Twenty-Six

IT WAS DUSK WHEN JOHNNY LEE, wearing plain clothes, same as Rick, opened the car door and slid in on the seat beside me. "Here," he said, opening a white paper sack and pulling out a cup of coffee. "It could be a long night." He pulled out another cup and gingerly pried loose the plastic lid. "Watch it," he said. "This stuff is hot enough to sterilize surgical instruments." He blew on the coffee. "Too bad I couldn't bring Rick some, too."

"He brought a thermos," I said. "Must have been a Boy Scout in his youth."

Johnny Lee laughed. "As long as *I've* known him, he's been a *girl* scout." He blew on his coffee some more and peered down the street. "Where is he?"

"He's moving again. Pulled off just before you got here. We've been here since five o'clock, and every thirty minutes or so he moves to a new position."

As I said that, headlights flared at the other end of the street, and seconds later Rick's Trans-Am eased to the curb near the end of the block, and its headlights went out. He was parked about five houses down from Eve's house, on the other side of the street from us. We were parked about three houses up from Eve's, facing him.

We had a pretty good view of the house, which was one in a row of seven or eight neat bungalows and townhouses that stood not far back from the sidewalk, maybe 30 yards – unlike the houses across the street. Apparently built in an earlier era, they were larger and grander, and sat far-ther back from the curb atop expansive, upward-sloping lawns.

One minor problem we had foreseen in scouting the area was that the lot on which Eve's house sat was flanked by fairly tall shrubbery along the property lines. It partly blocked the line of sight from up or down the street – which was why Rick and I had taken up our respec-tive positions. What one of us might not be able to see, the other could.

Another potential problem we had spotted was that a screened porch on the front of Eve's house darkened the interior. But Eve had helped by turning on all the lights in her house so that much of the interior was visible through the wide, uncurtained French windows and front door. We were not particularly concerned about the back of the house, for there was no back door, and Eve's lot, though deep and wooded, was effectively sealed off by a high wall at the back and her neighbors' tall wooden fences on each side.

But we were taking nothing for granted. By pre-arrangement, Connie paraded through the rooms on the front of the house every fif-teen minutes as a signal to us that all was well inside. If she didn't show on time, in we went. Moreover, she was also acting, willingly, as bait in case other eyes were watching and all of us hoped the right ones were. It was our only chance. Risky. Iffy. But if this didn't work, we had no other tricks up our sleeves.

"You've been here since 5 o'clock?" Johnny Lee said. "Sorry, but I had promised to take my little girl to the zoo, and I don't get to see her that much."

"Yeah. Rick told me. You did the right thing. Nothing going on here anyhow."

"Well," he said, "the night's still young." He set his coffee on the floorboard and slid low in the seat, knees propped on the dashboard. "Better make a low profile," he advised. "We don't want to spook our man." He reached up and threw the switch on the dome light to the off position. "Don't want to shine a spotlight on yourself, either, if you open the door after dark."

I shook my head at my own stupidity.

"Watch the coffee, though," he cautioned. "Spill it in your lap and, presto, you're a soprano."

I slid down in the seat, too. "I guess you've done a lot of this — stake-out, I mean."

"My share. Gets old in a hurry. Watch, wait, and then watch and wait some more — but you've already found that out, I'm sure." He sipped carefully at his coffee. "Who's she with, anyhow? Your girl, I mean. I never saw a newspaper today."

"A friend," I said, sipping, too, and trying to sound nonchalant. "Name's Eve something-or-other. An older woman. Thirtyish."

"And what did your story say? I mean, how's the killer supposed to find her?"

"Well, after saying that the police would question Connie soon, probably tomorrow, about Sims' murder, I wrote that she was staying with a friend, this woman, and gave the friend's name and told what street she lived on. All the killer needed after that was a phone book."

"Talk about long shots," Johnny Lee said.

"It's the only shot we got."

"Let's hope he thinks it's the only shot *he's* got."

Johnny Lee and I made small talk as the minutes crept by, but after a couple of hours the conversation wound down, and we watched in silence. Traffic was light on the street and getting lighter as eleven o'clock approached. Houses up and down the street were going dark, too, one by one, and the waiting became oppressive. Time seemed to move so slowly that frequently I thought my watch must be stopped. I'd check it in the dim glow of a street light, sometimes against my will, and then find, when I checked it again after what seemed like a long time, and again against my will, that only two or three minutes had passed.

"And I thought time stood still in the waiting rooms of doctors," I said softly.

Johnny Lee squirmed. "I can't even feel my ass anymore," he grumbled.

Mine was numb, too, except that my tail bone actually hurt from such prolonged sitting, and my legs felt stiff and crippled. But I forgot all that when Johnny Lee said, as a gray van passed, "That's the second time around for him. Georgia plates, but I couldn't make 'em."

I hadn't even noticed, but Rick had. After the van turned the corner at the end of the street and disappeared from view, Rick flashed the headlights on his Trans-Am. Johnny Lee reached across me and flashed our headlights too.

"Don't hold your breath," he said. "There are a hundred innocent reasons for going twice around a block. But if this is our man, I want you to send in my entries in the Publishers Clearinghouse Sweepstakes from now on 'cause you'd be one lucky son of a gun."

"Actually this was Rick's idea."

"Figures. He could walk by a candy machine, and a Hershey bar would fall out."

"I want a killer to fall out — from wherever."

"Well, you just might get your wish," Johnny Lee said as headlights swung into the street again, behind us. "Stay down."

This time, as the headlights closed in on us, Connie appeared again in a window of one of the front rooms. The van slowed, nearly stopping, and then moved on. It was him again – same van – and as soon as its taillights swung around the corner beyond Rick, Rick blinked his lights again and I blinked ours.

Minutes later, the van was back. Now, time really seemed to stand still as the van stopped just past Eve's house, and then, in reverse, began to ease back into her drive.

"Get ready," Johnny Lee said, moving his hand to the door handle.

He backed up nearly as far as the porch, and that's when I first noticed how dark Eve's driveway was near the house. The nearest street-light was three doors down and obscured by trees, and a tall, thick bush loomed on the far side of the drive, near the corner of the house.

I opened my door slowly and was about to ease out, and Johnny Lee cracked his door, too, but just as we got ready to go, the van pulled out of the driveway and headed up the street the way it had come.

"Jesus Christ!" I said, slumping into my seat as the tension snapped. I felt like a tire going flat.

"Lost," Johnny Lee said in disbelief. "The guy's simply lost, just turning around. Of all the driveways in Atlanta—"

Johnny Lee never finished that sentence. We both sat straight up when we heard Rick cry out, and saw him running across the street toward the house. "The porch! The porch!" he yelled.

I bolted from the car, and so did Johnny Lee, but I didn't know why we were running until Rick, ahead of us, got near the drive. When he did, I saw a sudden movement in the shadows of the porch, and then the screen door flew open as a dark figure bolted from the porch, leaped into the driveway, and ran toward the back of the house. All I could tell was that he was tall and fast. Rick raced after him, yelling, "Cover the front, JL! Come on, Ben!"

It was very dark around the back of Eve's house, and for a moment I lost sight of the fleeing figure as he ran into a thicket of pine trees and scrub oak. But Rick plunged on, and a split-second later yelled, "The wall! He's on the wall." I saw him then, about thirty yards away, outlined briefly in a vagrant beam of moonlight. He was clambering atop the brick wall at the back of Eve's yard. An instant later, scrambling like a big rat, he disappeared on the other side of it.

"Come on!" Rick yelled, racing to the wall, but when I got to it, I saw that it was too high, well over six feet, for either of us to get over easily – and that even if we did get over, the man could be lying in wait on the other side. "Damn," I said, thinking we'd lost him.

But Rick wasn't ready to give up. "Here," he said, "give me a boost."

I locked my fingers together, palms up, to form a stirrup for Rick's foot, and braced myself as he stepped into it. The moment he did, we heard underbrush rustling on the other side of the wall, and then the sound of running feet. Our quarry had been hiding in the shadows.

Rick, standing in my hands, said, "Lift! Lift!" And as I hoisted him to the top of the wall, I heard a loud splash. "Hurry!" Rick said, jumping to the ground on the other side. Seconds later, groping blindly along the wall, I found a couple of chinks in it, enough for a foothold, and climbed to the top, myself.

Help!" a voice cried out.

I heard more splashing, but I couldn't tell where the cry was coming from. The outline of a house loomed in the distance, but its backyard, which I presumed lay before me, was swathed in shadows. Soon, however, movement caught my eye, and I jumped to the ground and ran toward it as the cry for help rang out again.

"Watch it, Ben," Rick said as I got close to him. He was kneeling at the edge of a swimming pool, a big one, extending a long pole with a skim net on the end to a figure thrashing in the water. "Seems our friend here decided to take a moonlight swim."

I could see better now with no trees around, and better still a second later when a light came on in a house next door. We were in somebody's backyard, but apparently they were not at home, for the house remained dark. The man clutched at the pole, missed, flailed some more, and finally grasped it. "I can't swim!" he sputtered, breathless. "Pull me out!"

I moved to Rick's side and knelt, saying, "Here, let me help."

"Thanks," Rick said, "but that's close enough for now."

"Pull! Pull!" the man said, frantic.

I started to pull, but Rick stopped me with a hand on my forearm. "He can't swim," I said urgently, thinking that he must have misunderstood.

"Yeah, I know," Rick said, giving me a pointed look, "but we have *our* problems, too." He let go of the pole and stood up. "Just hold him there. I think I saw a raft or something over on the grass."

"No! No!" the man wailed as Rick stepped away from the edge of the pool. "Get me out of here."

"*You* want out; we want answers," Rick said as I strained to hold the pole high enough to keep the man's head above water. "Here," he said, and an instant later a big inner tube whirred over my head and hit the water near the man. The man let go of the pole and grabbed the inner tube.

Rick came back to the edge of the pool. "What were you doing at that house?" he asked.

"Get me out," the man said. "I can't swim."

"Talk or drown," Rick said simply. He pulled a gun from his back pocket, his police .38 revolver. A tiny diamond of light glinted on the barrel. "You're in eight feet of water there. If I plug that inner tube and walk away, you're a goner."

Holding onto the inner tube with one arm, the man whipped his head right and left, looking all around. He was a good four feet from the sides and the end of the pool. "Who *are* you? You must be crazy. You a cop?"

"What were you doing at that house?" Rick said.

"I was lost. I wanted directions. That a crime or somethin'?"

"You slipped out of the back of the van and sneaked onto that porch," Rick said. "I want to know why."

"Who? Me? You crazy? What van?" The man looked at me. "Who *is* he? Who are you? What is this?"

"I'll start with something simple," Rick said. "What's your name?" Rick sounded calm, but I could hear the restraint in his voice.

The man hesitated for a second or two. "Darryl. Darryl Owens."

"Where do you live?"

"Tenth Street. 1220 Tenth. Now what is this?"

"Well, Darryl, I *am* a cop. Good guess. And I'm investigating a murder."

"You're crazy!"

Rick smiled. "That was another good guess, Darryl. I *am* crazy. Ever meet a crazy cop before? Crazy cops do crazy things." He raised his gun and aimed it at the man. "Guy gives him any shit, he just shoots him."

The startled man flailed in the water a bit, and the inner tube bobbed up and down. "Wait a minute!" he said, sputtering again and wiping water from his face. Then he looked at me as if for explanation. "He *is* crazy enough to do it," I said. "You wouldn't be the first."

"Wait a minute," Owens repeated. "All right. I was gonna break in and rob the place. Satisfied? That make you happy? Now get me outta here, all right?"

Rick lowered the gun and waved it in a helpless gesture, looking at me as if to say, "I tried." Turning back to Owens, he said, "Darryl, you told me only half the truth, the part about breaking in. The other part was a lie, and if there's one thing I can't stand it's a lie." He raised the gun again.

"Hold it! Hold on!" Owens said.

"I really have to go now, Darryl," Rick said, "but I *will* do this much for you. I'll either shoot the inner tube and let you drown or I'll just go ahead and shoot you. Which will it be? Drowning is a terrible way to go." Rick took aim.

"No!" Owens shouted, kicking his feet to try to wheel the inner tube around in the water, to put it between him and Rick.

Rick's began counting. "One . . ."

"No! Okay. Ask your questions. Ask 'em."

"What were you doing at that house?"

"I was gonna rape her."

"Who?"

"The broad who lives there. I don't know who she is. I saw her through the window."

"You're still lying to me, Darryl." Rick said, his tone one of frustration close to igniting anger. He turned to me. "He's still lying to me. You heard him." He turned back to Owens and aimed again. I was beginning to think he really might shoot him.

"Aw right. Aw right," Owens said. "I was gonna hold her. That was the plan. A guy paid me. Five big ones. 'Get into the house and hold 'er 'til I get there,' he said. He didn't say why, 'n' I didn't ask. There: I confessed. Get me out. Take me in."

"Hold her?" Rick said.

"Hold 'er," Owens said.

"And who was this guy?" Rick asked. "The guy driving the van?"

"That's him," Owens said. "But I don't know him. Never seen him but twice in my life: this morning and tonight."

"Does this guy have a name?"

"Smitty. He said just to call him Smitty."

"Great," Rick said, lowering his voice; "that really narrows the field." Then he looked at me. "But you know something? I believe him. You believe him?"

"Yeah, I do. But let's get him out of there and pump him for more on this other guy. We can take him back to Eve's."

Rick picked up the skim net again and extended it toward Owens. "All right, Darryl," he said, "everybody out of the pool." In an aside to me, he added, "Too bad it's not the *gene* pool."

Chapter Twenty-Seven

STANDING AT THE EDGE OF THE POOL, Rick patted Owens down and found a cheap .22-caliber revolver stuck in one hip pocket and a wallet in the other. Owens, water streaming from him, puddling at his feet, submitted meekly to the search.

"Popgun," Rick said, sticking the pistol into his pocket. "You're lucky you didn't get a chance to use that, Darryl. It might've gone off in your face." Then, backing away from Owens, he flipped the wallet open and held it to the light. "Georgia driver's license," he said. "The name checks." Then he opened the wallet lengthwise: "Five C-notes," he said, glancing at me. "Guy paid him up front." He stuck that, too, in his pocket, and then we marched Owens around the block to Eve's house and took him inside, stopping in the living room.

Still holding Owens at gunpoint, Rick tossed his car keys to Johnny Lee and told him to drive around the block to see if the van was waiting nearby and, on his way back, to fetch a pair of handcuffs out of his glove compartment. As Johnny Lee left, Rick turned to Owens. "Shuck those clothes off." He turned to Eve, who, with Connie, was standing in the doorway to the next room. "You've got a dryer, haven't you?"

She nodded, looking Owens up and down. About six feet tall, he was slender but powerfully built, along the lines of a greyhound, I thought. Lank dirty-blond hair, still wet, fell over his face, which looked older

than his body. I figured him for 30 going on a hard 40. He pried off his
sneakers and peeled off his T-shirt, but when he got to the snap of his
blue jeans, he darted a furtive look at Connie and Eve, and then a questioning one at Rick.

Rick laughed. "A modest rapist? This may be a first."

"Rapist?" Eve said.

"That was only *one* of his stories," I said.

Rick waved the gun at Owens. "Take 'em off. A guy as modest as you
will think twice before making a break for it in his skivvies."

Owens unsnapped his jeans, but turned his back to Eve and Connie
before pushing them, or rather peeling them, down his legs. While he
was doing that, Eve sent Connie to get a blanket.

When the jeans lay in a puddle at Owens' feet and he stood there in
nothing but Jockey shorts, Rick said, "Good. Now kick 'em over here –
nice 'n' easy." When Owens did, Rick slid them with his foot toward
Eve. "Now," Rick said, "get on the floor, face down, hands behind your
back – and stay that way." After Owens was down, Eve scooped up the
T-shirt and sneakers, and left the room as Connie returned with a blanket. "Just hold it for now," Rick told her, meaning the blanket. "I don't
want him getting too comfortable down there."

Just then, Johnny Lee came through the door. "No sign of the van," he
said. He held up the 'cuffs. Rick signaled for him to put them on Owens.

Rick looked at Connie and nodded toward Owens. "He the one?"

She shook her head, no.

"Ever seen him before?" he asked Eve, who now stood in the doorway with Connie.

"Never," she said.

Rick turned his attention to Owens. "All right, Darryl; now tell us
your story again."

Owens raised his face from the floor. "I was supposed to get into the
house and hold 'er. That's all. He said he'd call later to see if I had 'er."

Rick looked at Eve.

"The phone hasn't rung," she said.

"Then what, Darryl?" Rick asked.

"He didn't say."

"What does Smitty look like?" I asked.

"Tall. Six-two or so. Well-built. Big shoulders. Good suntan. Blue eyes. Peroxide blonde. Moustache."

We looked at Connie. She nodded yes, and Rick and Johnny Lee and I exchanged quick glances.

"What does he do for a living?" Johnny Lee asked.

"He didn't say."

We all looked at each other. Another dead end was looming.

"There's always the mug file," Johnny Lee offered. "Maybe he got a better look at him than she did." He indicated Connie.

"Waste of time," Rick said. "He won't be in there."

"Think he saw us," I asked.

"I doubt it," Rick said. "He was already up to the corner before I spotted ol' Darryl here. But I wouldn't bet on it."

Johnny Lee pointed to Owens. "What about him?"

Eve spoke up. "You don't have anything on him that will stick, do you? He didn't actually break in. He'll be out on bail by morning, won't he?"

"Small stuff," Rick conceded. "Prowling. Trespass. No gun permit."

I could almost see the wheels turning in Eve's mind. "Tell you what," she said. "Why don't you take those handcuffs off him, let him get dressed, and then leave? Not him; you." She indicated Rick, Johnny Lee and me. "I'll wait 30 minutes or so, so you're nowhere around."

"Then what?" Johnny Lee asked, plainly puzzled.

Eve shrugged. "He's in my house, isn't he? This prowler is in my house. After you're gone, I'll shoot him and then call the police. That'll get rid of him and send a message to his friend, too. And to anybody else who's got ideas."

She meant it. Owens knew she meant it, too. "Hey, wait a minute!" he said, stirring on the floor, straining at the 'cuffs. He glanced at Eve and then looked at Rick as if to say, "You wouldn't really do that, would you?"

"Sorry," I said. "I can't be a party to anything like that."

"I'm a cop," Johnny Lee said simply. "Far as I'm concerned, you're talkin' murder one."

Rick made a face that said he didn't think it was a bad idea, but he said, "Eve, I don't think you've got to worry about Darryl here. He hasn't put two and two together yet, but I'm about to have a little tutorial with him that'll make jail seem like a fine and private place." He turned to

Owens. "Darryl, you don't know how lucky you are that you ran into us tonight. As I see it, this was shaping up as your last night on earth."

Owens looked up at Rick as if he thought he were crazy.

"That's right," Rick said, shaking his head. "Ol' Smitty was gonna wax you. You were set up for a one-way ride. He's wanted for murder, two of 'em, and he set this up tonight to get rid of the girl over there." He pointed to Connie, and Owens swung his head around to look at her, and then turned back to Rick. "She's the only one who could finger him." Rick paused, apparently for effect. "But then, of course, there'd be you. *You* figure it out."

Owens' eyes got wide.

"You were a decoy," Rick said. "*He* couldn't take the risk of coming to this door, but you could. Didn't you wonder why he paid you in full in advance? Think, Darryl, *think!* Are you thinking? Are you connecting the dots?"

Owens nodded. The expression on his face said that he might not be convinced, but that he'd better give the matter his full attention.

"Is jail sounding better and better, Darryl?" Rick asked.

"Yeah," Owens said. "Yeah, it is."

"What about bail?" Rick asked. "You've got the money to make bail."

"Uh, no," Owens said. "Take me in. No bail. I'll stay."

"You're sure?"

"I'm sure."

Rick turned to Eve. "Those clothes about dry?"

"No. But I want him out of here." She left the room to get his clothes.

"This suit you two?" Rick asked, looking at me and then at Johnny Lee. We said yes, and Rick helped Owens to his feet and unlocked the cuffs.

Eve brought in the clothes, and soon Owens was dressed.

"Okay, Darryl," Rick said, "Now we have to make sure some nice judge doesn't spring you too soon. Prowling and no permit might strike him as too tame to waste a cell on." He turned to Eve. "Didn't you say he broke in by jimmying the lock?"

Taken aback, Eve said, "Well, uh—"

Rick moved to the front door and opened it. "Yeah, the marks are here, plain as day," he said. Pulling out a pocketknife, he opened it and made some scratches on the door, around the lock. "Breaking and entering. That all right with you, Darryl?"

"Yeah," Owens said.

"Now," Rick said, looking around. "I need something—" He spotted a letter-opener on a table near the door. "Is this gold, Eve?"

"Yes."

"I'll return it. But for now, Darryl, be so kind as to put your finger-prints all over it." Holding it by the point, he extended the handle to Owens, who clasped it briefly and then let go. Rick wrapped it in his pocket handkerchief and stuck it in his hip pocket. "Eve, you're also missing a genuine pearl necklace, and $200 is gone from your purse, am I right?"

"Right," she said.

Rick smiled. "Prowling, breaking and entering, the weapon, grand theft. That ought to hold you awhile, Darryl. In a few days, the lady will find her pearls and her money, and I'll help you plea-bargain down to prowling, and you can walk. Deal?"

Owens, looking a bit dazed, nodded and said, "Deal."

Rick put the 'cuffs back on Owens, and Johnny Lee walked him outside. We were about to leave, too, when Eve asked the question that was on all our minds. "What next?"

"He'd have to be crazy to come back here," I said.

"There are other places," she said. "We can't live like this forever."

"We're not through with Darryl yet," Rick said. "Could be he knows more than he knows he knows. And first thing tomorrow we start look-ing for that van."

"Lotsa luck," Eve said dryly.

"You go with what you've got," Rick said, shrugging. "Look at it this way: We know a heck of a lot more tonight than we knew this morning."

"All right," Eve said reluctantly. Looking at Rick and then at me, she added, "Call me tomorrow, both of you."

As soon as we got off the porch, Johnny Lee, standing outside with Owens, said, "I know that woman from somewhere, and it's driving me crazy that I can't place her."

"Beats me," I said as we walked up the drive.

"Me, too," Rick said, giving me a conspiratorial nudge. Changing the subject, he said, "JL and I will deposit Darryl in the pokey — after I take one more swing through the neighborhood to see if our friend has come back. Then, what do you say we meet at the Majestic for some food?"

I said, "Okay," and stopped as something caught on my foot. I bent down to pull it off as the others walked on, and was surprised to see that it was a string of some kind, tied in a loop. I kept it, thinking I'd find a trash can somewhere nearby to toss it into, and when I got out to the sidewalk, where the light was brighter, I saw that it was a piece of twine. I also saw an open trash can by the curb near Eve's drive, and was about to try my luck at ringing it with the loop of string, now wadded in my hand, when suddenly a vivid image flared in my mind.

Poised for the toss, I froze, startled at the connection my subconscious mind had made, was still in the process of making. It was as if the brain, working its mysterious calibrations at lightning speed, were calculating the unlikely odds of such a coincidence and had sent an urgent courier to tell me to wait, to hold up, to stop, as if to say: *Message follows.*

All at once, as if surfacing from the deeps of murky memory, there it was: The twine in my hand was the same kind I had seen on Sims' wrist – and now I remembered where else I'd seen it before.

Excited, I started to hail Rick and Johnny Lee, and tell them what I'd found and the possible connection. But they were already pulling away from the curb. I stuffed the loop of twine into my pocket and ran to my car.

Chapter Twenty-Eight

IT WAS WELL AFTER MIDNIGHT and I was on my third cup of coffee when Rick and Johnny Lee showed up at the Majestic. Johnny Lee slid into the booth, opposite me, saying with outstretched, imploring hands, "Where have I seen that woman before? It's driving me nuts."

"What woman?" I said, knowing full well whom he meant. I glanced at Rick, who rolled his eyes as he slumped into the booth, beside Johnny Lee.

"Eve," Rick said. "He means Eve."

"I've got a better question," I said, pulling the loop of twine from my pocket and stretching it taut in front of them. "This came from Eve's driveway. Tonight. Just about where Owens rolled out of the back of the van. Ring a bell?"

Johnny Lee just stared at it, but Rick said, "Sims' wrist. *Son of a bitch!*"

"Yeah!" Johnny Lee said. "Let me see that." He took it and examined it, rolling it between his fingers. In the fluorescent lighting of the Majestic, the twine was a dull yellow, but we all knew that it was actually a brighter yellow, near the color of straw, with hints of orange here and there in its fibrous strands. "But now what?" he said, looking up.

I started to speak, but the waitress showed up at our booth, shoving glasses of water in front of us, along with utensils wrapped in paper napkins. "Ya'll ready to order?" she asked.

We were. Eggs, bacon, grits, toast, coffee. She wrote it all down and went away.

"My diet's gone to hell since I started hanging around with you two," I said. "Know that? If it isn't burgers and fries, it's fries and burgers. And now grits and eggs. Don't you guys ever eat a square meal? Good, solid food? Remember vegetables? Your mother was right; they're good for you."

"I ate a vegetable once," Johnny Lee said, yawning, stretching. "That was enough. It was green. I don't like my food green."

"Look who's talkin'," Rick said, meaning me. "Mr. TV dinner, himself. Cardboard *au gratin*. No thanks. I need real food. Now, you were about to say?"

"That kind of string. I remembered where I've seen it used."

"Yeah?" Rick said, not really interested.

"Well," I continued, "I'm no expert on string, but I don't think that kind of twine is used much anymore. They use baling wire instead. Or plastic bands. But when I was a kid, blocks of ice used to come encircled with string like that. Made it easier to handle."

"Gawd," Johnny Lee said, "I couldn't tell you where an ice house is located in Atlanta."

"Right," I said. "But news distributors are still around, and that's the other place I used to see a lot of this kind of twine — not at the distributors, mind you, but at newsstands, when stacks of papers and magazines had just been delivered."

"Jesus!" Johnny Lee said. "There must be 10,000 newsstands in Atlanta."

"But not news distributors," Rick said, flashing a slow smile. He looked at the twine and then at me. "You just may be onto something, m' boy." He jumped up and went to a pay phone just inside the front door. He opened the phone book, turned to the yellow pages, flipped through them and stopped. A minute later he was back in the booth. "Five," he said. "Four look legitimate, or at least straight; the other is a porn dealer. We can hit all five tomorrow."

"Not too early tomorrow," Johnny Lee said. "I'm bushed. Let's not forget, too, that there could be a thousand uses for this twine that we don't know about. I mean, we're really grasping at straws here."

"When haven't we been?" I asked, putting the twine in my pocket.

"Yeah. When haven't we been?" Rick said as the waitress brought our food.

"That's my whole point," Johnny Lee said, reaching for the salt. "Defense rests."

"But I remember," Rick said, "when we had nothing. Right, Ben?"

I nodded, but Johnny Lee picked up the pepper shaker and said, "And that's still what we got. We found a runaway who wasn't really a runaway, just a girl who left home. She'll prob'bly have a pimp and be turnin' tricks in the next 30 days—"

"Hey, wait a minute!" I said.

But he held up a hand to stop me and, sprinkling pepper furiously on his grits and eggs, went right on. "And we found a prowler who — if he's tellin' the truth, a big 'if,' I might add — doesn't know dick about any of this—"

"Hold on there," Rick said, trying to interrupt.

But Johnny Lee, under a full head of steam, put the pepper down hard, as if to underline what he'd said, and sailed on. "And now all we gotta do is find a tall, muscular, bottle-blond with blue eyes and a suntan. Tell you what," he said, pointing at me, "you take the first 50,000 suspects and," turning to Rick, "you take the next 50,000. And both of you call me when it's my turn." With that, he plunged his fork into his grits and began eating, ignoring both of us.

"Ahhhgh!" Rick said, throwing up his hands.

"Must be all that pepper he eats," I said to Rick. "Look at that." I pointed to his plate. "Black grits. "

"It is," Rick said. "Makes him feisty. Kills brain cells, too. Burns 'em right out."

Johnny Lee struck an impervious pose, looked away, and bit into a piece of toast. "Sticks and stones," he said in a singsong voice.

Rick continued. "But what can you expect of a guy from Cow Patty, Ga.? Down there, they think cosmetology school is higher education. *Haute cuisine* is chit'lins under glass."

"Your food's gettin' cold – to say nothing of your humor," Johnny Lee told Rick. "But don't forget to cross yourself and say the blessing, and then cross yourself again before you eat." He raised his right hand, fork and all, and made the sign of the cross, intoning solemnly, "Abracadabra, alikazam, hocus-pocus, pass the ham."

Rick recoiled in mock horror, and pushed his plate and cup over to my side of the booth. Getting up, he said, "Move over, Ben. I don't want to be too close when the lightning strikes." He moved in beside me.

Johnny Lee laughed and stretched elaborately. "That's what I wanted all along — the whole booth to myself."

"Good," Rick said. "And now that you're happy, are you going to help us tomorrow, or what?"

Johnny Lee shrugged. "Why not? Beats staring at four bare walls."

"Nine o'clock," Rick said.

"Twelve o'clock," Johnny Lee said. "Not a minute sooner."

Rick looked at me. "High noon it is," I said.

Chapter Twenty-Nine

BY 4 P.M. THE NEXT DAY, I was beginning to see what Johnny Lee had meant. Looking for a guy named Smitty with no strikingly different physical characteristics was like looking for the proverbial needle in a haystack — with no assurance that we were looking in the right haystack. People wanted to help us, but again and again we got the same look, a look that asked first if we were serious, and then shaded to one of dutiful indulgence.

"A nickname? No photograph?" said the office manager at the Blue Ridge News Agency, her eyes two oversized, puzzled orbs behind lenses as thick as Coke bottles. "Sorry." She looked us up and down. "What's he wanted for?"

Along with "What'd he do?" and "He a crook or somethin'?" we had been getting that question all day, though we never said he was wanted for anything.

This time, though, a saucy redhead in the office, maybe 25, chimed in. "Tall, blond, blue eyes, and well-built? Guy look like that, I know what I'd want him for." She flashed a brilliant smile at Johnny Lee, and then turned and walked toward the back of the room, swiveling her shapely hips, and perfectly aware that all three of us were watching.

"Your move, Johnny Lee," I said softly as the office manager turned away.

Embarrassed, Johnny Lee mumbled, "I don't go for redheads."

"A bare redhead beats bare walls, JL," Rick said.

"Let's get out of here," Johnny Lee said, going on out the door.

Rick and I looked at each other and shook our heads.

"He just won't let go of that wife of his," Rick said.

"What happened there, anyhow? I know you said it was another woman, but there must have been more to it than that."

"Didn't I ever tell you?"

"You know damn good 'n' well you never told tell me."

Rick took a deep breath, the kind that often breaks bad news. "Caught 'em in bed together."

"Ouch!"

"Yeah, a man would have been bad enough, but a woman — that really hurts. A real kick in the balls. She should've just shot him; it would've been more humane."

WE SAT OUTSIDE IN RICK'S CAR FOR AWHILE, watching people come and go at Blue Ridge, and then we circled through the news agency's parking lot, but we saw no gray van and nobody who resembled our Smitty.

"Fucker prob'bly gave us a bum description," Johnny Lee groused from the back seat. "Guy's prob'bly short, fat, dark and ugly — like somebody else I know," he said pointedly, "and ol' Darryl's sittin' in jail laughin' his ass off while we traipse around Hotlanta looking for one of the Beach Boys."

Rick laughed. "I may be as ugly as you implied, but I ain't dumb — at least, not dumb enough to pass up what you just did. That gal was table-grade."

"Yeah?" Johnny Lee said. "Well, there's more to life than girls and sex — something you dagos wouldn't understand."

I turned in the passenger seat up front. "Well, I'm not a dago, and I don't understand it either."

Johnny Lee smiled in spite of himself.

"Yeah," Rick said. "Name one thing more important."

Johnny Lee waved us off with one hand and turned to gaze out the window. "You wouldn't understand — neither one of you. Let's move on to the next place."

The Triplex News and Novelty Company was housed in a long, squat building of cinder block and brick on Marietta Street. One of the strangest streets in Atlanta, Marietta, for six or seven blocks stretching north and south, was typical of any main thoroughfare running through the heart of a big city. It was a concrete canyon lined with tall, imposing buildings and routinely clogged with traffic. But once it crossed International Boulevard and turned northwest, Marietta narrowed like a diseased artery to four tight, sparsely traveled lanes, and veered sharply into the past. Here, for block after block, small rundown buildings, relics from another era, hunkered close to the street and squeezed together as if holding tattered ranks against the advance of time. Even the casual observer could see that the future had long ago taken a detour and moved on. This part of town, doors closed, windows painted over or boarded up, was trapped in an urban time warp, the 1940s frozen in amber. In all, it struck me as a good place to locate a business that needed a low profile.

"Don't tell me; let me guess," Johnny Lee said with exaggerated weariness, looking all around as we pulled into the parking lot. "This is the porno place."

"Right," Rick said. "Wanna stay in the car?"

"What? And miss meeting all the nice folks who run such a place?"

A sign on the small loading dock advised visitors to enter through the office, off to the left, toward the street, but Rick ignored the sign, climbed onto the loading dock, and went in through another door. Johnny Lee and I followed.

Two or three workmen inside stared at us as we entered a large room filled with stacks of boxes, but as we moved on through, a man in a small office spotted us, did a double take, and hurried out to stop us.

"Hey!" he said, coming toward us with quick, determined steps, his face red behind wire-rimmed glasses. "Can't you guys read? The sign says enter through the office, and that's what it means."

We stopped and let him catch up with us. Rick ignored his question and asked one of his own. "You the owner?"

"Who wants to know?" The man, who appeared to be about 50, was balding and carrying a slight paunch, but he looked able to take care of himself. About 6 feet tall, he had a barrel chest and big, wide shoulders.

"Police," Rick said.

The man didn't look surprised. "Again? You were here just last month. And the month before that, and the month before that." He looked toward the ceiling and raised his hands in exasperation.

He was referring to efforts by the Fulton County solicitor's office to harass the city's pornography dealers — porn movie operators, nude dancing bars, adult bookstores — with the goal of driving them out of business. A determined do-gooder, the solicitor had appointed himself as Keeper of Atlanta's Morals, and made case after case against offenders. The cases amounted to no more than nuisances, because the courts repeatedly threw them out. But he kept right on making them.

"This isn't a bust," Johnny Lee said. "We're looking for somebody."

Rick gave the man the description and name, and I think all three of us were startled when he said casually, "You just missed him. He gets off at 4." The man looked at us, from one face to another. "What'd he do?"

Rick lied smoothly. "We think he can help us identify a holdup man. Convenience store. He wasn't there when it happened, but he had just left the store. We're hoping he saw the guy come in."

"Oh."

Rick asked for Smitty's full name and address, and when the man went into his office to look up the information, Rick followed him as far as the office door. Johnny and I began to look around. Here and there around the large room was box after box of porn books and magazines, and along one wall were boxes overflowing with various sex merchandise: French ticklers, cock rings, dildos, vibrators, cartons of X-rated movies, inflatable dolls, the same kinds of things Johnny Lee and I had seen in our visit to the No Exit. But, of course, such items were widely available in Atlanta.

"Makes me wanna throw up," Johnny Lee said. "S'pose you worked in a place like this and your kid asked you what you did for a living. What would you say? What could you say?" He snorted in disgust.

"I suppose there are worse ways to make a living," I said.

"Not to me," he said, turning away.

I walked across the room to have a more thorough look around, and there, on the lower shelf of a long, waist-high table in a far corner, I spied cones of twine. Snippets of it littered the floor, and I picked up a piece about six inches long and stuck it into my pocket.

As SOON AS WE GOT OUTSIDE AGAIN, Rick said, "I think this is our man. Fits the description, drives a gray van. But — get this — Smith is his *first* name, not his last. Smith Brinson." He kicked at some gravel as we walked across the unpaved parking lot. "If we hadn't gotten lucky, we'd've been looking till hell froze over for a guy with the last name of Smith. I tell ya, you can't assume *anything* in working a case."

"You better back up, then," Johnny Lee said. "He may *not* be our man."

"I meant our van man," Rick said. "One step at a time. That's the way any who-done-it comes together, and that's the way you solve it."

As we got into the car, I said, "Well, Dr. Holmes, I think the next step is to tell us where we find this guy."

"Lives in Midtown. 709-B McFadden."

Midtown was an old intown residential neighborhood not far from my own. But unlike Virginia-Highland, whose residents were mainly older, retired folk, Midtown attracted young professionals, both married and single, and a disproportionate number of homosexuals. Not far from The Strip, Midtown offered the excitement of city nightlife, as well as the tranquility of Piedmont Park, and the gays probably liked it because so many establishments that catered to them were close by: bars, restaurants, nightclubs.

"McFadden's off Ponce, near North Highland," Johnny Lee said. "Two to one this guy's a fairy."

"They aren't called fairies anymore," Rick said. "Or fags. Or pansies."

"Or queens," I said.

"'A rose by any other name . . . ,'" Johnny Lee said.

Chapter Thirty

BRINSON'S APARTMENT BUILDING RESEMBLED two tall boxes held together by a staircase, with two apartments on each side, one up, one down. The rest of McFadden seemed to consist of small wooden homes in need of new paint and repairs. Atlanta's urban pioneers, the advance guard of the regentrification movement, had either skipped over McFadden or hadn't gotten to it yet, so it sat there, dozing in the afternoon sun, apparently content to be left alone. Rick parked the car and we got out.

"I don't see the van," Johnny Lee said, looking up and down the street, "and there's no driveway to the back."

The two downstairs apartments were "A" and "D." We checked behind the building for the van, saw nothing, and then moved to the stairs.

"Cover us from here, JL. Ben and I will go up."

At the door to "B," Rick pushed me away from the front of the door and took up a position on the other side. Then he reached out and knocked. When nobody answered and we heard no stir, he knocked again. Nothing. Stealthily he tried the doorknob, but it didn't turn.

"I think the doorknob is the only lock," Rick said. He took out his key chain and fingered through keys until he found a small metal probe, hooked on the end and resembling an Allen wrench, only flatter, more flexible. He moved it toward the keyhole and smiled. "Look the other way, Ben."

"Wait a minute," I said, taken aback. "Isn't that illegal entry?" I had seen of course that Rick didn't go by the book, but until now his corner cutting had made a kind of practical good sense. It might even have saved Darryl Owens' life. But this was clearly breaking the law — and I would be an accessory.

He shrugged. "Who's gonna know? 'We knocked on the door, Your Honor, and it came open all by itself,'" he said.

"I'll know — and I'm a reporter."

He gave me a dubious look. "You mean reporters tell everything they know?"

"Well, no."

"So? How else are we gonna get in?"

He was right. I didn't like it, but he was right. I struggled with it for a moment, but finally said, "Do it." The words cost me, though. I felt some of the paint flake off my ethical armor.

Rick bent over the doorknob, stuck the probe into the keyhole, jiggled it a bit, and the door opened. "Piece of cake," he said.

I started to enter, but he pushed me back against the wall. "Take nothing for granted," he said. Crouching away from the door, he reached out, pushed it open, and waited. Then, standing, he reached inside his coat, and took out his pistol, and swept into the room. A moment later, he said, "Come on in. Nobody home."

The apartment looked surprisingly neat for what I took to be the home of a bachelor. The living room, where we stood, was tidy except for a work shirt flung over one end of the sofa, and I could see into the kitchen and small dining area, off to the right, and they looked clean, too.

"That's the bedroom," Rick said, pointing to my left. "You start in there. I'll start in here. I'd love to find a gun, but we probably won't, so just look for anything that strikes you as not quite right. And leave everything exactly as you found it. I don't want this guy getting too nervous — just yet."

The bedroom, blinds drawn, was dark, but I could see well enough without turning on lights. Nothing but clothing was in his dresser drawers, and nothing at all was in the drawers of his bedside tables. The guy really was neat, I concluded. Even his king-size waterbed was neatly made up.

I thought the closet might tell another story. Many people simply hid their untidiness from view. But the closet was neat, too, neater than my own, I reflected with a twinge of guilt. We were going to have trouble pinning anything on this man, I saw; he was too careful to leave loose ends. I walked back into the living room. "Nothing in there," I told Rick, who was going through a desk in a corner of the room.

"Here, either, unless you count dirty pictures." He pointed to a stack of photographs on top of the desk. When I picked them up, he said, "Don't change the order they're in."

I shuffled through the stack, twenty-four of them. They were of poor quality, simple snapshots by an amateur, taken indoors with a flash. They featured a man and two women, all wearing Lone-Ranger masks and engaged in bondage and discipline. Wielding a whip, or in some cases a riding crop, the man seemed to be menacing the women as all of them performed sex in various combinations: man-woman, woman-woman, man-two women. In some, the women were bound. "Think it's our man?"

"I'd bet on it. Wouldn't you?"

I nodded, put the pictures down and pointed to the desk. "Anything else there?"

"Not yet," he said, closing one drawer and opening another. "And I already checked the kitchen." He looked around. "Try those doors up there." He pointed to a cabinet in the built-in bookshelves along one wall.

I went over and opened them. "Record albums," I said, glancing at a stereo set nearby. "A couple of porn novels. A stack of adult magazines."

"Umm," Rick said, engrossed in his search of another desk drawer. "He banks at Phoenix National," he said in a ho-hum tone of voice. "Keeps all his receipts — nothing unusual among them. A shoe repair claim ticket. Postage stamps. Canceled checks." He rifled through them. "Routine. Guy doesn't throw anything away. That could be a break for us." He went on looking.

"Think this guy knew we were coming?" I asked, opening another door. "The place is awfully clean."

"It would be even cleaner if he'd thought that." Rick was examining the contents of another drawer. "He knows something went wrong last night, but if he had thought it involved the police, we wouldn't find porn here, even though it's perfectly legal. You'd come away thinking he was an Eagle Scout."

"Think he's our man? Not just our van man, but *the* man?"

Rick turned from the desk. "Don't you?"

"Yeah, I do. If he's *not* the man, he can *lead* us to the man — that's what I think."

Rick smiled. "Then keep looking." He turned back to the desk. "Nobody can hide everything. We already know ol' Smitty likes his sex kinky. That's not a crime, but it is a clue, and one clue has a way of leading to another."

I turned back to the cabinet and opened another door. "Video cassettes." I looked at a VCR on top of his TV. "Some X-rated, some not. Three or four unlabeled."

Rick came over to look at the cassettes, lined up end on end, like books. Among the X-rated titles were some well known ones I recognized: "Talk Dirty To Me," "Deep Throat," "I Like To Watch," and "Behind the Green Door."

"Are you thinkin' what I'm thinkin'?" Rick asked.

"Yes. Connie said the man came to see Sims about making a porn movie."

"Here," Rick said, taking the unlabeled cassettes. "Let's have a quick look at these things." He went to the TV, turned it on, and slid a cassette into the VCR.

The first tape appeared innocent enough, showing musicians that he had probably picked off MTV or the televising of a rock concert, and the second tape was blank, or seemed so. We didn't have time to check out all of each tape. But when Rick put in the third videocassette, and the face of a young woman popped onto the screen, we stood as if transfixed. The young woman, eyes wide with fear, a red ball gag in her mouth, was Bonita Catledge.

Rick lunged at the VCR to cut if off and eject the film. "Sonofabitch!" he said, excited. "Here." He handed me the first two cassettes. "Put those back and let's get out of here." He held up the third tape. "This baby's coming with us."

"Thought you didn't want to make this guy nervous just yet," I said dryly.

"That was then; this is now. If this tape is what I think it is, I hope he sweats pellets."

I was as eager as he was to see what else was on that tape, but I had to ask: "Don't you need a search warrant? Suppose the tape does turn out to be evidence — evidence in a murder case."

Rick held up the tape again and wagged it at me. "This may be the break we've been waiting for. Come back with a warrant and it may be gone."

"But if you take it without a warrant, the *case* may be gone."

"No, it won't," he said slowly, precisely. "If it *does* link Brinson to Sims and the girl, I'll come back with both the tape *and* a warrant, and nobody but you and Johnny Lee will ever know the difference."

He gave me a quizzical, conspiratorial look, and I knew he was waiting for me to say yea or nay. It was a hard call, a damned hard call. This went way beyond lock picking — which was bad enough. I was a reporter, trained to remain objective, uninvolved, enjoined by every canon of journalism to back away from anything that would compromise my role, my journalistic ethics – not to mention my employer, *The Phoenix*. Moreover, I despised all forms of official wrongdoing and was obligated to report it without fear or favor. Before today, I had simply blinked at Rick's disregard for the letter of the law. The ends seemed to justify the means and, after all, technically it was Rick, not I, who was doing these things. But now he was talking about something that might convict a man of murder, send him to the electric chair.

And then I thought of Sims, his crumpled body lying in the woods, his life snuffed out as if he were no more than a cockroach. And of Bonita Catledge, left to rot in a shallow grave, buried as if she were so much garbage. And of Connie, threatened with the same fate if the killer ever got hold of her. Which was more important, I asked myself: the killer's rights or theirs? I didn't know the answer to that question. I doubted that I'd ever know. But the answer I gave was: "Take it."

Chapter Thirty-One

WE GOT TO MY APARTMENT in about five minutes, turned on the TV, and slid the videocassette into the slot of the VCR. Johnny Lee sat on one end of my couch, I sat on the other, and Rick pulled up a chair from the small dining area, just off the living room.

Soon, Bonita Catledge's face appeared again on the screen, and, as it faded the film's title, *The Big 'O,'* rolled up and a soundtrack featuring spooky organ music began.

The movie was disjointed, had no dialogue and no discernible plot, resembling at times mere raw film footage. It opened with a shot of Bonita, naked, hands tied behind her, kneeling in front of a hooded male figure dressed in nothing but cowboy chaps and wielding a short leather whip. He was standing and the girl was performing oral sex on him.

As she continued, the camera moved away periodically to pan the room, which was bare except for a table strewn with various implements of bondage and discipline — chains, ropes, dildos, whips, handcuffs, harnesses, a chair, an upholstered bench, and an odd-looking contraption resembling a sawhorse with a small saddle on it, and with manacles attached to each leg. A mat lay on the floor in one corner of the room and black curtains covered the only window shown.

Soon, following a knock on the door, another male entered the scene, and I was gripped by a great sense of dread as I saw that it was

Clifford Sims. Rick, Johnny Lee and I exchanged anxious glances.

Sims, apparently playing the role of a pizza delivery boy, looked shocked but also aroused by what he saw going on, and soon he, too, was nude and standing in front of the girl. Menaced by the hooded figure, the girl began performing oral sex on Sims.

The film rolled on, getting rougher and rougher, and soon both Sims and the girl were either tied up or bound in chains as the hooded man moved from one to the other to engage in sex of various kinds.

I saw no evidence of real coercion or intimidation, and all three participants entered into the acts with evident enthusiasm. Still, I felt uneasy watching all this. I had seen porn films before. Most of them were too artificial, too silly to be taken seriously, mere chronicles of mindless exhibitionism and self-indulgence. But this film seemed to be a blatant appeal to the baser emotions in man — and not just an appeal to them, but an ugly exultation in them, and watching it made me feel somehow diminished as a human being. *The Big 'O'* seemed determined to rub the viewer's nose in its depravity, saying, in effect, "I am a pig — but so are you underneath."

Rick watched with an impassive face, but Johnny Lee seemed to be suffering. He had slid down on the couch as if cringing, and one hand was cupped above his eyes to shield them from time to time. When Johnny Lee saw me looking at him, he said, "I don't know how much more of this I can take."

"Don't watch with your emotions; watch with your mind," Rick said without turning his gaze from the screen. "This is work, not recreation."

"It damn *sure* ain't recreation," Johnny Lee said, "and if it's work, I'd rather be unemployed."

At that moment, the girl left the room and the film went blank for a second or two. When the picture resumed, Sims was astraddle the sawhorse and bent over, his feet chained to the rear legs and his hands tied together in front of him. Straddling the sawhorse behind him was the hooded figure, still wearing cowboy chaps, a whip in one hand, and his erection in the other. He eased forward, seeking contact with Sim's rearend, and then eased forward some more as the camera moved around to show the pleasure on Sims' face.

"Jesus Christ!" Johnny Lee said, disgust twisting his face into an ugly mask. "This is more than I bargained for. This ain't police work; this is sick work."

"Same thing," Rick said.

"Next time the camera shows Sims hands," I said, "see if that isn't twine on his wrists." I reached into my pocket and pulled out the two pieces of twine – the loop I had picked up in Eve Garland's driveway, and the piece I had found at Triplex News Agency. I tossed them onto the coffee table near Rick. Pointing to the six-inch piece, I said, "Picked this up at Triplex, where Smitty works." Next, I pointed to the loop of twine. "You already know where that piece came from."

They were a perfect match, and they looked exactly like the twine used to tie Sims' wrists.

"Years ago, when I was a teenager, I worked one summer at a news-stand in Augusta, my hometown," I said. "The magazines and newspapers were delivered in stacks tied in that kind of twine. All the news dealers used it. I must've cut a million pieces of the stuff during that summer. It's the kind of thing you do on automatic pilot, but it definitely rang a bell when I saw it on Sims' body. I just couldn't place where I'd seen it."

Rick glanced at the twine and then back at the screen. "It'll be another knot in his noose," he said, meaning the hooded figure on the screen. He nodded his head solemnly. "The guy in the hood is Smitty, all right. I'd bet the farm on that. But how do we prove it?"

"And *what* are we proving?" Johnny Lee asked. "If you could bust somebody for sodomy, half the waiters in Atlanta would be in jail."

I tried to brighten Johnny Lee's mood by quipping, "I hope not; service is bad enough already."

Rick said dryly, "It wouldn't hurt the service; half the straight population would be in jail with them. Ass-fuckin's been around since Adam and Eve. Guarantee it."

Johnny Lee snorted. "Not where I come from."

"Let's debate it some other time." I pointed toward the screen. "If we can prove that's Smitty, then we've got a suspect."

"He'll have to convince us he wasn't the last person to see Sims alive," Rick said. "That should be an interesting conversation."

"Homicide would never pick him up for questioning on this kind of evidence," Johnny Lee said, pointing at the twine and then nodding toward the screen. "No judge would sign the warrant, and even if he did, Smitty's lawyer would make us eat that hood right there in court."

"Who said anything about Homicide?" Rick asked, grinning.

Distracted, we had not been paying attention to the film. I knew only that Sims and the man wearing the hood were still engaged in anal intercourse. But when Johnny Lee, looking at the screen, shouted, "Goddamn!" and sprang to his feet, I looked toward the TV and saw that the man had looped the whip around Sims' neck and was strangling him, apparently at the moment of orgasm.

My heart in my throat, I leaped to my feet and stared at the screen in disbelief.

"Mother of God!" Rick said. He was standing and staring, too, a look of horror disfiguring his face.

There was no mistaking it as play-acting. It was vividly, undeniably real, and the camera recorded it all in obscene close-ups. The muscles in the hooded man's arms stood out rigidly and his arms trembled with the effort of murder as he strained and pulled. Sims' eyes bulged and his tongue lolled out of his mouth as he clawed desperately with bound hands at the leather gripping his throat. Soon his hands shook violently and fell away, and his body slid off the sawhorse and slumped to the floor as the picture faded to black.

"A snuff film!" Rick said. "Holy Jesus!" He punched the stop button on the VCR and stood there staring at the blank TV screen, looking stunned and ashen.

"I think I'm going to be sick," Johnny Lee said, weaving a bit on his feet and looking around desperately.

"That way," I said, pointing toward the bathroom, just off the hall outside the living room. Johnny Lee darted in that direction, and seconds later I heard sounds of retching.

I felt numb and realized that I was bathed in sweat. I wanted to speak, to express somehow the sense of outrage, of violation, I felt — that I knew all three of us felt. But all the words I summoned stopped at my lips and turned back, wouldn't come out, inadequate to the task, quailing at the challenge. Finally, pointing to the TV screen, I managed to say something else, the words thick in my mouth: "Rick, I want to be there when that sonofabitch gets his." I meant Reidsville. I meant the death chamber there, the electric chair.

"Don't forget the cameraman," he said, still staring at the blank screen.

"Him, too."

"And there may be others."

"All of them."

A voice behind me said, "Well, don't hold your breath, Ben." It was Johnny Lee, standing in the doorway, dabbing his face with a wet wash-cloth. "The best you can hope for is prison, which is no punishment at all to a cocksucker like him, the guy in the mask. He'll love prison. Might as well sentence a dog to a meat locker. Tell 'im, Rick."

Rick shrugged. "Nowadays a lot of people look to the courts for jus-tice and get sociology instead. So what else is news? Let's leave all that to a jury and concentrate on nailing these guys. That's our job."

"I say it's Homicide's job," Johnny Lee said. "Turn it over to them."

I didn't like the sound of that. At the moment, the story was all mine, an exclusive, first-hand account. Turn it over to Homicide, and not only would the story go up for grabs, I'd be pushed to the sidelines, become a mere onlooker. "I say we find out who the guy in the hood is and then turn it over to them."

"Me, too," Rick said. He held up his right hand, with the thumb and forefinger nearly touching. "We're *that* close to solving this baby our-selves, JL. I feel it in my bones. Don't quit on me now."

"All *I* feel is sick," Johnny Lee said, wiping his face with the washcloth again. Looking first at me and then at Rick, he added, "I'm not like you two. You've got some crazy need to know things. Anything. Everything. But there are some things I don't want to know. I could have gone the rest of my life without seeing what I just saw, and been perfectly happy."

"We need you, JL," Rick said. "And you're a cop."

"Not your kind of cop," he said. "You never heard me say I wanted to work Homicide, or be a detective of any kind, or even work vice. Uh, uh. I'd rather work fender-benders any day. That, and drunks and dis-orderlies. Domestic squabbles. Break-ins. The routine stuff. Somebody's gotta do it. Life is shitty enough without volunteering for jobs that rub your nose in it."

"We need you," Rick said.

"Hey, I signed on to find a missing girl. We found her."

"You also found Sims' body," Rick said. "What about that?"

"He was a cocksucker. A pervert. A sicko."

"He was a human being" Rick said.

"I ain't so sure about that."

"He was just a kid," I said. "A dog deserves better than he got."

Johnny Lee gave me a level look. "With that I agree."

"Just a few more days," Rick said. "We're close. I know it."

Johnny Lee shifted his weight to one leg. He was thinking it over. "What about the girl? This Bonita What's-'er-name?"

"What about her?"

"Well, I figure she's next on the film. I won't sit through another one."

"Go out there. Get some air." I pointed to a small deck on the back of my apartment, visible through sliding-glass doors from where we stood. It overlooked a small wooded area and caught the shade from some of the trees. Johnny Lee went out, taking the washcloth with him.

When he was gone, I looked at Rick as if to say, "What do you make of all that?"

"All cops get like this, each in his own way, at one time or another."

"And?"

He shrugged. "They either pull out of it or they go down in flames."

"Anything we can do?"

"Not until he's ready to let us help. And most cops never get ready. They go it alone. Big mistake."

"What about you?"

"Me?" He was taken aback. "I'm fine. Don't I look fine? Act fine?" Suddenly, as if a light bulb had come on in his head, he said, pointing to the TV set, "Oh, you mean *that.*"

"No. I mean all of it."

He made a helpless gesture with his hands. "'Man is a wolf to man.' What else can I say?" Then he smiled weakly. "Whatta ya think of that, Mr. Writer? Pretty literary, eh?"

I couldn't manage a smile, not even a weak one. "I think it gives wolves a bad name. Hit the play button and let's get this over with."

"No," Rick said, a strange look in his eyes now. "First, let me tell you what I *really* think. Put this in your story about cops: every time — every fucking time — I think I've seen the worst, something comes along, something like this—" He pointed toward the TV set, meaning the film. "—that says, 'Stick around, pal, you ain't seen nothin' yet.' And you know what hurts the most?"

I shook my head.

"It's all so goddamn ordinary," he said slowly, wearily. "People think murder is glamorous. Wrong — but glamorous. They can't read enough about it. Or see enough movies about it. But nine times out of 10, it's just one pea-brain knocking off another pea-brain. Hell, murder ain't nuclear physics, and murderers ain't rocket scientists. Murder's not at the high end of the I.Q. scale — just the opposite: it's stupid. So maybe, just maybe, it's nature's way of weeding out the pea-brains among us. So help me, Ben, the police department is nothing but a branch of the Sanitation Department. The boys on the dump trucks pick up the stuff in cans; we get the stuff on two legs."

For a moment I said nothing. He had a point. Murder often seemed to be the predictable explosion after stupidity combined with amorality had reached critical mass. Still, I was amazed at the new depths of cynicism Rick had plumbed. Finally, taking into account what he had just seen on the film, I said, "Thought you said you were fine."

"I am," he snapped. "Roll the tape."

THE FINAL SCENES WITH THE GIRL were just as brutish as those with Sims, lacking only the gut-wrenching surprise of her murder. Her hands bound behind her by a chain attached to leather wrist straps, she performed extended fellatio on the hooded man, who then laid her on a table, groin-high, and stood at one end of it, moving between her dangling legs, to enter her. Soon, when she began to orgasm, he suddenly gripped her throat with his hands and choked her to death as the camera captured in merciless detail the change of her facial expression from ecstasy to surprise to alarm, and finally to pain and panic before dissolving into an ugly mask of death as the screen went black.

Neither Rick nor I spoke for a few moments after the film ended, but again I felt the violation and outrage — that and an unreasonable help-lessness. I could not stop a murder happening right before my eyes, because it had already happened. And I could not help but wonder at the malevolence of a fate that could mark two youngsters — or anybody else — for such an obscene death, and then decree that it be recorded so they could die the same way, publicly, over and over and over.

Wearily, Rick got up, turned off the TV and punched the rewind button on the VCR.

If only life had a rewind button, too, I thought. "And to think," I said, "that I used to be opposed to capital punishment."

"Me, too."

"I used to think all men were basically the same, merely variations on a theme," I said, thinking out loud. "But they're not. They're sure as hell not."

"You can say that again. And finding it out is the toughest thing about being a cop. No — *handling* it is the toughest thing. It can make you so cynical that after awhile you're not much better than the scum-bags who made you that way."

"Is that where Johnny Lee's heading? I think he meant something like that in saying he wanted to be a plain, ordinary, everyday cop, han-dling fender benders and domestic disputes."

"He did. But that's town-constable stuff. This is Atlanta PD, not Mayberry RFD."

"But Johnny Lee's a veteran," I said.

"And paying for every minute of it. I've seen it again and again, Ben. Twelve months or 10 years - doesn't matter; JL's been on the job too long. For some people, thirty days is too long. The lucky ones hang it up in a hurry and segue to another line of work. The Johnny Lees hang in there and let the job eat 'em alive."

"What about the Rick Casenellis?"

"I grew up on the streets of south Philly. Illusions don't last long in an environment like that. They move out — maybe to the suburbs; who knows? — and reality moves in."

"Illusions don't last long in a newsroom, either."

Rick shrugged. "Illusions go to live with people like Johnny Lee —

and that's fine until he brings them back to the Big City. They wave bye-bye again, and guys like him are left holding the bag — an empty bag. But Johnny Lee won't change."

"Maybe he can't."

"I think you're right. I don't understand it, but I think you're right. Time and again, he's seen reality stomp the shit out of his ideals, but he goes right on thinking they have some fight left in them. But after awhile, what you've got is a punch-drunk fighter who won't go down, and a manager who refuses to throw in the towel. Until it's too late."

"Well, let's work on Johnny Lee by nailing this hooded SOB, and nailing him good. That ought to revive his spirits a little, give him some hope."

"Now you're talking," Rick said. He looked at his watch. "Here's the plan: The guy moonlights as a barkeep at The Back Door, a gay bar on The Strip."

"I knew it!" said Johnny Lee, coming back into the room. "This whole case is like a bucket of shit: the more you stir it, the more it stinks." He gave us a woebegone look. "Why didn't you tell me earlier?"

"Slipped my mind," Rick said, lying so obviously that complaint seemed pointless. "But hang in there; it's almost over, I think. Now, as I was saying, we'll pick him up late, say, midnight. Not arrest him, mind you — just pick him up. I'll think of something — just go along with me. And we'll take him to the station on Piedmont. Place is all but deserted at that hour. "

"And if we're seen?" Johnny Lee said.

"We're just having a late-night chat with a snitch."

Johnny Lee looked at me and shot his eyes to the ceiling. "What we're headed for is a daylight chat with the captain — probably the review board too."

"It's our only chance," Rick said. "You said it yourself: everything we've got is circumstantial."

"What are you gonna do?" Johnny Lee said, sighing.

"Mess with his mind. Do a number on him." He smiled. "Guilt, like God, moves in mysterious ways — or didn't you non-literary types know that?"

"Us non-literary types know how to keep our noses clean," Johnny Lee said drolly, "—and how to hang onto our jobs - and pensions."

"We," I said, correcting him: "*We* non-literary types."

"Fuck you, too," Johnny Lee said; "I'm talkin' common sense, not grammar." He pointed toward Rick with a jabbing thumb. "Slick the Spic here is about to lead us right over a cliff, I think. Lotta good your grammar will do you then."

"Yeah, but you'll do it, won't you?" Rick said, giving him a look that said, "Say yes."

Johnny Lee looked worn down. "Yeah. I just wish I had a good reason."

"Well, if you don't do it," I said, again trying to make him laugh, "Rick and I won't let you hang around with us anymore."

He threw up his hands. "Well, that settles that. Why in the hell didn't you say so to start with?"

"Good," Rick said, clapping his hands. He told Johnny Lee he'd drop him off at his apartment and pick up both of us around 11:30. He picked up the pieces of twine. "Got any scissors? Never mind."

He went into the kitchen and searched through drawers until he found a knife. He cut the six-inch piece of twine in half and stuck all three pieces into his pants pocket. Patting the pocket, he looked at me and at Johnny Lee, and then pointed a finger to his temple. "Part of the plan," he said mysteriously. "Now with a few other things, which I'll pick up while you two are eating supper and generally lazing about, we'll be ready for Mr. Hood."

Chapter Thirty-Two

NOBODY COULD ACCUSE THE BACKDOOR CLUB of false advertising in its name. It was located on Peachtree and had a Peachtree address, but it did not open onto the street. Not even a window broke the front exterior of the long, low-slung wooden building, and no sign indicated what lay behind the wall. The entrance was around back, opening onto a dark, unpaved parking lot that was still full when we arrived, about midnight — full and active, too. The headlights of Rick's Trans-Am raked across one figure after another, all male, as he swung into the lot, and for a moment I wondered if there had been an accident, or maybe a fight. But then I saw the activity was merely an extension of the club, a part of its ambiance, one of the club's attractions. What began inside could be finished outside in the parking lot, if the patrons were so inclined — and evidently many were.

Rick grabbed a parking space as somebody was leaving, and we walked toward the club, spotting Brinson's gray van by a fence near the door. Rick looked at the license plate and then said, "Stay loose. If Brinson is the same guy on that film, he's a cold-blooded bastard. One slip and he could take us all out."

THE CLUB WAS PACKED. Booths, all full, ran down two long walls, and men stood five deep at the bar, which had no seats. Smoke rode the air lazily above their heads, moving in serpentine undulations as if it could hear the slow-dance music that broke now and then above the din of crowd noise. At the other end of the room, a few couples danced dreamily in a shower of tiny lights reflected from a mirrored ball turning overhead.

We spotted Brinson right away. With three other bartenders, he was working quickly but smoothly, serving up beer and mixing drinks, plucking empty bottles and glasses from the bar, raking up money, and making change.

At a signal from Rick, Johnny Lee drifted back to cover the door, and I watched as Rick pushed right through the crowd at the bar, got Brinson's attention and held up his wallet, letting it fall open to show his badge.

Brinson looked surprised, but not startled. Rick nodded his head toward the door, and Brinson, who seemed to be in charge of the bar, called one of the other bartenders over, spoke to him briefly, and then looked at Rick again and headed out from behind the bar, toward the door. Rick moved down the bar with him, parting the crowd in his way as if he were a human plow, and kept his eyes riveted on Brinson.

Outside, a few steps away from the door, we stopped and Rick told Brinson we were investigating a robbery in which his van had been implicated. "You do drive a gray van, don't you? Georgia license OYM 606?"

Brinson showed only mild surprise. "That's it right over there." He pointed to the van. "But it's been here all evening."

"This was last night," Rick said. "Lafayette Avenue. In Ansley Park."

"Yeah, I know where it is," Brinson said. "Dropped a hitchhiker off there last night. Could be your man, but he didn't seem like the type to me."

"His name?" Rick said.

"Search me. Picked him up on Piedmont — Piedmont at Ponce. Dropped him off on Lafayette. Never seen him before."

"Say where he worked? Anything?"

"Nope."

"Would you recognize him again if you saw him?"

"Uh, yeah, I guess so."

"Then we'd like you to come with us."

That surprised Brinson. "Now?"

"Now."

"You want me to pick him out of a line-up or something?"

"Something like that. Let's talk on the way to the station."

Brinson looked toward the door as if he wanted to go back inside, but Rick said, "This way, please. We'll bring you back to your van."

Chapter Thirty-Three

WITH BRINSON AND JOHNNY LEE on the back seat and me up front, Rick headed for the station on Piedmont, driving in silence except for once, when Brinson, apparently trying for levity, said, "What kind of cop drives a Trans-Am?"

"One who's up to his eyeballs in car payments," Rick said.

Along the way, I thought about Brinson, trying to size him up. But try as I might, I couldn't make what I believed about him coincide with my impression of him. It was like looking in the viewfinder of a camera, seeing two images of the same person, and being unable to make them resolve into one. In person, he seemed absolutely ordinary. On the other hand, I told myself, if we could pick out the murderers among us by how they looked, there'd be no need for police.

When we got to the station, Rick fetched a bulging briefcase out of the trunk of his car, and then we entered the building, which appeared deserted except for a watch sergeant asleep in a small office near the entrance. Following Rick, we walked through an empty squad room and then down a hall of darkened offices to one with lettering on the door that said: Lt. A. C. Bartholemew. Rick opened the door, switched on a desk lamp, and waved us into the room as he adjusted the blind on the window overlooking the hall, opening it a bit, but not all the way.

"Have a seat," he told Brinson, indicating a chair in front of the desk.

Rick sat down behind the desk and put the briefcase on top of it. Johnny Lee took a seat near the door, and I sat off to the side on a small couch.

The room looked less like an office than a study. Most police offices I had seen looked depressingly Spartan, with file-cabinet green or battleship gray as the predominant color. This one was painted in a pastel yellow, and was decorated and downright homey. Framed photographs and certificates hung on the wall above my head, house plants sat atop file cabinets and on the ledge of a window that looked out over a side street, and a hook rug lay on the floor at my feet. Lt. Bartholemew apparently looked at his office as a home away from home. The only odd note in the whole decor was a miniature electric chair that sat on his desk among family photographs and other odds and ends. A grim little thing, it was highly detailed, with touches of polished brass that gleamed in the light from a desk lamp. Rick moved it casually from the side of the desk to the center, putting it alongside the briefcase. I saw Brinson glance at both and then at Rick. The mind tricks had begun.

"Your hitchhiker's also wanted for attempted rape," Rick began, lying with apparent ease, "and he roughed up one of the women pretty bad."

"Gee," Brinson said, "I had no idea the guy was such a bad dude. He looked kinda, well, wimpy to me."

"The important thing is that you got a look at him," Rick said.

"Well, it *was* dark."

"But you said you could identify him," Johnny Lee snapped.

His tone of voice surprised me, but then I realized that he was role-playing. He was the tough guy to Rick's good guy — a standard technique in police interrogation, designed to keep the suspect off guard, off balance, to play ping-pong with his emotions.

"I said I *guess* so," Brinson said.

Johnny Lee snapped again. "Well, can you or can't you?"

"Yeah, well, he was short and stocky. Red hair, I think. A beard. I took him for a hippy."

Almost gently, Rick said, "That doesn't match our description."

"Shit," Johnny Lee said. "It ain't even close."

"Well, hey," Brinson said, "maybe it's not the same guy." He looked from Rick to Johnny Lee as if beseeching them to join him in this obvious conclusion.

"But it was the same guy," Rick said softly, almost apologetically. "You backed into the drive and he eased out the back. This was witnessed."

"Hey," Brinson said, "guy tells me where to drop him off, how am I supposed to know?"

Johnny Lee shot up out of his chair, a look of disgust on his face. "We're talkin' about what he looked like, not where you dropped him off. We *know* where you dropped him off."

Brinson stiffened. "Well, what am I, a fuckin' camera?"

"You got eyes," Johnny Lee said, pointing to his own and stepping toward Brinson.

"Hey," Brinson said, turning around in the chair to face Johnny Lee. "Did you go to lunch today?"

"What if I did?"

"Describe your waitress."

Johnny Lee had said earlier that he ate lunch at home, but now in almost a military manner, he said, "Five-feet-two, three. Dark brown hair, cut short, to the ears. Brown eyes. 130, 140 pounds. String of moles on the neck, left side."

Brinson raised and dropped his hands, and turned back toward Rick. "Okay, so you're a cop. You been trained to notice. But I'm not. And I haven't. And obviously I didn't."

"Still," Rick ventured, "that's a funny way to drop somebody off, backing into the drive, him going out the back."

Brinson heaved an exaggerated sigh. "Why? I needed to turn around. I overshot his house, or what he said was his house. And after I back in, the back door is the nearest way out for him." He rolled his eyes and looked around the room. "Say, is there a water fountain around here?" A thin film of sweat on his forehead reflected the light from the lamp.

"We'll get you some," Rick said. He nodded to Johnny Lee, who made a great show of being put upon and left the room.

As soon as he was gone, Rick told Brinson, "Try to overlook my partner. This happened on his beat and he's taking some heat from the brass."

"Well," Brinson said, looking somewhat mollified, "we all take our turn in the barrel."

"Speaking of which — not that it's any of my business, but what's it like working in a place like that?" As Rick spoke, he reached out and ran his fingers idly over the tiny electric chair.

Brinson's eyes followed the move. "You mean the Back Door?" he said, sounding surprised by the question. "What the hey, it's a job. I serve 'em drinks, I take their money, I close up, I go home."

"Actually, I meant the porno agency – Triplex."

Just then, Johnny Lee came back in carrying a paper cup filled with water. Small and cone-shaped, it held no more than a swallow, but Brinson took it, said, "Thanks," and knocked it back as if it were a shot of whiskey. Looking at Rick again, he said, "That's just a job, too." He crumpled the cup in his hand. "I see you been checking."

Rick reached out a hand, took the cup and tossed it into a wastebasket. Then, fiddling with the tiny chair again, he said, "Routine. You sure know how to pick 'em, though — jobs, I mean." He said it in an off-handed manner and while smiling, but he was probing.

"Same guy owns both places. Other places, too."

"Oh, yeah?" Rick said. "Who's that?"

"Bruce Davenport."

Rick merely nodded. I knew Davenport, at least by reputation, and I figured Rick did, too. Davenport, about 35, was a hot-shot entrepreneur who had come to Atlanta from Florida and made a splash in the city's nightlife. He opened a gay bar at Pershing Point, near the Coach and Six Restaurant on Peachtree, and it had proved so successful that he soon owned three or four more gay bars, as well as a posh restaurant near Colony Square.

Davenport was a go-getter — brash, pushy — but he must have pushed the wrong people at some point in his mercurial rise, because a couple of years back, his gay bars had been plagued by a series of fire-bombings. One of them was especially nasty. Somebody poured gasoline through an exhaust fan on the roof and then torched it. In seconds, the bar, packed on a Saturday night, was engulfed in a ring of fire. Seven were burned alive, and 15 or 20 others were injured. An investigation, played big for awhile by *The Phoenix*, uncovered a blood feud among factions in the gay-bar business, but the arsonist was never caught, nobody was arrested, and soon the police and the newspaper turned their attention to other things. Maybe Davenport had turned his attention elsewhere, too, deciding to expand into areas where the competition was less fierce.

"What's Davenport like?" I was asking Brinson, but Johnny Lee answered: "A sleazeball."

Brinson ignored him. "Smart. Ambitious."

"And kind to little old ladies," Johnny Lee said, smirking. "Now let's get on with it. You gonna help us or not?"

"What more can I say?"

For a moment we were silent. Then Brinson spoke again. "Didn't the broads get a look at this guy?"

"They were in bed, lights out," Rick said, lying again.

Brinson nodded. "Lights were *on* when I dropped my guy off. Sure we're talkin' about the same house?"

"How many fuckin' driveways did you back into on Lafayette?" Johnny Lee said. "It was the same house. The guy waited 'till the lights went out, is all, for Christ's sake."

Brinson leaned back in his chair. "Just trying to be helpful."

Nobody spoke for a moment, but then Rick said nonchalantly, "Well, see if you can help us with this: The guy says all of this was your idea."

Startled, Brinson sat straight up and almost bellowed. "*Who* said?"

"Darryl. Darryl Owens — that's his name."

"He's outta his fuckin' mind. I don't know nobody named Darryl." Brinson whipped his head around the room, looking from me to Johnny Lee, and then back at Rick. "When did he say this? You catch him?"

"He's cooling his heels in the city jail," Johnny Lee said. "And there's an extra bunk in his cell for you."

"Hold on, JL," Rick said, affecting a reasonable posture for Brinson's sake. "Every jailbird says it was somebody else's fault. You know that."

"Never saw him before in my life," Brinson said. "So help me God." He shook his head. "Try to be a nice guy and where does it get you?"

"Tell me when you tried and I'll give you the answer," Johnny Lee snapped.

"Hey," Brinson said, looking at Rick for help, "no need to get nasty. I work. I pay taxes. There are people who will vouch for me. But what is he, this Darryl whozit? Fuckin' hippie. Drifter, for all I know."

Johnny Lee scoffed. "Yeah, and you're Young Man of the Year. Pillar of the community. Porn dealer by day, gay den mother by night. When's the last time you knew anybody normal?"

"Well, it wasn't after I met you."

Johnny Lee ignored him. "I'm tellin' you, Rick, he's a fag." He nod-ded toward Brinson. "Works for a fag, hangs out with fags . . ." He stopped, his conclusion obvious.

"Hey! I don't have to take this." Brinson told Rick. "I give a guy a lift, he gets into trouble and then blames me. Well, it's my word against his." He squirmed in his chair, agitated. "Tell you something else. I think you guys are fishing. If you had anything on me, I'd already be in the slam." He stood up. "So I'm leaving. *Caio.*" He looked at the door but didn't move. Johnny Lee had stood up and was blocking the doorway.

"Please," Rick said. "Sit down. We're almost through here. Promise. And JL will mind his manners so we can wrap this up. Right, JL?"

Johnny Lee didn't speak, but when Brinson eased back down into his chair, Johnny Lee sat, too, and Rick continued. "You're right, Mr. Brinson, we haven't been completely straight with you. But try to see it from our point of view. Cops usually have a few answers and a lot of questions. If we revealed our answers too soon, we'd wind up with noth-ing but questions. You've been around; you know that."

"OK, OK. Let's get on with it," Brinson said in a weary voice.

"Good," Rick said, slapping both his hands gently on the desktop. "What we really want from you is help in solving a murder case."

Brinson jumped as if he had been hit. "Murder? Me?"

Rick smiled. "Yes. Hear me out. On the morning of August 5, two bodies were found in North Atlanta, in the woods near Brookhaven, off Windsor Parkway. A young man, a young woman. Both had been stran-gled and shot. Are you with me so far?"

Brinson seemed to have trouble speaking, but finally managed a yes. A bead of sweat trickled down the side of his face, and his T-shirt seemed to cling to his torso.

Rick opened the briefcase on the desk and took out some eight-by-eleven photographs. Spreading them on the desk in front of Brinson, he said, "These are crime-lab photos of tire tracks at the scene."

Brinson looked at the pictures, but said nothing, merely cleared his throat.

Very businesslike, Rick took more photographs from the briefcase and put them in front of Brinson. "And these are lab photos of footprints at the scene."

Brinson stared at those, too, as if he found them absorbing, but I got the impression that he was mainly avoiding eye contact. He was nervous. He kept fidgeting with his hands, clasped in his lap, and then rubbing them along the tops of his thighs as if to dry his palms on his pants.

"Still with me?" Rick said cheerily.

"Uh, yeah," Brinson said as if snapping out of a daze, "but could I have some more water? It's hot in here."

Rick said, "Sure," and nodded to Johnny Lee, but I needed a drink myself and said I'd get it.

When I stepped into the hall, I was surprised to see Eve and Connie there, and closed the door quickly.

Rick had called her earlier in the evening, Eve said, and asked her to bring Connie over around 1 a.m. to see if she could identify a suspect — identify him without his knowing she was there. They had just arrived.

"Is that the suspect?" Eve asked, looking through the blind.

I told her it was.

She turned to Connie. "Recognize him?"

Connie peeped through the blind, too, and said, "Yes. He's one of the two I saw with Cliff that day." She quickly stepped away from the window.

Brinson was still looking at the photographs, but Rick and Johnny Lee saw us, and Rick raised his eyebrows as if to say, "Well?"

I stepped in front of the door so he could see me better through the glass and raised my hand, thumb and forefinger forming an 'O'. Bingo!

"Who is he?" Eve asked

"Smith Brinson."

She gave me a look that asked for more.

"Bartender at The Backdoor. Works for—"

"Bruce Davenport," she said. "Gonna lock him up?"

"I don't know. This is Rick's show — but I need to get back in there."

"Call me later."

She and Connie left, and I got some water and went back into the room, this time taking a chair nearer the desk, but still off to the side of Rick and Brinson.

"Are you squeamish?" Rick was asking Brinson. Not waiting for an answer, he added, "You might want to see what the victims looked like when we found them." He put more pictures in front of Brinson, but Brinson took one look and flinched, and then turned away as if in pain, almost dropping his water.

"Oh, I'm sorry," Rick said. "Wrong pictures. Those are of the autopsies. Even surgeons have been known to lose their lunch at autopsies."

On reflex, I leaned forward to look at the photographs and immediately wished I hadn't. The picture on top of the stack — the only one I saw, thank God — showed the cadaver of what had once been a female, lying on its back on a long metal table. The body had been laid open from sternum to pelvis as if excavated by a backhoe, and the top part of its head was missing, sheared off, I assumed, by the surgical saw plainly visible in the background. The scene reminded me of a hog killing I had witnessed as a boy of 10, and I wondered anew what Bonita Catledge — Sims too, for that matter — could have done to deserve such a fate. Again the answer came back: nothing.

Rick whisked the photographs away and replaced them with others. "Here. These are the ones."

Brinson looked at them, but showed no sign of recognition. Pulling out a handkerchief and wiping his brow, he managed a strained laugh and said, pointing to the pictures, "Gee, I don't how you guys do it."

Rick slumped back in his chair and fixed Brinson with a steady gaze. "*We* guys don't know how *you* guys do it."

Brinson appeared thrown, uneasy. Darting his eyes left and right, he said, "What do you mean?"

"I mean cold-blooded murder — and for what?" Rick sat up, reached into the briefcase again and pulled out the videocassette. He placed it on the desk alongside the miniature electric chair. "For this?" he asked.

Brinson's eyes got big as saucers as he stared at the videocassette. It was clear that he recognized it.

Rick then reached into his shirt pocket, fished out the three pieces of twine, and tossed them onto the desk alongside the videocassette and the tiny electric chair. "This one came from Triplex," Rick said, pointing. Moving his finger, he added, "This one came from Sims' wrist." Here he paused, obviously for dramatic effect, and pointed to the third piece of twine. "And this one came from the back of your van." As Brinson stared mutely at the desktop, Rick said softly: "Perfect match on all three."

Time stood still in the room, and for a long time Brinson said nothing. He simply mopped his brow and stared at all the evidence on the desk — and maybe at the little electric chair, too. Finally, he looked away and said in a hollow, flat voice, as if retrieving a thought from a hiding place in his mind, "They were nothing, you know — just a punk and a cunt." A moment later, appearing refocused on the present, he asked, "Who fingered me?"

"You did," Rick said. "When you sent Darryl Owens after Connie."

Seeming more relaxed now, Brinson said, "Yeah, I knew that bitch would come back to haunt me."

"Want to tell us about it?"

Brinson ignored Rick's question. "I want to deal."

"Fair enough," Rick said. "But first: JL, read him his rights."

Johnny Lee took a card out of his billfold and read from it: "You have the right to remain silent. Anything you say can and will be used against you in a court of law . . ."

As Johnny Lee's voice droned on, I flipped to a clean page in my reporter's notebook and waited for Brinson's confession.

When Johnny Lee finished, Brinson said to Rick, "Deal?"

"Do you want a lawyer?"

"Fuck a lawyer; I want a *deal*."

"If you cooperate fully, we'll do all we can. That's the best I can offer you."

Brinson said nothing for a moment or two and then offered lamely, "It wasn't my idea."

"You've got the floor," Rick said. "It's now or never."

Brinson looked from me to Johnny Lee to Rick, heaved a great sigh, and then it all came tumbling out. Hungry for more power, more money, Davenport wanted to break into the porn-movie business, producing, not just distributing. He figured he could do that by beginning with X-rated films for a very select clientele, the rich and jaded. Snuff films would attract their attention, and their money, right away. Snuff films were being written about in the national media; several people claimed they had seen one, but nobody had yet come forth with proof that they existed. Davenport would provide that proof, circulating the films quietly for $5,000 per copy, and then use the money to bankroll another X-rated film for general distribution. For the snuff movie, he had needed both a male and female so he could fashion three movies out of the raw film footage and cover all the sexual bases: homosexual, heterosexual, and those who liked both.

"Who was the cameraman?" Rick asked.

"Ike Pomeroy," Brinson said. "He works for Davenport, too. He's a gofer at The Backdoor. Works in the office."

"Anybody else involved?"

"No."

"Who processed the film, edited it?"

"Pomeroy. Photography's his hobby."

"Were the films circulated?"

"No. All that editing and splicing for three films takes time, is what they told me. I don't know. I just acted in the thing."

Johnny Lee guffawed. "Acted? You're a sick sonofabitch; you know that, don't you? You and your two bum-hole buddies."

"They were trash," Brinson said, meaning Catledge and Sims.

"So all you're guilty of is littering? That the way you see it?" Johnny Lee said, bristling.

"Who shot them?" Rick asked, sticking to business.

"Davenport. He wanted to be sure."

"And you hauled away the bodies," Rick said.

"You got pictures of the tracks," he said matter-of-factly.

"I meant who helped you."

"Me and Pomeroy did it. Too much like real work for Davenport. He might mess up his nice clothes."

"Where'd you shoot the film?"

"In a room upstairs at Triplex. It's deserted down there at night."

"Thought of everything, didn't you?" Johnny Lee's voice was dipped in sarcasm.

Brinson turned and looked at Johnny Lee. "What is it with you? You got a hard-on or something?"

"Why? You interested, if I do?"

"I'm no fag."

"Tell it to somebody else," Johnny Lee said. "I've seen the film."

"Hey, you don't like a blowjob now and then? You never gave it to your ol' lady in the ass?" Brinson now turned his full attention to Johnny Lee. It was as if he had detected something there that he could rattle, a dropped stitch in Johnny Lee's makeup that he could pull on to unravel. "What kind of woman you got? Women love to gobble a root." He smiled obscenely. "Only thing they like better is to take it in the ass. You just prop 'em up on their knees and slide it in. There's no other feelin' like it. Nice and tight. Hugs and squeezes your dick like a milkmaid pullin' on a cow's tit."

"Shut up."

"And after you get it all the way in, up to the hilt, that little asshole just goes crazy and starts to quiver and quake."

"Shut up!"

Brinson laughed. "Hey, if you won't ream your ol' lady, somebody else will. I can tell you ain't been doin' your homework. You prob'bly think eatin' pussy's perverted too. Where the fuck did you grow up, East Jesus or something?

Johnny Lee stood up, his cheeks fiery red in an otherwise pale face. Eyes fixed on Brinson, he said, "You better shut him up, Rick."

Brinson said, "Hey, if you haven't tried it, don't knock it," and that's when Johnny Lee charged.

Brinson looked startled and tried to brace himself, but it was too late. Johnny Lee caught him halfway up out of his chair, and both men went sprawling onto the floor, rolling and punching. Johnny Lee was the larger of the two men, but Brinson was both strong and quick as a cat. He broke Johnny Lee's hold on him and sprang to his feet, but Johnny Lee lunged and tackled him low, sending both of them crashing into tables and lamps and filing cabinets.

Rick and I were on our feet, looking for some way to help Johnny Lee, but the two men were wrestling so furiously that we saw no opening. Neither seemed to be landing effective punches, but their wild gyrations hurled them back and forth across the room until one end of it looked as if a small tornado had struck it. Furniture tilted crazily this way and that, shattered picture frames and whatnots littered the floor, and potted plants, looking startled and forlorn, lay strewn in small explosions of crock and dirt.

Somehow, though, when the two men crashed to the floor again, rolling over and over in a desperate struggle, Brinson came up on top of Johnny Lee holding a gun in his hand.

"He's got my piece!" Johnny Lee yelled, grabbing Brinson's wrist as Brinson struggled to aim the gun at Johnny Lee.

Johnny Lee was fighting for his life, but Brinson was the stronger man, and slowly he was able to turn the pistol in Johnny Lee's direction. I don't remember doing it, but I flung myself at Brinson and knocked him off Johnny Lee. When the gun went off , it sounded like a cannon firing, and for a second I lay there, ears ringing, wondering if I had been shot, and if not I, then who? An instant later, I realized that Brinson and Johnny Lee, rolling this way and that, were still locked in a ferocious struggle. When Brinson rolled up on top again, another shot rang out, but this one was fired by Rick, who finally made his move firing a bullet into the ceiling.

Darting behind Brinson, Rick grabbed the man around the neck with one arm and gouged the barrel of the gun into his temple. "If you so much as twitch," Rick warned in a tight, low voice, "you'll wake up in Hell."

Brinson froze and I snatched the gun from his hand.

"Get up," Rick snapped, backing away.

Brinson got to his feet. Johnny Lee did, too.

"You okay, JL?" Rick asked. He was breathing very rapidly and had his gun trained on Brinson's midsection.

"Yeah," Johnny Lee said, moving away from Brinson and straightening his clothing. Neither man appeared harmed except for a scratch or two and the usual signs of a scuffle: flushed faces, mussed hair, heaving chests, clothing in disarray.

In a small, tight voice, Rick said to Johnny Lee, "Why don't you go to the head and wash up?"

Still brushing himself off, Johnny Lee left the room.

Rick glanced fiercely at me. "Why don't you make sure JL's all right?"

I almost left the room, too, but something in Rick's voice, something in the rigid way he was standing there, in the way he was looking at Brinson, made me hesitate. I stopped at the door.

"Go on," he said, his back to me.

"No," I said. "JL will be okay."

"Get outta here!" he snarled, tossing the words over his shoulder at me.

"No," I said. "I don't like the look of things here. I'd better hang around."

By now, Brinson had caught on, too. "Yeah, stay," he said, fear unfurling behind his eyes, a small plea in his voice. He was talking to me, but he stared anxiously at Rick the whole time.

"I'm not staying for you," I told Brinson. "I'm staying for him."

"One more time," Rick said. "Go."

"No. I'm gonna stay until you come off that adrenaline high. And don't forget: I'm holding a gun, too, and I've got the drop on you."

He didn't look around. He knew better than to take his eye off Brinson. Instead, he snorted a cynical laugh. "You wouldn't shoot me."

He was right, I wouldn't – but I had learned a thing or two from him. "Maybe not," I said, "but the price of guessing wrong seems mighty high. I'm not going to let you make me an accessory to murder – and that's what this would be, you know, cold-blooded murder."

For a moment, I thought he was going to shoot Brinson anyhow. He stood there looking so taut, almost aquiver with rigidity, that I knew he could snap like a towline at any second. But suddenly he relaxed, flashed a slightly abashed smile and said, "I would've called it hot-blood-ed instead of cold-blooded. But all right, where were we?" Looking around the room, he said, "Gee, I wonder if the lieutenant will like the way we redecorated his office."

"What I wonder," I said, "is how that sergeant up in the front office slept through all this."

But just as I said it, the sergeant came rushing through the door — and did a double take as soon as he saw the wreckage. "Damnation," he said. "This must've been one hell of a party. Fireworks, even. I'd've got here sooner, but I was tied up on the radio."

Rick introduced us. He was Sgt. Matt McCray, a large, bespectacled, white-haired man who appeared to be near retirement age. We shook hands.

"Sarge," Rick said, getting handcuffs from a drawer of the desk, "we got a live one here. How 'bout calling the wagon and holding him up front till it comes?" He snapped the 'cuffs on Brinson, who showed no resistance. "But don't turn your back on him."

"Come along, sonny," McCray said, and Brinson followed.

When the door closed again, Rick looked at me and said, "Thanks."

"Forget it."

"I was gonna waste him, you know."

"I know."

"I had it all doped out: He put up a struggle and tried to escape."

"Might've worked."

"JL was right, you know: Guy like him will be in hog heaven in prison and be back on the streets before you know it."

"Yeah, there's gotta be a better way — but this wasn't it," I said.

"I kept seeing in my mind's eye what he did to Sims and that girl."

"It was different for me," I said. "I had to keep reminding myself of that. The guy, Brinson, I mean, looked — I don't know — so normal. I guess I was expecting two heads or something."

"No conscience," Rick said. "*That's* what you couldn't see." Abruptly he added, "I'd appreciate it if you didn't tell Johnny Lee about this."

"My lips are sealed."

Rick went to the desk and began putting things back into the briefcase.

"By the way," I said, "where'd you get all that stuff? Pictures of his tire tracks, footprints?"

Rick smiled. "They aren't his. He just thought they were. I simply went to the files and pulled out the first ones I came across."

"Clever," I said, marveling again at his ingenuity. He'd make a hell of a detective, I thought, if he could learn to play by the rules. "What comes next?"

He opened a drawer and pulled out a tape recorder. "It's all on here — and you're a witness." He put the tape recorder into the briefcase. "Now I'm gonna take Mr. Hood downtown and book him, murder one, two counts, lay it all in the lap of Homicide, and let them take it from here."

"What about Davenport? And what's-his-name, Pomeroy, the cameraman?"

"All Homicide has to do is pick 'em up — which I'm sure they'll do first thing in the morning."

I didn't like that idea — and it didn't sound like Rick. As I saw it, we weren't through yet. I wanted him to go right then and arrest Davenport and Pomeroy — especially Davenport. His arrest would make a better story; more importantly, it would give me a satisfaction that I ached for in the deepest reaches of my mind and heart.

As usual, Rick was ahead of me. Looking pained, he said, "I feel the same way you do. But, one, if we don't let Homicide have a piece of this, Johnny Lee and I will pay with our asses. It's police politics, pure and simple. Two — and you can write this down — we've got nothing on Davenport except the word of that amoral idiot who just walked out of here in handcuffs. Sure, Davenport'll be arrested soon after daybreak. But by noon he'll be eating lunch at the Driving Club on Piedmont or some other posh watering hole. He'll never be convicted. I'll be surprised if he even goes to trial."

I knew he was right, but something curdled inside of me anyhow. "Shit!" I said.

"My sentiments exactly, pal. But at least we got Brinson — and, tell you the truth, I wanted him worse than Davenport. Davenport is scum, but Brinson's a homicidal maniac.

"I want 'em all."

"You'll get Pomeroy, too, mark my word. His fingerprints are all over this crime. And, like the song says, two outta three ain't bad." He glanced at his watch. It was 2:30 a.m. "I'm whipped. How 'bout you?"

"To a frazzle," I said as Johnny Lee came through the door.

He looked none the worse for wear, but I could tell he was angry. His face was puckered into a scowl and there was fire in his eyes. "You bastards!" he said. "I just remembered where I saw that woman, the one with the girl, Connie."

Rick and I raised both our hands, hoping to shut off his anger or at least deflect it, but he sailed right on. "She's a goddamn bull dyke. I got a call to her club one night, few years back, to break up a brawl between two lezzies. She's queer as a three-dollar bill."

Rick tried bluffing. "So?"

Johnny Lee bellowed, "So what does that make Connie Phillips, a goddamn Girl Scout?"

Rick tried for humor. "So they like to eat each other. Who gets hurt? A pussy's like a Timex: takes a lickin' and keeps on tickin'."

"You bastards fooled me," Johnny Lee was so angry that he couldn't stand still. "I knew it. By God, I *knew* it!" Now he was nearly dancing in anger and frustration. "This case was fishy from the word 'Go.' A damn queer! I busted my ass, worked on my time off, risked my job — even my life — and all for a fuckin' lesbo, a muff diver, a snatch snorkeler. Jesus fuckin' Christ! "

We tried to stop him, tried to reason with him, but he wouldn't listen.

"After tonight," he said, pointing to each of us, "both of you can kiss my ass. Some pals you turned out to be." He whirled and left the room, slamming the door so hard the glass rattled.

Rick and I looked at each other glumly for a moment or two, but then — we couldn't help it — we started laughing. We laughed until our sides ached. Johnny Lee was right, of course; we had deceived him. And it wasn't that we didn't value his friendship. We did. But his anger seemed so disproportionate to the cause that it was funny.

Sex in all its variations was just a fact of life. You didn't have to like all the variations or approve of them, but they sure as hell weren't going away because some people huffed and puffed about them. Might as well curse the sun for shining, the wind for blowing, the moon for circling the earth.

"Let's get out of here," I said. "I've got one hell of a story to write tomorrow and I'm worn out."

"I'll be lucky to get to bed at all," he said. "I've got to sneak that tape back into Brinson's apartment and then head downtown to file my report." He stretched and yawned. "Ah, 'To sleep; perchance to dream.'" He looked at me slyly. "Eddie Guest, right?"

His yawning was contagious. I did it too. "Guest wrong," I said, risking a pun. "Stick to police work."

"Dammit," he said, picking up the briefcase and heading for the door. "At this rate, I'll never get on 'Jeopardy.'"

"You *are* jeopardy, pal, and anybody around you is in jeopardy up to his hips."

He laughed, and when he dropped me off at my apartment, he said, "Risk jeopardy one more time. Ride with me tomorrow night — or, rather, tonight. I'll fill you in on how it went."

"If I can find a rabbit's foot and a four-leaf clover before then, I will."

He laughed and drove off, but then stopped and backed up. I bent down to the open window on the passenger side, and he leaned over and said, "Would you really have shot me?"

"I didn't even have a gun on you. It was in my pocket the whole time. In fact, here." I took out the gun and handed it to him. "Johnny Lee will need this, and you'll see him before I will."

He took the gun and roared off again, laughing like a loon.

Chapter Thirty-Four

BY NOON THE NEXT DAY, the newsroom was abuzz over the story of Brinson's confession and arrest. Though I was only halfway through writing it, Owens and other editors stopped by my computer terminal every now and then to read over my shoulder, and others in the newsroom were calling the story up on their screens so they could read it, too.

We were going to the front page with it, playing it above the fold with a Judgment-Day headline — and right beside it would be Morgan's sidebar, a first-person account, already in the computer system, of her undercover work as a Peachtree prostitute. Even the managing editor came by, grinning from ear to ear, to say, "Hell of a story, Ben. Morgan's, too."

I thanked him and continued working, but soon I saw Morgan coming in to work and walked out to the newsroom to speak to her. "Great story," I said. "Read it first thing this morning."

She was all smiles. "Thanks," she said, hanging her purse over the back of her chair at the copy desk. "It worked, too; I'm now a reporter, thanks to you." She opened a drawer and began taking stuff out. "I'm moving to that empty desk back there." She pointed to a desk three rows past the city desk. "General assignment."

I congratulated her and scooped up some of her belongings to help her move. "But you don't owe this to me," I said. "You earned it. Your sidebar is terrific."

"Let's call it teamwork," she said, leading the way to her new desk. "You're to be congratulated, too. I heard about the latest story on my way in. I ran into some copy editors in the lobby, on their way to lunch."

"Suppose I tell you all about it after work. Say 11 p.m." I figured that would give me enough time with Rick.

"It's a date," she said.

I went on back to the features section, and was surprised to see Connie's mother waiting at my desk.

"I just wanted to come by and thank you," she said, rising as I approached. She wore a neat two-piece navy blue linen suit with white piping, and had a new hairdo.

I complimented her outfit and added that she didn't look like the same woman I'd seen about two weeks earlier.

"Oh, I'm not. I can rest easy now, knowing that killer is in jail, that Connie is safe."

I couldn't resist asking. "How are things with you and Connie?"

She bit her lip and gripped her purse. "You mean that woman, Eve." She sighed. "It's hard to accept, very hard. I don't think Joe will ever accept it. He keeps asking what we did wrong, and at first he kept saying she was no daughter of his." She looked out the window. "Maybe, in time . . ." Then she brightened and gave me a look that seemed forced but jaunty. "But I thank the Lord for my blessings. All I asked was that Connie be found alive and well — and she was, thanks to you." She smiled.

"And to two very helpful policemen," I added.

"I saw one of them on TV this morning, an Officer Casenelli. When you see him and the other one, Officer Cook, I believe, please tell them how grateful I am for what they did." She started to leave, but then turned back to me. "How can I ever thank you?" Her eyes were misting over.

"You just did," I said.

She left and I went back to work. The story all but wrote itself except for Davenport's denial, which I saved for last because he was taking his time getting back to me. I had phoned his home and office first thing this morning and left messages at both places — pointed messages: "You've been implicated in a double murder that I'm writing a story about for tomorrow's *Phoenix*. Please call me right away at my office, 692-4808."

At 2:15 p.m., I finally heard from Davenport, but only through his lawyer. I wasn't surprised to see that he had retained J. Howard, one of the best defense attorneys in Georgia. All business, Howard said: "I have a statement for you. My client is innocent. The charges leveled against him by Mr. Brinson are utterly without foundation. Mr. Davenport is a highly respected businessman and citizen of Atlanta, and he will have no further comment on this matter." He hung up.

"'This matter,'" I muttered scornfully – as if it were a speeding ticket or jaywalking or operating a business without a license instead of a depraved murder.

I plugged the denial into the story, high up near the lead, told the city editor that the story was ready for publication, and walked out onto Marietta Street in search of a late lunch.

It was a brilliant day, unseasonably cool, and for a moment I thought I detected a hint of autumn in the air, though surely it was still a few weeks off. It felt good, however, to be thinking ordinary thoughts again after the intense involvement of the past several days, and it felt strange but good to be doing something as ordinary as strolling out from the office for a bite to eat.

The street was crowded, as usual, and as pedestrians flowed around me in both directions, going about their business, I couldn't help wondering if any of them had experienced anything remotely resembling what I had been through in the past month or so. Sure, the odds said that somebody in this throng had either lived in a private hell at some time or was lost in one now, but most of them, I knew, lived very tame lives, never venturing outside their quotidian routines. This observation made me feel somehow special, but it also made me feel tired. No, not tired – drained. And it wasn't the pleasant exhaustion one feels after an exertion that brings triumph. Instead, it was a flat, dull feeling of defeat somehow. It was as if things were at last resolved, or nearly so, but the resolution wasn't satisfying. Or maybe it was that the ending brought no satisfying resolution. Yes, that was it.

I took a quick inventory: Connie was found, but in truth she was still lost, at least to her parents. She'd never be their little girl again. And

Sims was dead. We simply got to him too late. Brinson would go to prison, but he'd adjust and feel quite at home there, just as Johnny Lee had said. And Davenport – well, Rick was almost certainly right about him. He'd beat the rap.

"Oh, well," I told myself, fully aware of the cynicism I was feeling, "I guess all's well that ends well."

Dammit! Dammit! Dammit! I thought.

Chapter Thirty-Five

RICK STARTED TALKING A MILE A MINUTE as soon as I got into the car, around 8:15 that evening, Davenport had been arrested and was already out on bail. "He denies any involvement," Rick said, "and a search of his house and office turned up nothing to connect him to the crime. It's his word against Brinson's, just like I said it would be, and Davenport can afford the best lawyers in town."

We were cruising around Central City Park and heading toward Margaret Mitchell Square on Peachtree. "They didn't find the gun?"

"Not a trace — so far."

"What about the cameraman?"

"He's in the can — but he says it was all Brinson's idea, that Brinson did the shooting, and threatened him if he didn't go along. He says nobody else was in on it."

"Think he was bought off?"

"That's *my* guess. But look at it from his point of view: The heaviest weights are tied to Brinson — the van, the attempted kidnapping, the videocassette, the stranglings. Pomeroy can turn state's evidence and watch Brinson slip beneath the waves. *Sayonara*, beach boy. At worst, he draws 10 and is out in seven, maybe sooner with good behavior."

"And Davenport?" I already knew the answer.

Rick made a face. "He gets another blot on his reputation."

"Damn!"

"Of course, the gun *might* still turn up, and *if* it belongs to Davenport, we *might* have a case. But don't hold up supper waitin' for that to happen."

"Something tells me that gun is long gone, hacked to pieces, maybe, and scattered from Hell to Halifax."

"He wouldn't have to travel far to dump it. More than one murder weapon is hidden forever right here in town — at the bottom of the Chattahoochee River."

"Damn!"

"The good news is that we've got Brinson by the short hairs."

"I already knew that," I said. "I was hoping for *better* news."

"Welcome to the world of law enforcement."

We drove past 10th Street on Peachtree, entering The Strip. Traffic picked up, though it didn't seem as heavy as usual.

As if reading my thoughts, Rick said, "It'll be quieter here tonight. Weekends after the first and the 15th of the month are the worst. They're paydays for a lot of people, especially the first; that's when the eagle flies — all those government checks."

"So, in a sense, the government supports all this," I said glumly.

Rick laughed. "Is this a great country or what?"

But my thoughts were focused elsewhere. "I wanted all three of those guys put away."

"Don't feel like the Lone Ranger. But, for all we know, come right down to it, Brinson was lying about Davenport."

I gave him a long, blank look. "Nice try."

He shrugged. "Well, I said for all we *know.*"

"What about the master tapes? Find those?"

"Not yet — and I thought sure we'd find them in Pomeroy's darkroom. But Brinson could've been lying about that, too."

"I don't think so."

"I don't either."

Still on Peachtree, we drove past Colony Square and headed toward Buckhead. "I was supposed to call Eve," I said. "It's just as well. She's not going to like all this one little bit."

"Don't bother. She reached me at the station this afternoon. I told her more than you could have. She wasn't happy with developments, especially with the outlook on Davenport, but it's not over yet."

"Have you been to bed at all since I saw you last?"

"Grabbed a couple of hours on a couch in the captain's office."

"Captain's office?"

He looked at me and grinned. "Yeah. You are not riding with just any ol' cop here, son. I am now Detective Sgt. Rick Casenelli, Homicide. This is my last week in Atlanta blues; next week, I trade in the uniform for a coat and tie. *And* a raise. *And* an office. *And* daytime hours." Lifting both hands off the steering wheel, he snapped his fingers and began to sing: "'R-e-s-p-e-c-t, find out what it means to me . . .'" He laughed like a lunatic and shouted, "Look out, Aretha!" Turning mock serious, he said, "She wrote that, you know."

"Try Otis Redding," I said. "Poet laureate of Macon, Georgia."

"Oh, no," he said. "That's Little Richard." He raised his hands, and shimmied and shook again. "'A wop mop a lu bop, a lop bam boom!'"

"What about Johnny Lee? Same deal for him?"

"If he wants it. But he wasn't around all day, and tonight, after line-up, he got away before I could talk to him. Still got the red-ass, I think."

"No. I think Johnny Lee has the *real* Atlanta blues. Remember that old tune by Jimmy Rogers and, later, Grampa Jones, and countless others: 'Rather drink muddy water and sleep in a hollow log...'"

Rick finished the line: "'... than to be in Atlanta, treated like a dirty dog.'" He laughed. "Surprised you, didn't I? Hey, Philadelphia has country music stations, too. I tell you, I am definitely ready for Jeopardy, don't you think?"

"I already told you, boy; you *are* jeopardy, and I don't mean maybe." Suddenly the police radio squawked, and as usual I couldn't make out what the dispatcher said. Her voice was a monotone, as if the wires through which it flew had squeezed it flat, and static exploded around each word like enemy flak. Instantly Rick was all business. "Officer needs backup," he said, interpreting for me. "That'll be Johnny Lee." He picked up the microphone and acknowledged the call. "I'm on the way."

We were approaching St. Phillips Cathedral, an Episcopal church that sat high on a curve in Peachtree Street and, to traffic moving uptown, loomed out of the dusk looking like a great, gray ship sitting smack in the middle of the road.

"Balboa Street. That's in Garden Hills," Rick said. "There's St. Phillips. We're pretty close. Hang on." He switched on the blue light, turned right at the next side street, and floorboarded the cruiser, its siren piercing the night like the cry of a large, terrified bird.

Garden Hills was a residential neighborhood of nice homes inflated in value by the benign proximity of Buckhead, one of Atlanta's most affluent addresses. The streets of Garden Hills wound around small parks and ponds, interconnecting like the strands of a huge net, and running first uphill and then down. Like a giant pinball, the cruiser rolled this way and that as Rick negotiated the maze of narrow, curving streets, zigging and zagging to get to Balboa as fast as possible.

"There it is," I yelled, glimpsing a street sign as we streaked through an intersection.

Rick slammed on brakes, threw the cruiser into reverse, roared back through the intersection, braked again, and then swung left and barreled up a hill. "Look for a black-and-white," he said, meaning Johnny Lee's cruiser. But he no sooner said it than we saw it, parked at the curb, maybe 50 yards ahead on the right.

Rick raced up behind the cruiser, stopped on a dime, and both the front doors flew open like steam valves. We ran toward the house, which looked for all the world like a mountain home — set into the side of a hill, steeply pitched roof, long front porch with rocking chairs, and high steps — but stopped when we saw Johnny Lee sitting on the bottom step, elbows on his knees, hands clasped together. He might have been taking the evening air, he looked so calm. But when we got close to him, we saw that he was dejected, and when we got closer still, we saw that he was crying.

"What's up, partner?" Rick asked.

Was that surprise or concern in his voice? I wondered. Both, I decided.

Johnny Lee had trouble speaking. Motioning toward the house, he finally managed to say, "Go up there and arrest those bastards." His voice was one of exasperation beyond endurance. "If I have to go back up there, I'll shoot 'em instead." Then he buried his face in his hands.

Rick and I looked at the house. A couple of lights were on, and somebody, a man, was standing in the doorway, watching from behind a screen door.

Rick started up the steps. "Better stay here, Ben."

"No way," I said, and went up right behind him.

As we got to the top of the steps, the man in the doorway said over his shoulder, "It's another one, Ethyl." He appeared to be about 40 years old, and was of medium height and thin, but what struck me about him was the expression on his face: tight, scornful, indignant.

Rick paused at the door to speak to the man, but it was his wife, a woman of about 35, with whom he had to deal. A thin, pale woman with a hatchet face, she sprang to the door and launched into an agitated harangue that offered no opening for Rick to speak.

"She's got the devil in her!" she said in a loud voice. "She *must* be disciplined. She's *our* child, and it's nobody's business how we raise her. 'Spare the rod and spoil the child,' sayeth the Lord." Spewing words as if they were arrows aimed at infidels, she fixed first Rick and then me with a sharp, jut-jawed look through wire-rimmed glasses and said, "I know who called the law. I know who it was." She pointed across the street. "That hussy who parades through the neighborhood in her tiny little shorts, and sunbathes right out on her front lawn in front of God and everybody in her tiny bikini. We're surrounded by heathens here, and God will tolerate it only so long. Mark my word. Mark my word! We know what's best for our daughter, and no court is going to tell us how we can raise her. We never should have come to this God-forsaken city. So you go right on back downtown—"

Rick reached for the handle of the screen door. "Stand back, ma'am; we're coming in." He swung the door opened and the couple retreated, the woman still talking. "I gave *birth* to that child. I am her *mother*. I will not have my home invaded like this. That child's got the devil in her, but we will root it out if it's the last—"

Rick ignored her. To the man, he said, "Where is the child?"

Like a mute, the man pointed toward the back of the house.

"Show me," Rick said.

The man, followed by the woman, walked to a hallway, went down it about halfway, and then stopped at a door. "The basement," he said.

Rick and I exchanged glances. Most Atlanta homes didn't have basements.

"Lead the way," Rick told the man. "You, too," he told the woman.

The man opened the door and started down the stairs. From below, we heard the moaning of a small voice, and when we got farther down the steps we saw on the floor, at the foot of a bed, a girl of about 8. She was chained to the bed, the only furniture in the room.

Rick and I stopped in our tracks. "Jesus Christ!" he said.

The woman screeched, "Don't you take the name of the Lord in vain in my house."

We pushed past the couple and hurried to the little girl. Dressed in dirty, ragged clothes and with bruises all over her body, she sat dazed, head bowed, in her own excrement.

Down on his knees beside the girl, Rick looked up at the parents, still on the steps. "How long's she been here?" he barked.

"Since Sunday," the woman said. "She violated the Sabbath. God says—"

As she spoke, Rick stood up straight and advanced toward her. "Shut the fuck up," he snapped, glaring at her. "Just shut the fuck up."

The woman looked stunned, but she shut up.

I looked at the man. "Get these chains off," I told him. He hesitated until I snapped, "Do it now!" Then he reached into his pocket, pulled out a set of keys, and walked toward the bed.

"You two are under arrest," Rick said, "for cruelty to children and whatever else I can make stick against you. I'll read you your rights when I get time. But for now —" He looked at the woman. "— get some hot water and a wash cloth, and clean her up. Clean up that mess she's sitting in, too."

The woman gave him a hateful stare, but turned and went up the steps.

Rick looked at the man as he fiddled with the chains. "You ought to be horsewhipped," Rick said.

The man gave us a disdainful look. "'Vengeance is mine,' sayeth the Lord."

"Good thing for you," Rick snapped. "If vengeance were mine, I'd kick your ass till your nose bled."

As soon as the man opened the lock, Rick and I turned our attention to the little girl, who was conscious but too weak to respond. Whispering words of comfort, we gently removed the chains from around her waist. "Everything's gonna be all right. It's all over. We'll take care of you."

I looked at the man, "How long since she had anything to eat?" When he didn't answer, I guessed. "Sunday?"

He nodded.

I stood up. "You have milk, juice?"

He nodded again.

"Get it," I said, "Get both." I scooped up the girl. "Lead me to your kitchen," I told the man. On the way up the stairs, we met the woman coming back with a basin of water. "Follow us," I said.

In the kitchen, I put the girl down in a chair at the table. "Give me that wash cloth," I told the woman. "Now go run a bath and get out some clean clothes for her."

I began wiping the girl's face, hands and arms, rinsing the cloth frequently in hot water at the kitchen sink. Underneath the grime, she was a pretty thing — one of nature's little ironies, I told myself: a rose sprung from two dung heaps. Her hair was matted in places and stringy in others, and the bruises marred her complexion, but her eyes were the color of jade, and her lips were a perfect little red bow around perfect little white teeth.

Rick came into the kitchen. "I called for a policewoman and some juvenile authorities." He looked at the man, who was pouring orange juice into a glass. "They'll take care of your little girl," he said. Then he added pointedly, "And then they'll take care of you and your wife."

More aware now, the girl tried a sip or two of the juice and then drank it down. "Pour some milk," I told the man.

The girl drank the milk, too, gulping it down hungrily until we cautioned her to sip it instead.

As soon as the policewoman arrived, bringing another officer with her, we turned the case over to them and left, telling the girl, whose name was Vivien, that we'd see her the next day. She nodded numbly, nibbling on a graham cracker, but looked at us with grateful eyes.

Johnny Lee was still sitting on the bottom steps, but he got up as we approached. Unpinning his badge, he handed it to Rick. "Here," he said, "turn this in. I'm through."

"Naw, naw," Rick urged, refusing to take the badge.

Johnny Lee handed it to me instead and unbuckled his gun belt. "This belongs to them, too," he said, handing it over. "The uniform's mine. I paid for it. But anybody who wants it is welcome to it."

"Wait till tomorrow," Rick said. "Hell, you can't just quit in the middle of a shift. Too, you've got 10 years on the force. Better think it over. Sleep on it, at least. I'll tell 'em you got sick and had to go home."

Johnny Lee shook his head. "I got sick, all right. But I don't *want* time to think it over. I might get scared and change my mind, and *that* would be the wrong decision for me. This is it. Over and out."

"You've been promoted to Homicide," Rick said. "Didn't you hear?"

"Thanks, but no thanks. I've already told 'em that."

"But why quit altogether? Why?" Rick said. "The brass'll give you anything you want."

"I couldn't begin to add it up for you," Johnny Lee said. "But what I saw in there was the last straw. That could have been my little girl, you know. I don't know where people like that come from." He pointed toward the house. "But this much I do know: They don't come from Claxton, Georgia. I'm going back to my own kind. No more big city for this country boy. These goddamn people here are ape-shit. It may be Atlanta to you, but to me it's Sodom and Gomorrah combined. Anything — and I mean *anything* — goes in this town. It's the queer capital of the whole Southeast, you know. If they could all suck at the same time, they could pull San Francisco as far east as Chattanooga. No. I gotta go. I can't do this anymore."

"Get some help," Rick pleaded. "You said yourself, you made a mistake when you didn't go for counseling last time."

"Ha! If I went for counseling — if I told 'em how I *really* feel — I'd wind up in a rubber room, waiting for my next shock treatment. The only therapy I need is a one-way ticket out of Atlanta. Hey! They could light me up like a Georgia Power substation, and I would still want out."

He leaned down and got in Rick's face. "Didn't you see me? I turned my back on those two yo-yos up there." He pointed to the house again. "How's that for proper procedure? They could've grabbed a gun and blown me away. But when I saw that little girl, I just came unglued. A cop who comes unglued is worse than no cop at all. And if he doesn't see that, he'll soon be a dead cop. Like Riley." He shook his head vigorously, his cheeks trembling. "Uh, uh. Not me. Not *this* ol' boy. Drop me by my place, will you? Here're the keys to the car." He handed them to Rick. "They can pick it up anytime they get ready." He waved toward the car. "Good riddance."

Chapter Thirty-Six

WE DROVE IN SILENCE to Johnny Lee's apartment, said our goodbyes, and then rode until 10:30 with so little happening that our dejection was compounded by boredom. Around quarter to 11, Rick dropped me off at the newspaper's parking lot. It had begun to rain, and the rain, while a welcome respite from the heat, did nothing to elevate our spirits.

"Keep in touch," I said, getting out of the car.

He didn't hear me, though. The radio crackled and diverted his attention. "Hold on," he said, raising a hand to shush me. When the radio was quiet again, he said, "Get back in. I recognize the address. It's Davenport's place. I was there just this morning."

I scrambled in and buckled up. "What's going on?"

Rick was already rolling. "Somebody reported gunfire there. Maybe the bastard shot himself. Hold on again." He picked up the radio's microphone and spoke into it. "This is Bravo 4. I'm close by. I'll take it." He hung up the microphone and looked at me. "It wasn't my call, but I want it."

The radio blurted again, the dispatcher telling Bravo 3 to ignore the call.

"Where does he live?" I asked.

"Fairchild. It's off Lenox Road."

Lenox Road ran past Lenox Square, Atlanta's premier shopping mall, a mile or two beyond Buckhead. The neighborhoods around there were premier, too. I looked askance at Rick. "Thought you said it was close by."

He grinned. "It is, the way I drive."

MINUTES LATER, WE PULLED INTO THE LONG, WINDING DRIVE of a big, Tudor-style house set well back from the street and at the crest of a long, sloping lawn. In the moonlight, I could see that it was a beautiful house, the kind that betokens money, though in an understated way.

"This is it?" I asked, surprised. Good taste and the business Davenport was in had trouble fitting together in my mind.

"Haven't you heard, m'boy?" Rick said. "There's money in sex." He opened his car door. "Sit tight while I have a look around."

As usual, I ignored him and got out, too.

The house was nearly dark, but we could see through the glass panels alongside the front door that a light was on somewhere inside. Rick rang the doorbell, but before anybody could answer, we heard footsteps behind us and turned. Coming up the driveway was a young woman wearing jogging shorts and a T-shirt.

"I tried that," she said, meaning the doorbell, "but got no answer." She stopped at the steps to the front porch.

She was a blonde, about five-feet-four, with a pixyish face and an eye-catching body that her outfit did little to conceal. I guessed her age as twenty-five.

"Who are you?" Rick asked.

He liked her looks, too. I could tell.

"Bunny Ramsdale. I live across the street." She pointed out into the darkness. "I'm the one who called you."

"I'm Officer Casenelli. This is Ben Blake, a reporter. You say you heard gunshots?"

"Just one," she said. "At least, I think it was a gunshot. I didn't call until I couldn't get anybody to the door."

"You know who lives here?" Rick asked.

"Not well. Only to speak to. But it's Bruce Davenport. He keeps pretty much to himself."

"Maybe he's not home," I said.

"Well, that's just it," she said. "I saw him drive up not 10 minutes before I heard that noise. And his car's in the garage. I looked."

"See anybody else around?"

"No."

Rick rang the doorbell again and said, "When did all this happen, Mrs. Ramsdale?"

"Miss," she corrected, coming up onto the porch, giving Rick a radiant smile. "I'm a grad student at Georgia Tech, but I live at home with my folks." She took a deep breath, one that did interesting things to her T-shirt. "Anyhow," she continued, "I went out at 10:30 to run. I like to jog at night, when it's cooler. While I was warming up in my driveway, I saw Mr. Davenport pull into his drive and go into the house. Soon after that, I started my run, but I wasn't two houses up the street before I heard that noise. I knew where it came from, but by the time it registered that it must have been a gunshot, I was halfway up the block. I stopped, came back, looked around here some, and then rang the doorbell. After that, I called the police. You think I'm nosy?" She flashed the smile again and then laughed, a bit embarrassed.

"You did the right thing," Rick said, smiling, too. He looked at the door and then back at Miss Ramsdale. "I'm not having any luck raising anybody, either, so I'm gonna have to look around. You'd better go on home, though."

She backed away, looking a bit apprehensive.

"But first," Rick added, "give me your phone number. I might need to check with you later."

Her face lit up and she gave him the number, which he jotted down in a small notebook. "That's my number," she said, "not my parents'. They're not at home now. Want theirs, too?"

"Yours will do. I'll be in touch."

She began walking down the driveway. "If I'm not there, leave a message," she said.

Rick waved and said under his breath, "I sure will, Bunny, honey. I sure will." And then he was all business again. "First," he said, "let's not overlook the obvious." He reached for the doorknob and turned it. The door opened. "You better stay here," he told me, stepping inside, "until I see what's what."

I said OK but moved right in behind him.

"Anybody home?" he called out from the foyer.

When nobody answered, we moved down a hallway toward the light we had seen from the front porch. Soon we were at the doorway of a den, or maybe a study. There, seated in a high wingback chair, was Bruce Davenport. He was dead. Head tilted to one side, resting against one of the chair's wings, he looked as if he had merely fallen asleep, except that his eyes were open. We moved closer and saw that a hole had been drilled into his forehead. It sat like a rosebud just over the right eye, blooming atop a thin stem of blood that trailed down the side of his nose. No gun was in sight.

"Don't touch anything," Rick said. He went to a telephone that sat on a roll-top desk against a wall. "I'll phone this in and then look him over."

I moved around the body, studying it. Davenport was dressed in street clothes — nice but casual, with slacks and a blue blazer, a sport shirt and loafers. He was smaller and shorter than he had appeared on television; his feet barely touched the floor, and his small frame was dwarfed by the big chair in which he sat.

Then I studied his face. It was youngish, unlined, and his blue eyes appeared fixed in an odd mix of wonder and horror, as if at the instant of death he might have glimpsed what lay beyond for him. I hoped it was the deepest pit of Hell. The cynicism of that hope surprised me until I remembered how Clifford Sims and Bonita Catledge had died. Compared to the way they died, Davenport's death was an easy one. *Boom! Goodbye.* When I moved on around the body, I saw with a sense of malicious, unsettling satisfaction that the back of the head was missing, and that some of the pieces were spattered on the chair and on the wall behind him.

"Hollow point," Rick said. I hadn't heard him come up. "Neat going in, messy coming out."

"Ugh!" I said.

"Couldn't happen to a nicer guy," he said. He leaned closer to examine the hole in Davenport's forehead. "Hard to tell what caliber." He moved around to the wall behind the body. Pointing to a hole in the wallpaper, he said, "Here it is. Lab'll dig it out."

"What do you think?" I asked.

"He had lots of enemies."

"You think maybe there was somebody else in on the snuff film, somebody who wanted to make sure Davenport didn't talk?"

"I don't think so. Do you?"

"No."

"Well, anyhow, I'm going to leave this to Homicide. Officially, I'm not a detective until next Monday, and somebody else is welcome to *this* murder. Brucie-boy's, I mean. What do you say?"

"I say Amen. Two of the bastards are in jail, and the other is dead. Case closed."

WE WAITED OUTSIDE UNTIL A DETECTIVE ARRIVED, followed closely by an ambulance. Rick briefed the detective while I watched the medics haul out that damned gurney again. We left as it was rattling up the walkway.

Rick drove me back to my car again, and I got into it and headed for Morgan's place. It was late, past midnight, but when her apartment, lights aglow, appeared out of the night, I gave thanks she had waited up and that I wasn't going on home to an empty apartment. When she came to the door in a red teddy and holding two glasses of wine, I decided not to go home at all that night.

Chapter Thirty-Seven

I DIDN'T HEAR FROM RICK for about two weeks. He was busy, I knew, learning a new job, and I went back to my regular routine, writing feature stories. I stayed in touch with the case, but only through the police reporters, and when the grand jury returned indictments against Brinson and Pomeroy, I put it out of mind altogether.

One crisp Saturday morning in late September, however, I heard a knock at the door and opened it to find Rick standing there.

"Where the hell have you been?" he said, grinning.

"Savannah. Doing a story on shipping. Got in late last night."

"Man, I have been wearing your phone out." He glanced at the coffee cup in my hand. "Got any more of that?"

I went into the kitchen, and Rick climbed up on a stool at the breakfast bar. As I poured, he said, "Wanted to bring you up to speed on Davenport. One shot — a .32 hollow point right between the baby blues at close range." He pointed a finger with a cocked thumb and made a popping noise with his mouth as the thumb snapped forward. "Never knew what hit him. But you knew that."

"Except for the caliber. Any suspects?"

He took the coffee and sipped it gingerly. "Only 200 or 300."

"You working the case, after all?"

"No. More than anything else, I've been working on Bunny

Ramsdale." He smiled. "We're dating."

"I could have told *you* that."

He laughed. "But about the case: I read the report, talked to the detectives. Just curious, you know. Did I say it was a neat job? No witnesses. No sign of a struggle. No forced entry. Nobody seen coming or going. No prints, either. They don't even have a neighbor, except for Bunny Ramsdale, who heard something go bump in the night. Clean as a whistle, this one was. All the earmarks of a professional job, maybe even a contract. Don't be surprised if they never find out who done it."

I nodded and made a face as if impressed. "Sounds like you planned it well."

He affected a wounded look. "You are confused, m' boy; I, your humble civil servant, am sworn to *uphold* the law. Besides, if you are not *too* far gone in senility, you may recall that I was with you."

"Only after 8 p.m." I was enjoying this.

He smiled. "And where were *you* before I picked you up?"

"Seriously. What was the time of death?"

"Around 10:30, they say — but TOD is hard to peg closer than, say, two hours. Me, I think he got it when Bunny Ramsdale heard the shot."

"Me, too. But I keep remembering that you were going to shoot Brinson."

He surprised me by turning serious. "Yeah. Actually that's why I dropped by." He took a deep breath. "I'm not going to play detective, after all. I turned it down."

"You're not?"

"No. I've been giving a lot of thought to what happened that night. *I would have shot him.* I've tried to tell myself I wouldn't have, but it's no use. If you had left that office when I told you to, I would now be a murderer." He sipped his coffee and then gave me an earnest look. "You've seen me. The adrenaline starts pumpin' and I get higher and higher. I crave action. I crave excitement. I see now that's a big reason I became a cop, in the first place."

"You're a great cop." A bit unorthodox, I was thinking, but still a great cop.

"No," he said, shaking his head vigorously. "I'm a *dangerous* cop. I spun out of control that night. And I see now that it started some time ago." He held out an open hand. "You've seen how hyper I get. A really good cop keeps his cool. Heck, Johnny Lee wised up to himself. If he can do it, so can I."

"So what'll you do?"

"I laid it out for the captain, pretty much as I've laid it out for you. He offered me a job at the police academy, and I grabbed it. I think I'll like that. I start first of the month. Until then, I'm taking a few days off."

"Congratulations. You'll make a hell of a teacher."

He grinned. "Yeah — in what *not* to do."

I had some news too, which I told him as I poured us another cup of coffee. I was moving in with Morgan. And I was leaving *The Phoenix*. I was going to write a book, a book about him and Johnny Lee and Connie Phillips — all of it.

He raised his coffee cup. "I'll drink to all of those moves. Good luck, Ben."

The doorbell rang and Rick answered it. Soon he was back at the breakfast bar, saying, "Postman. Package for you." He handed it to me and sat back down.

I examined the package idly, my thoughts elsewhere. "What happened to Darryl Owens? Still in jail?"

"They're holding him as a material witness. But he'll be all right. I talked to the D.A." He snapped his finger. "That reminds me, though. Remember that kid, the one with the Corvette, the one Jane Kimball told you about?"

"The guy I thought might be involved in Connie's disappearance?"

"That's the one."

"What was his name? Oh, Brooks Creighton. Rich kid."

Rick pointed a finger at me. "He *was* involved. Not criminally — but not innocently, either. That boy *does* get around, just as Kimball told you. He was pals with Davenport, and he was the one who told Sims to look up Davenport for work. He knew Davenport was looking for a certain type of talent for his new film venture."

"And it was Creighton who gave Sims and Connie a ride into town when they left home," I said. When he looked at me quizzically, I added, "Connie told me that much. I didn't think it was important."

"Sonofagun. Guess we dropped the ball on that one, didn't we?" Rick said. Then, shaking his head, he added: "Hell, he wouldn't've told us anything. Swears he didn't know they would be in any danger — and there's no proof that he did."

"Well," I said, "it's all water over the dam now."

Suddenly Rick made a gesture of exasperation. "Are you going to open that package or aren't you?"

I looked at it. It was a box about eight inches long and five inches deep, sealed with masking tape. "I didn't order anything," I said.

"Who's it from?"

It bore no return address. "Atlanta postmark," I said.

Rick threw up his hands. "Why do people stare at packages, wondering what's in them? Open it, dummy."

Inside were three videocassette tapes and an embossed business card that read: Davenport Film Productions, Bruce Davenport, president, and gave an address and phone number.

"Jesus Christ," Rick said. "Those must be the missing master tapes, the ones Brinson told us about, the ones we couldn't find."

I was mystified. "But who sent them? And why send them to me?"

Rick caught my eye and stared. "Are you thinkin' what I'm thinkin'?"

"Yeah — and it ain't the first time it crossed my mind."

"Mine, either."

At the same time, we said, "Eve Garland."

"It's the only thing that makes sense," Rick said. "Motive, means — remember, she had a .32, and she said she knew how to use it. That leaves only opportunity. And what do you want to bet she was at her club all night the night Davenport was killed, and could get 40 witnesses to swear she was there and didn't leave all night?"

"Tell you the truth," I said, "I hope they would give her an airtight alibi."

"Then I'll tell you the truth: I hope it doesn't even come to that."

"Will it?"

"Not unless you tell it." He grinned. "You're the loud-mouth reporter — and, as I recall, the guy all broken out with ethics."

"Not anymore," I said. "Besides, I told you: My reporting days are over. I hear the fat lady singing, and she's singing loud and clear." I poured myself more coffee. "Anyhow, what good would it do?"

"So a scumbag got exactly what he deserved," Rick said. "Got it the only way he was ever going to get it — in this world, at least. We never could have pinned anything on Brucie-boy. Remind me, though, never to cross Eve Garland."

I looked at the tapes. "But why would she send them to me?"

"Nice lady," he said. "She wanted you to know you were right. She figured, too, that you'd know what to do with 'em."

I pointed to the tapes. "Are they needed for the case?"

"No. The one we already have is plenty."

I looked at Rick and he looked at me. "Now what?" I said.

"They're *your* tapes," Rick said pointedly.

I thought for a moment, and then I decided. "I say somebody has sent me some tapes that I didn't order. I say I don't know what's on them — and don't want to know."

"Got a screwdriver?" Rick said.

I got out a couple of them and we began to pry open the plastic casings. I also turned on a gas burner on the stove.

It took a while and stank up my kitchen, but soon the film was charred to ashes.

Epilogue

SMITH BRINSON WAS SENTENCED TO DIE in the electric chair at the State Penitentiary in Reidsville, in South Georgia. He died in the shower there instead, in May 1982, stabbed repeatedly with a homemade knife in a dispute over the sexual favors of a young inmate. His killer was never caught.

Eisenhower (Ike) Pomeroy, sentenced to a life term in Reidsville, was paroled in 1988 after serving seven years. They tell me he was a model prisoner.

I never see Eve Garland or Connie Phillips, but I hear they are still together.

Johnny Lee Cook went back home to Claxton, and is now chief of police in Hazlehurst, a small town in south Georgia. Married again, he has a son, Rick, who is 7 years old. I hear from Johnny Lee at Christmas, when he sends me a card with a picture of the family. He has gained a few pounds, but looks happy.

Rick Casenelli now heads the police academy. He and his wife Bunny have three children, twin girls aged 5, Angela and Teresa, and a son, Benjamin, 3. I am the boy's godfather, and Rick and I still get together about once a month for beer and auld lang syne.

Morgan Matthews and I got married and have two children, Richard, 7, and John, 5. Morgan still works at *The Phoenix*, where she is now managing editor of features.

I stay home and write, mostly freelance journalism, but this was a story I had to tell. I dedicate it to all — and they are legion — who have ever had the Atlanta Blues.

–Benjamin Blake